PRAISE FOR LOREN
NEVER STREET

A *NEW YORK TIMES* NOTABLE BOOK OF THE YEAR

"For all the Chandleresque contortions . . . Estleman never compromises form for cleverness. His language is strong enough to support the weight of its metaphors, his characters can't be pigeonholed, and his hero doesn't faint under stress."
—**Marilyn Stasio, *New York Times Book Review***

"Estleman's back with NEVER STREET . . . [and] settling in with an Amos Walker book is like peering over the shoulder of a man who's lovingly admiring the lines on a classic car. . . . No one else writes about Detroit with the deep personal knowledge and hard-bitten romanticism of Estleman. . . . His Detroit novels are the finest ever written about that unique American city."
—***Washington Post Book World***

"Detroit's summer of power outages provides a brilliant backdrop for Walker's Chandleresque storytelling at its most gaudy and orchestral, with enough lush villainy for three ordinary novels."
—***Kirkus Reviews* (starred review)**

"The best film noir I've read in a long time."
—***Boston Sunday Globe***

more . . .

LOREN D. ESTLEMAN is the author of the heralded Detroit series of novels that include *Whiskey River*, *Motown*, *Edsel*, and *Stress*. NEVER STREET is his first Amos Walker novel since *Sweet Women Lie*. Loren Estleman lives in Whitmore Lake, Michigan.

NEVER STREET

LOREN D. ESTLEMAN

WARNER BOOKS

A Time Warner Company

WARNER BOOKS EDITION

Copyright © 1997 by Loren D. Estleman
All rights reserved.

Cover design by Rachel McClain
Cover photo by Alexa Garbarino

Warner Books, Inc.
1271 Avenue of the Americas
New York, NY 10020

Visit our Web site at
http://warnerbooks.com

W A Time Warner Company

Printed in the United States of America

Originally published in hardcover by The Mysterious Press.
First Paperback Printing: May, 1998

10 9 8 7 6 5 4 3 2 1

To those who lived:

Curtis K. Stadtfeld
Ray Puechner
—mentors—

To those who live:

Jim O'Keefe
The Gang at Sigma Video

And to those who will live forever:

Humphrey Bogart	Orson Welles	James Cagney
Lizabeth Scott	Ida Lupino	Virginia Mayo
Dick Powell	John Garfield	Dana Andrews
Gloria Grahame	Lana Turner	Joan Crawford
Alan Ladd	Fred MacMurray	George Raft
Veronica Lake	Barbara Stanwyck	Lauren Bacall
Glenn Ford	Burt Lancaster	Richard Widmark
Rita Hayworth	Ava Gardner	Marlene Dietrich
Robert Mitchum	Cornel Wilde	Kirk Douglas
Claire Trevor	Gene Tierney	Jane Greer

. . . Roll 'em!

REEL ONE
Mise-En-Scéne

One

IT WAS THE SUMMER of darkness.

It was the summer of darkness, and Ula McAdoo was responsible.

It happened this way. The previous autumn, Detroit Edison had made a brave effort to trim all the trees in Wayne County that waved to one another during windstorms, taking down electric lines and pitching most of southeastern Michigan back into the Mesozoic. The workers had polished their yellow hardhats, pressed their blue coveralls, buffed the steel toes of their work boots, gassed up their chainsaws, and hit the woods. Then Ula, aged seventy-four and living in Dearborn Heights with a cat named Buster, came home from the Monday night meeting of the Committee to Suppress Satanism at Disneyworld, found the top four feet missing from the cedar in her front yard, and sued Edison for a million. She settled for ten thousand and a bundle of striplings.

After that the chainsaws fell silent. Summer came, bringing its handy sampler of thunder, lightning, tornadoes, and gale-force winds, batting the trees about and twirling and snapping the electric lines like the threads in a fifty-dollar suit. By August, Wayne and Oakland counties had experi-

enced fourteen major power blackouts; rumor had it some
residents had been waiting for their service to be restored
since before Bastille Day. A couple of the dicier neighbor-
hoods in Detroit had taken to burning Edison's chief executive officer in effigy for the illumination, when what they
should have done was torch Ula's cat.

The latest outage struck just as I was about to push the
button of my snazzy new microwave oven for dinner. The
ceiling light flickered twice, then died to an amber glow.
After five minutes I unplugged the oven, refrigerator, and
television to avoid a surge, left the dish of frozen lasagna to
thaw on its own, snagged a bottle of Scotch and a bowl of
doomed ice from the dark refrigerator, and went out on my
toy front porch to plaster myself quietly in the dewy evening
cool. The days had been cracking ninety, with the humidity
just behind. I figured I had twenty minutes of peace before
the first of my neighbors fired up his portable generator.

It was a time for taking stock and reflecting. Business was
off, as it always was in vacation season, when George and
Marian loaded the kids and the luggage in the car and left
behind their regular extramarital affairs to make room for
the cabana boy and the anonymous divorcee with the tattoo.
All the best sins—adultery, employee theft, credit-card
fraud, Neil Diamond on the neighbor's stereo—were out of
town. All the private investigators, too; those who hadn't
blown the Tahiti fund on a space-age oven now pulling single duty as a cupboard, anyway. In the morning I would
make some calls. Cold calling was always something to look
forward to on a gummy August day when all the air condi-
tioners were down and there was nobody to take it out on but
the stranger on the other end of the telephone, looking for
work. I refilled my glass.

As I did so, a pint-size breeze lifted my hair where I sat
on a demoted kitchen chair and sucked the front door shut

behind me. There was a hint of brimstone in it. Another storm was on its way.

After a while a two-cycle motor started up down the block with a noise like marbles bouncing off a bass drum. In another minute or two, that mating call would be answered, and before long every generator on the street would be coughing up its lungs. I was thinking about taking my drinking paraphernalia inside when a black Jeep Grand Cherokee with green neon running lights turned the corner and boated my way, slowly, as if the driver was trying to read addresses in the steepening dark. It rolled along on jacked-up tires and a cushion of grumbling bass from a pair of speakers that were using the space where the back seat belonged. Rap, of course. I wondered, not for the first time, if anyone listened to those expectorated lyrics in his own living room with his slippers on.

The Jeep stopped in front of my house, rocking in place on the thick waves of sound washing out of its open windows, and the driver poked out his head. It was shaved at the temples, but long-haired in back, with a trailing moustache and pointed goatee and two or three gold rings glittering in one ear. In the green light coming up from below, the face looked like it belonged to Boris Karloff, Junior.

"Yo, Zeke!" he called to me. "Know where I can find a dude named Walker?"

I rubbed my chin, which needed scraping nearly as badly as his—but then it generally did from noon on—and spoke through my nose like Jed Clampett. "Wal, I believe if you was to turn left at the house where Wilbur Klumpp died, and went on past where the Bodie place used to be before it burned down, and turned right at Olson's Swamp, you'd find him plowing his pasture as like as not."

He scratched his nose, squinting at me against the dark of the house. "You're him, right?"

I said I was him. He might have been seventeen or twenty-three. The Auschwitz haircut put on as many years as it took off.

"Don't you answer your phone? My sister's been trying to get through to you for a half hour."

"The line's probably down. We had a storm earlier. Didn't you hear it, or were you listening to Snoop Doggy Dog?"

"Blowfish," he said. "She wants to see you." He gave me an address in West Bloomfield.

"She got a name?"

"Catalin. Gay Catalin. I'm Brian Elwood. I'm her brother."

"I guessed that when you told me she's your sister. This business, or does she want somebody to hold her hand until the lights come back on?"

"She had lights when I left. You're like a private eye, right?"

"Just like one. Only taller."

That one buzzed right past him. "A private eye's what she needs. Her husband split yesterday. She wants him back, Christ knows why. He's a major feeb."

The pickings there were too lean for me. I lit a cigarette. The air was still, and it had begun to heat up. Nothing like a breeze had ever come down that street. We were in for a big banger.

"I'll ride you on over," Brian Elwood said.

I pointed in the direction of the noise coming from the Jeep. "That a tape?"

"CD. I got Hammer, the Fat Boys, Rectal Itch—"

"Marcus Belgrave?"

"Who?"

"I'll drive my own heap, thanks. Tell her half an hour."

"You tell her. I'm off to Cherie's. Tits and ass."

He flashed me his pearlies and took off with a blat of twin pipes. Seventeen, definitely.

Lightning flickered in sheets over Windsor when I pulled out of the driveway. We had had a load of rain that year. The guy who read the weather on Channel 4 had traded his sport-coat for a white beard and cassock like Noah's. The mos-quitoes were as big as DC-3s. Doors stuck, freeways flooded, and a puddle had formed on the floor on the driver's side of my big Mercury. I was thinking of stocking it with trout.

The streets were dark, with here and there a light showing in a window like the outthrust tongue of a homeowner with a generator. The traffic light was out at Caniff. While wait-ing for the other drivers to work out who had the right of way, I punched a Sarah Vaughan tape into the deck. "Ain't No Use." The theme song of the professional information broker in the age of the hard drive.

West Bloomfield was nearly inseparable from Bloomfield Hills and Birmingham—"Bloomingham" was the local coinage—which had started out as the waiting room for Grosse Pointe, where auto money aged in big colonials fac-ing Lake St. Clair with lawns the size of small European countries. Now it was an end in itself, with its own waiting rooms in Farmington and Farmington Hills. Paved streets wound among modern homes with Sevilles parked in the driveways and security lights burning all night atop twenty-foot poles, shaming the stars. Well-dressed white children pounded basketballs off the concrete pads in front of the garages in the daytime, looking to fight their way out of the upper middle class with nothing but their trust funds and a dream.

The power failure had missed the Catalin neighborhood. It happens that way sometimes, democracy to the contrary.

All the windows were ablaze in the cool, sprawling ranch-style of brick and frame, the only house in a cul-de-sac that ended in a berry thicket and a chainlink fence. Four huge oaks were arranged on the lawn in such a way that the house would always be in shade. The brimstone smell was strong during the short walk from my car to the front door. It wouldn't be long now.

A thick-waisted woman in a gray dress and white apron, with her brittle black hair caught up by combs, listened carefully to my spiel, then shut the door in my face. A minute or so later she came back, led me into a large sunken living room with a conquistador's breastplate and weapons mounted above the stone fireplace, and went away. They aren't called maids anymore, but they still don't speak much English.

"Thank you for coming on such short notice, Mr. Walker. I'm Gay Catalin."

She'd come in through an open arch from a brightly lit room at the rear of the house when I was looking in another direction, a small compact red-haired woman with a forest of flowering plants behind her. That put her over forty, assuming she'd planned her entrance, with the light at her back. She had large eyes mascaraed all around, a pixie mouth, and a fly waist in a pale yellow dress tailored to show it off. The scent she wore was light and euphoria-inducing, like stepping out of a dank cellar into the sunshine; or it might just have been the flowers in the other room.

"I like your home." I borrowed a warm, slightly moist hand with light calluses—the kind you get from gardening—and returned it. "They don't design them this way since air conditioning."

"Neil has an instinct. He produces home-improvement videos, among other things."

"Neil's your husband?"

"Yes. Can I get you something to drink? I'm sorry to say Angelina has narrow ideas about her housekeeping duties."

"No, thanks. I left a pitcher of Scotch back home and it's the jealous type."

She laughed, a nervous little preoccupied laugh, and put her hands in the pockets of her skirt. She didn't know what else to do with them.

"I hope Brian wasn't rude. He's a good boy, essentially; he just runs with the pack. He's been living here ever since our mother died, and I suppose he finds us boring. Your office phone didn't answer, so I looked up your residence. When I couldn't get through, I didn't know what else to do but send him over."

"He was okay. He said your husband's missing?"

"It's official now. Twenty-six hours. I trust the police, but they're outnumbered by their cases. That's why I tried you."

"This puts me neck and neck with mine. Why me?"

"I saw your picture in the paper last year, when you testified against that man Matador. The killer. I remembered your name. I liked it; I still do. I don't know very much about hiring a private detective, Mr. Walker."

"I take it Neil isn't in the vanishing habit."

"No. He's never been gone without an explanation except for the time he was in the hospital."

"Accident?"

"No."

I was starting to get the idea. "Is that where you think he is this time?"

She shook her head. There was a tight vertical line between her eyebrows. "May I show you something?"

I said okay. She turned, taking her hands out of her pockets, and I followed her through another arch. We crossed a stainless steel kitchen hung with yellow curtains to match her dress and went down a quiet flight of open steps swathed in silver pile. At the foot we stood in a dark underground room smelling of furniture oil and new plastic. The only light came from the fixture in the stairwell.

She picked up a long black object from a table and pushed a button. Three black tubes mounted under the ceiling glowed and shot three colored shafts of light, red, green, and blue, at a forty-five-degree angle across the room, where they illuminated a screen six feet square. It was the first front-projection television set I'd seen outside of photographs in home theater magazines.

"Impressive." I waited.

Gay Catalin's face looked sickly in the reflected glow. "Neil's in there, Mr. Walker." She pointed at the empty screen. "That's where he's gone. I'm sure of it, and I want you to go in and bring him back out."

Two

SOMETHING SHOOK THE HOUSE to its foundation. There was a concussion like a sonic boom, followed by a rattle of caked mud or plaster falling between joists. The moment wasn't that dramatic; it was just the first sharp peal of thunder crossing the river from Canada. I groped at the wall near the stairs and tripped a switch. A row of indirect lights mounted behind a soffit came on, reflecting off a pale gray ceiling.

The room measured about eighteen feet by twelve, with a medium gray tweed carpet laid wall to wall and dark gray paneling on the walls. The panels were covered with some kind of spongy fabric that absorbed sound. There was a wet bar, two big recliners and a Chesterfield upholstered in charcoal Naugahyde, and a built-in cabinet containing stacks of video and sound equipment twinkling their digital readouts behind smoked-glass doors. The blue-green numerals provided the only color beyond the labels on the bottles behind the bar and a frieze of movie posters in gray steel frames continuing unbroken along all four walls. They looked like originals, and I was younger than the newest of them. Below them, a set of built-in shelves that I thought at first held books was packed instead with videotapes in gray plastic containers. There must have been a thousand of them, and twenty or more laser discs in the bottom of the smoked-glass cabinet.

"My husband's favorite room," said Gay Catalin. "He spends most of his time here when he's home."

I read the labels on the tapes. They were all hand-lettered in the same neat block capitals. Movie titles: *The Dark Corner, Edge of the City, Double Indemnity, Detour, The Asphalt Jungle*—not a Technicolor title in the pack, and none of them made after about 1955.

"I see he likes murder mysteries."

"Not just murder mysteries. Dark films with warped gangsters and neurotic heroes and dangerous women. Shiny wet streets and big black cars with their headlights on. There's a name for them." She hesitated. "My French isn't very good."

"*Cinéma noir.*"

"That's it. It means 'black films,' from the lighting and the mood. I don't think collecting them and watching them is a very healthy hobby."

"I like old movies myself. So far it hasn't landed me in psychiatric."

"You don't know Neil."

"Tell me about Neil."

"He's senior partner in Gilda Productions, a company that provides video features to cable television stations. He started it just after he graduated from Michigan, filming local commercials and documentaries, and now the firm has clients in New York, Los Angeles, and Hong Kong. Neil's forty-two; he's done all this in twenty years, the last eight of them married to me. I suppose he was past due for his little slip last year."

"That would be the hospital?"

She nodded. Her hands were back in her pockets. "He committed himself to a sanitorium. That was eighteen months ago, when the government was talking about regulating cable rates. His business was in a slump. The firm's attorney advised him to declare bankruptcy, but Neil insisted on paying back every creditor in full. It was too much for him, the worrying, the long hours. One day he left for the office and never showed up. The police traced him to the hospital after three days."

"Which hospital?"

"Balfour House, on Mackinac Island. You won't find it listed; it's private. I have the number, if you want to check it."

"Didn't you?"

"I called every hospital I could think of, public and private. No one's seen a man answering his description."

"How's he been lately?"

"Wired. We're just now getting back on our feet. I didn't think it was serious until his partner called yesterday asking where he was. He walked out in the middle of a meeting."

"Does he get along with your brother?"

"They get along. They don't joke and slap each other on the back. Did Brian say something?"

I passed that pitch. I was curious about what she'd said before, about Neil having gone into the TV screen, but I had another question to ask before I put up the detective's handbook.

"Any reason to suspect he might be romantically involved?"

"Yes, but I called her and she swears she hasn't seen him in months."

"I think I will have that drink. Can I make you one?"

She raised a smile then. She had to go deep for it—deep as the *Edmund Fitzgerald*—and what she brought up hardly seemed worth the dive. "I must look like I need it. Bourbon and ginger ale, please. There's a refrigerator under the bar."

I made two. I found a bottle of tonic water in the dwarf refrigerator and substituted it for ginger ale in mine. When we
were both provisioned I took a long cool sip. I wasn't thirsty.
The handbook didn't cover her casual answer to my last
question. As a rule they either threw a cleaver at me or cried
all over my lapels. I took a seat on the Chesterfield. Mrs.
Catalin perched on the edge of one of the recliners with her
ankles crossed. From that angle the white screen dominated
the room.

"Vesta's the name she uses," she said. "Vesta Mannering.
She claims to be an actress. In any case, Gilda Productions
employed her to appear in some of its features. Never mind
how I found out about her and Neil. It's been over for two
years."

"Does she still work there?"

"I made him fire her. Oh, it's a cliché, I know. Gilda
would certainly never have anything to do with it. The market for that kind of thing dried up a long time ago. I'm in
love with my husband, Mr. Walker. I'll do anything to keep
him. I guess in a way that makes us just alike."

I had some more bourbon. The quinine in the tonic water
transported me to a folding campstool outside a tent in the
Punjab, holding the frontier for Victoria. In another minute
a couple of thousand Bashi-Bazouks, mounted on camels
and swinging scimitars, would come pouring out of that
naked screen.

Gay Catalin leaned over and touched my wrist, and I was
back in West Bloomfield. The light found hairline creases in
her face. "I should explain something. The doctors at
Balfour House diagnosed Neil as an obsessive personality.
He's subject to binges."

"Alcohol or women?"

"Neither." She swept a hand around the room. "You said
you like these old movies. Neil sucks on them."

I said nothing. The place was full of hidden speakers, crackling faintly for want of a soundtrack to sink their teeth into.

"I used to watch with him, when we were first married and the collection was less than half this size. They're interesting, and many of them are as good as or better than anything they make today. But not as a steady diet. I don't think he even noticed when I stopped watching. Lately he's been spending every spare minute in front of that screen, exposing himself to I don't know how many murders, deceptions, and acts of sadism. It can't be healthy for someone with his history."

An empty cassette sleeve lay on the end table by the Chesterfield. *Pitfall,* starring Dick Powell, Lizabeth Scott, and Raymond Burr. I got up, opened the cabinet, and punched the EJECT button on the VCR. A tape licked out. *Pitfall.* It hadn't been rewound. "He was watching this one when?"

She looked at it. "Night before last. He disappeared the next day."

"When was the last time he got on this kick?"

"Just before he checked himself into the hospital on the island. That was six months after I found out about Vesta."

"Do you think there's a connection?"

"I called his doctor at the time and asked him the same thing. He said that was confidential. His name's Naheen, if you think you can do any better. Ashraf Naheen."

I made a note in my pocket pad and slid the videocassette into its sleeve. "All right if I take this tape with me?"

"Of course. You'll need a picture of Neil, too. And I suppose you'll want to look through his things." She stood, smoothed her skirt, and used the remote. The room seemed much bigger when the screen was dark.

"Where can I find Miss Manncring?" I asked on our way upstairs.

"She's listed in Iroquois Heights. But as I told you, she hasn't seen him. I believe her."

"I'd like to believe her in person. Who's your husband's partner?"

"Leo Webb. He's been with Neil much longer than I have. Almost from the beginning. Gilda Productions is in Detroit, the Consolidated Gas Building on Woodward. I'll give you a card."

Back in the living room she took a five-by-seven portrait out of its frame and handed it to me. Catalin was a representative specimen of middle-aging manhood, still youthful looking in an outworn way, like a necktie that's still in use after it's gone out of style; he had sad eyes, a jaw that lacked resolution, and dark hair thinning in front. Women that age tended to look hard, although Gay Catalin had dodged that bullet. Men just looked beaten.

There were some empty hangers on his side of the bedroom closet, but his wife couldn't say which of his clothes were missing. She summoned Angelina, who merely shrugged. Washington was recruiting its diplomatic couriers from the wrong class. Neil's home office, just off the bedroom, was small and windowless, with a desktop computer and printer on one of those homely assemble-it-yourself work stations. The computer didn't have anything to say to me, but then neither did a French waiter once he got a look at my suit. Catalin had the standard settings on his speed-dial: office, partner's home, 911, Little Caesar's Pizza. I punched his redial and got the time of day. That was more than anything I'd gotten so far.

He kept his checkbook and savings account passbook in an unlocked drawer. The last check he'd drawn had been made out to a video store in Birmingham for two hundred and change. Hard times weren't so hard he'd abandoned his obsession. He had twenty-seven thousand dollars in the joint savings account he shared with his wife. He hadn't made any substantial deductions in weeks.

That was it for the office. The room contained no personal items, nothing in the way of decoration. Setting it up wouldn't have taken him a tenth of the time he'd put into the movie room in the basement. I was starting to get a handle on Neil Catalin.

Gay was waiting for me in the upstairs hallway with her husband's business card. I glanced at it and put it in my wallet. While I had it out I said, "I get five hundred a day and incidentals. A day might be four hours. It might be twenty-three. It depends on what I pry up."

"Why just twenty-three?"

"I need more sleep than I used to."

She smiled then, and this one was worth getting wet for. Her face had a little color now. Score one for John Barleycorn. She went into the bedroom and came back out with a checkbook with a canary-yellow cover. Neil's was gray, like the cellar room. "Will a thousand do to start?" She began writing.

"If there's anything left over you'll get it back. It wouldn't be the first time I've delivered same-day service."

She tore off the check and gave it to me. "Where do you plan to begin?"

"First I'll touch bases with Webb. Then I'll give Doctor Naheen a whirl. I haven't been up to Mackinac Island this decade."

"He won't tell you anything."

"Who, Webb or Naheen?"

"Leo will talk your ear off if you let him. Naheen's a cold show. Most of those foreign-born physicians take that oath pretty seriously."

"There never was a horse that couldn't be rode."

She watched me put away the check. "What I said before, about Neil having gone into the screen downstairs."

"You were upset."

"I still am. I meant what I said."

I left space for her to fill. Lightning stuttered outside the window at the end of the hall, throwing one of the oaks in the yard into stark negative, white on black, with witch's fingers. The thunder was a while coming and might have been left over from another flash.

"You have to understand he might be unbalanced," she said. "The first time caught me off guard, but Lord knows I've watched enough of these things to recognize the plot. I think Neil wants to be one of those noir heroes, Mr. Walker. I think he thinks he's in a film."

I said I'd be in touch and went down to the ground floor and out. I wouldn't have taken that other flight of stairs that night for another thousand.

Three

THE RAIN HIT three blocks from the Catalins'. First came the wind, snarling through the leaf-heavy trees planted along the street with a noise like breaking surf. Then a great barbed fork of lightning turned the sky blue-white, thunder smashed, and the first drops struck the windshield, thumping like fingers on taut canvas and flattening out as big as rubber bathtub stoppers. Finally the clouds zipped open. Sheets of water slammed into the asphalt and wrapped themselves around the car like flypaper. I cranked the wipers up to Turbo, but it was like piloting the *Nautilus*. On Telegraph I drifted over to the right turn lane behind a dozen or so sensible drivers and set the brake. I smoked a cigarette while the car rocked in the gusts and other motorists— equipped, apparently, with periscopes—swept past down the remaining three lanes at normal highway speeds. If I had a cellular telephone I'd call my broker and invest in a body shop, if I had a broker and money to invest.

There was a chain video store in a strip mall up ahead on the right. I had an inspiration. I released the brake, crept around the cars standing in front of me with smoke creaming out of their exhaust pipes, and pulled into a handicap slot in front of the door. Ten minutes and twelve dollars later I ran back through the downpour with a rented VCR bundled inside my coat. On the off chance my power had come back on, I planned to put myself to sleep with the movie Neil Catalin had been watching just before he dropped out of sight. Maybe I could dream up his present location. Such things had been known to happen, although never to me.

The outlook was as dark as the streets. The rain had let up and Edison trucks were out, but the workers were all either sitting in the cabs waiting for the storm to pass or standing around in their shining ponchos trying to keep their cigarettes burning. Then I turned down Joseph Campau and the weather broke. It was still coming down on the Detroit side, but on the Hamtramck side where I lived, the stars were out and the puddles stood undisturbed on the pavement.

Two linemen in rain gear shared the bucket of a cherry-picker parked on my block, fiddling with the transformer atop the corner pole. As I cruised past I gave the thumbs-up sign to a third worker sitting at the levers. The bleak look I got back was familiar. I'd seen it often enough in mirrors to know the expression of a man who had no idea when he'd see his home again.

I carried Neil Catalin's video and the VCR in its satchel from the garage into the kitchen and flipped up the wall switch before I remembered, an automatic movement. Just at that moment the lights came on. I plugged everything back in and started the lasagna warming in the microwave. I hadn't eaten since late morning. The liquor I'd drunk was clawing at the lining of my stomach like feral cats tied in a gunnysack.

After supper I washed dishes, started a pot of coffee, and hooked the VCR up to the television set in my little cupboard of a living room. The job required written instructions and a number of venerable Anglo-Saxon words, but the coffee was ready by the time I finished. I set the tape rewinding and poured my first cup, yawning bitterly. It was just past 11:30 and felt much later. So far the forties were playing hell with my nocturnal inclinations. In another couple of years I'd be one of those people who ate breakfast.

The caffeine kicked in about the time the *Pitfall* title card pounced on screen with a burst of strings, and for the next ninety minutes I was nailed to the spot. It was a tense, tightly plotted crimer, made the way Hollywood made them in 1948 and then forgot how: Dick Powell, as a tired insurance agent slogging his way through midlife crisis, stumbles into an extramarital affair with smoldering Lizabeth Scott, running afoul of her boyfriend, a jailed embezzler, and a hulking, hormone-driven private eye played by Raymond Burr nine years before *Perry Mason* made him a star on television. Powell kills the boyfriend in self-defense, Scott shoots Burr, and Powell's marriage to Jane Wyatt is compromised, possibly forever. Scott, despite her sultry looks and husky voice the only true innocent in the triangle, gets the muddy end of the stick, arrested for defending herself from what today's criminal justice system would label a textbook stalker. There were plenty of tricky camera angles and lots of contrasty lighting, Burr in particular looming like an implacable ape in up-from-under shots with no fill.

It was a good movie. It wasn't worth stepping off the edge over, but then neither are most of the reasons men and women choose to turn their backs on a comfortable life and walk away into an uncertain night. When it was over I caught a rerun of *Green Acres* on Channel 20. After Perry Mason in a padded suit, even Mr. Haney looked good.

Morning was rain-scrubbed and cool. The cupola on top of the Fisher Building glistened like a copper bowl in the distance. The weather reader on the radio said that would all be over when a pressure center trundled in around noon—high or low never mattered in Michigan—dragging steep temperatures, thick humidity, and a fresh chain of thunderstorms. Up in Oakland County, fifteen hundred more households were without power since last night's blow.

I picked up the telephone to call Gay Catalin and ask if Neil had shown up, but the line was as dead as bell bottoms. That meant a trip to the office. On the way I stopped at the shrine of the clown for a cup of boiling coffee and sausage *tartare* on a biscuit with a frozen center. That didn't count as breakfast, so my record held. I parked in the defunct service station across from my building on West Grand River, gave the derelict who claimed he owned the spot a dollar to keep him from slashing my tires, and climbed the three stuffy flights to the Emerald City of Oz.

There were no bills or threatening letters on the floor inside the outer office, no Sicilians in sharkskins tossing the file cabinets, no flaming arrows stuck in the wall next to the print of Custer's Last Stand. On the other hand, there were no foreign princesses waiting to pay me a retainer in rubies or a harem, either: an atypical morning in the dangerous, glamor-soaked life of the globe-hopping P.I. I brushed the crumbs of yesterday's brunch off the swivel and put the telephone to work. Neil was still missing. Gay's voice did not belong to a woman who had ever smiled at me over a glass of Jack Black and Vernor's. Next I tried Leo Webb, Neil's partner at Gilda Productions, but a receptionist informed me Mr. Webb was away on business and wouldn't be available until tomorrow. Her voice dripped with air conditioning. She would have one of those plastic water bottles like runners drink from on the corner of her kidney-shaped desk.

I looked up Vesta Mannering in the outcounty directory and got a recording saying her telephone was out of order.

Those were the duty calls. I had a hunch about Dr. Ashraf

Naheen and the Balfour House. My hunches almost never worked out but they were nearly always fun to play. I called Detroit City Airport and got a ticket clerk named Alvin with a Memphis accent. I asked him for the best rate to Mackinac City.

"American Eagle's offering eighty-nine dollars round trip, but there's a catch."

"I have to ride outside?"

"Not quite that bad. You have to fly after ten P.M. and stay over two nights."

"Okay, book me."

"Sorry, sir. Everything after ten's full up. I could put you on standby."

"No, I'm all caught up in my reading. What else you got?"

"TWA has a commuter. One forty-three, with a penalty fee of fifty dollars for late changes."

"Any flights this morning?"

"Nothing today until four P.M."

"Four's swell. Book me."

"Sorry, sir. That one's been canceled."

"Hang on, Alvin." I parked the receiver, rolled back, opened the top drawer of the desk, picked up the .38 Detective's Special that lived there, and shook out all the shells. I put the revolver back in the drawer and the shells in the shaving mug where I keep my pencils and shut the drawer. I retrieved the receiver.

"Listen close, Alvin. I want a real seat on a real airplane, today if possible. Don't tell me about the ghost flights. If you do that to me one more time I'll feed you to a propeller."

Five minutes later I was ticketed for the 10:42 A.M. to Mackinac City, returning to Detroit at 8:15 P.M. I just had time to make one more call before leaving for the airport.

Dr. Naheen answered his own telephone, a surprise. He

had a colonial British accent and time to see me, if I didn't mind wasting my client's money since anything that had passed between Mr. Catalin and himself was cloaked by Hippocrates. I replied that no time spent on the island was ever wasted. That pleased him. Mackinites are proud of their little patch in Lake Huron.

It's a five-hour drive to the straits under the best circumstances. In late summer, with construction zones blooming like goldenrod all along U.S. 23, you mark your progress on a calendar. In the interests of time and Gay Catalin's money, I put up with an eighteen-seater with duct tape on the upholstery, a pilot whose voice was still changing, and no stewardess with a copy of *Forbes* and a glass of anything to take my mind off the engine shuddering on the left wing. We bumped around in the air for forty minutes, then drifted down through a tatter of clouds, and there was the tip of the mitten that is the Lower Peninsula, a dozen shades of green with blue water all around and the souvenir shops, confectionaries, and marinas of the resort city clinging to the mainland like kernels of colored glass.

That far north the air was noticeably cooler, with a stiff wind planing off the lake that bellied and popped the awnings over the store windows like sails. Even so, there wasn't a pair of long pants to be seen. Young women in cut-offs and blouses tied into big floppy bows under their breasts flashed their brown legs and flat bellies, old men in cocoa straw hats, madras shorts, and black socks complained to their wives that their feet hurt, and local youths with their shirttails out and their caps on back to front leaned against the light poles, belching and crumpling aluminum beer cans against their foreheads to impress the girls from downstate. The air was sticky with the sick-sweet smell of fresh fudge, a Mackinac trademark, and dirty white gulls swooped at crumbs on the sidewalk, crying like rusted hinges. Stalled cars, trucks, and RVs honked and overheated in every block. Autumn was on its way, and everyone in the Wolverine State was determined to get the last best out of the warm season if it killed him.

I was without a car, but in the only place in Michigan where it doesn't count. Ferries to and from the island measure the day into fifteen-minute blocks. From the moment you leave the gangplank until you get back aboard, you are in a different century. Automobiles have been banned from Mackinac Island for as long as there have been automobiles. Once there you get to where you're going by foot or bicycle or horse. Dogs die of old age on Mackinac Island.

During the brief trip over I smoked a cigarette in the bow, then took a bench seat to get out of the cold wind. The water was slate blue and shot with whitecaps to the horizon, where it turned brazen. I was the only passenger wearing a suit. I felt like a kid stuck in summer school.

At the dock a tanned teenager in running shorts and a T-shirt that read COED NAKED BROAD JUMP caught the rope thrown him by an old salt of twenty and tied it to a piling with a tire suspended from it. A rich brown odor reached my nostrils as I waited my turn at the gangplank. The sight of horses and carriages lined up on the other side of the dock told me it wasn't fudge.

I asked for directions to Balfour House from another veteran, wearing a retainer and handing out printed leaflets advertising Old Fort Michilimackinac. He said he'd never heard of it.

I had better luck with a driver waiting on the seat of a rubber-tired flatbed wagon for cargo. This one was absolutely decrepit, thirty if he was a day, in a tight maroon velvet vest with a white ruffle, white silk leggings, a black top hat, and his hair in a ponytail.

"That's a private house, mister. Nothing there for tourists."

"That's bad news for tourists." I waited.

"There's a bike rental up the hill. You don't look like a horseman."

"That's where you're wrong. I'm told I'm the spitting image of my great-grandfather. He was a U.S. marshal in Montana. Can I walk it?"

For no reason that I could see he leaned forward and patted the rump of one of the shaggy grays in the traces. Then he sat back. I never saw a man so far short of the half-century mark with so much time on his hands. "Work up a sweat. I'll take you there for two bucks."

"What about your load?"

He had a slow, easy grin. "Hell, mister. I was born here. There ain't nothing on this patch of grass won't wait an hour or a month."

"Isn't that the idea?"

He shrugged. It was like watching sand shift.

I thought a second, then climbed up beside him. When I sat down he gave me a worried look. "You don't live at Balfour, do you?"

I said I didn't.

"That's good. I can stand tourists okay. It's the professional crazies I can't hack." He gave the reins a flip.

Four

IT WAS A BRICK manor house, twenty or so rooms built on a stone foundation along lines more modest than either of its neighbors, a Queen Anne horned all over with gables and a Swiss chalet that looked like a cuckoo clock. A double row of narrow arched windows and a triangular lintel set on Doric columns flanking the front door gave the place an institutional air that may have influenced its sale. An embossed plaque set at the end of the concrete walk explained that the house was constructed on the site where Captain Henry Balfour was believed to have established his quarters while taking possession of Fort Michilimackinac in 1763. A professionally printed placard in the window to the left of the door warned visitors that it was a private residence.

A porter or something in a white coat and gray slacks let me into a blue-carpeted foyer and asked me to wait while he took my card into Dr. Naheen. There were no pictures on the walls, but a hall running straight through to the back of the house opened onto a picture window looking out on the lake, where boats with bright-colored sails skidded around, cutting white arcs in the blue water. Rembrandt couldn't have competed with that.

I waited five minutes. Nobody screamed, nobody in a white uniform hustled through carrying a butterfly net, nobody ran down the staircase dressed like Robin Hood. At the end of the wait the porter stepped in front of the view at the end of the hall and beckoned to me.

Ashraf Naheen rose from behind a big polished desk cluttered with executive toys and walked around it to take my hand. He wore a brown pinstripe three-piece suit tailored to make him look less small and less round. He had thick black hair combed straight back, showing the marks of the comb, round rimless glasses, and a moon face poured into the mold of a pleasant expression. I had a feeling a tidal wave wouldn't change it. A crooked scar above his lip, the result of an old surgery to correct a cleft palate, marred the smooth polished surface of his milk-chocolate–colored skin.

"I'm sorry I kept you waiting, Mr. Walker. I was just finishing a conversation with a guest."

"Not a patient?"

"We try not to use language that would make anyone feel he or she has been institutionalized."

"Which they are not."

"Admission to Balfour House is strictly voluntary. We are a private facility, and somewhat exclusive."

"That must explain why most of the locals don't know it from Brigadoon."

He adjusted his glasses and looked pleasant. "We treat cases of nervous disorder, as well as substance abuse. In some circles that is regarded as a badge of celebrity and fair game for the media. Our guests don't belong to those circles."

"I'm not a tabloid reporter, Doctor."

"You certainly don't look like one. Of course, that raises

the strong possibility that you are one. I assume you have the usual identification."

I showed him the investigator's license with my picture and my carry permit with my fingerprints. He wrinkled his brow at the latter.

"I hope you're not armed at present."

I shook my head. "I never met a horse I couldn't talk out of homicide."

The wrinkle vanished. "Understand, no one here is violent. Still—" He smiled pleasantly. "Will you have a seat?" He gestured away from the desk, in the direction of a cozy little conversation area in the opposite corner. This consisted of a brace of slingback chairs covered in coarse nubby green fabric, tough as steel, and a couch that was just a couch, not something to stretch out on while the nice doctor opened his steno pad and grilled you about your mother; that might have led to feelings of institutionalization.

The office was good-sized, not cavernous, and in an earlier incarnation had probably been a bedroom for the more important visitors, such as George III or Chief Pontiac. Cabbage roses bloomed on the pale green paper on the walls, which wore some good abstracts in rosewood frames and Dr. Naheen's diploma from the University of Michigan School of Medicine. The carpet was sculptured, a mottled pattern in beige and green, and the lamps on the desk and the glass-topped table in the conversation area were burning. They were necessary. Heavy curtains over the window behind the desk blocked out the sunlight, also the rest of the view of Lake Huron that began at the end of the hallway outside the room. No worldly distractions to upset the guests.

I sat down, found with surprise and pleasure a glass ashtray the size of a wheel cover on the low chrome-and-glass coffee table, and offered Naheen a Winston from the pack. He declined, slipping the band off a long green cigar he took from his pocket by way of explanation, and offered it to me in return. Having established that we were both satisfied with our own smokes, we fired them up and poisoned the air for a few seconds in silence.

I broke it. "Neil Catalin was a guest last year?"

"I'm afraid I cannot answer any questions about Mr. Catalin's case. I explained that when you called." He hiked up his trouser cuffs and sat on the couch, reinhaling through his nose the fumes he'd just exhaled. An addictive type, Dr. Naheen. Most cigar smokers didn't take the stuff into their lungs even once.

"You wouldn't be violating anything if you told me when was the last time you saw him."

"He left Balfour House February fifteenth of last year," he said. "I looked it up after you and I spoke. I haven't seen or heard from him since."

"I know a little about his case. I won't ask you to interpret his dreams. I need answers to some general questions about his particular psychosis."

He frowned pleasantly and cocked the hand holding the cigar; the tolerant judge allowing an irregularity to continue until he decided to throw it out of court.

"He's a classic crime film buff," I said. "His wife says he's loony on the subject. Day before yesterday he disappeared after bingeing on Bogart and Dick Powell and Fred MacMurray in the movie room in his basement. Mrs. Catalin thinks he's gone off to live the life of a Hollywood hero. How's that square with your experience and training?"

"That would be a classic schizophrenic reaction to a traumatic episode. Wish fulfillment. Freud coined the term. After he had subjected a series of his patients' recurring fantasies to analysis—"

"Doctor." I spoke gently. "I have a flight out in seven hours."

The eager gleam faded out behind his glasses. He drew in a chestful of smoke and watched it find its way back out. "Don Quixote complex. It predates the invention of the motion picture by several thousand years. Cervantes put a name to it when he wrote about his demented knight-errant. Whether because of abuse, sudden trauma, or long-standing feelings of inferiority, the victim decides that his own life has become unbearable, and so co-opts the life of someone he admires, preferably a creature of the imagination, since the genuine article is often a disappointment. We've all known the urge. James Thurber's fictional Walter Mitty represents us all, daydreaming while stuck in traffic of winning the big game, saving the great man's life, impressing the beautiful woman with one's swordsmanship; the sword, of course, representing—"

"Wilkinson razors. I'm not out to cure the guy, I just want to find him and bring him back to his wife."

"That would be a Sherlock Holmes complex. Another manifestation of the same obsessive compulsion."

"Yeah. Fortunately, mine pays the bills." I was beginning to have had enough of Dr. Naheen; a new record.

I went fishing.

"How often does Walter Mitty actually put on armor and duke it out with windmills?"

"Almost never. In fifteen years of practice I have yet to encounter an authentic case. If Mr. Catalin has begun to exhibit classic schizophrenic behavior, I hope he consults me. I'd like to publish a paper."

"So you think it's possible his wife is right."

"I didn't say that."

The water was too cold for worms. I threw it away and tried a spooner.

"You said it could have been triggered by a traumatic episode. Do severe business problems qualify as traumatic?"

"Only if you use the term very generally. By definition, trauma refers to life-threatening incidents. Freud to the contrary, the will to survive is much stronger than the human sex drive."

"That sounds like your pet theory."

He waved the cigar. "I've written upon the subject for the psychiatric journals."

"What about sex?"

"It has its importance. It isn't paramount. If you want my opinion, I think dear old Sigmund needed desperately to get laid."

I smiled; not for the reason he thought. A professional man who has been bitten by the competitive bug is already sniffing at the lure.

"A man struggling hard to avoid bankruptcy," I said, "whose marriage is in trouble because of an affair; could that make him suicidal?"

"In some cases, yes . . ."

I jumped in ahead of the *but* with waders on. "So his life can be said to be threatened."

He shook his head, trying to spit out the hook. "You speak as if the situations were simultaneous, when in fact six months—" His pleasant expression deserted him at last.

A hit.

He cleared his throat, leaned forward, and tipped a column of ash into the big glass tray, nodding, as if in approval of the perfect cylinder. "It's a pity you haven't a medical degree, Mr. Walker. I could use you on my staff."

"I can't even fix a toaster." I pretended to consult my notebook while he reassembled the elements of his professional imperturbability. If I rubbed it in now I'd lose him for good. It was enough to know that Catalin had felt sufficiently guilty over his fling with Vesta Mannering to confide it to his analyst half a year after the fact. That took him out of the casual philanderer category. I'd won myself a free game, and to hell with the angling metaphor. I was still seasick from the ferry.

"I guess the bonus question is does a Walter Mitty have it in him to become a Don Quixote? Can a dreamer be a doer?"

"Most definitely. That's the whole point of giving in to a fixation."

I looked up from the notebook. "There's a point?"

"Of course. It's always a matter of choice. On that one thing, Freud and I are in total accord. Nothing happens by accident."

He parked his cigar and braced his hands on his fat thighs, warming to the subject. He had stamped out his own brief flare of inferiority. In his case it would always be a temporary aberration.

"If you dislike the suit of clothes you're wearing strongly enough, eventually you will change suits. If you hate yourself—totally, violently, with the deep self-loathing of the true paranoid schizophrenic—you will become another person. Not just think. Become."

I was looking at my own double reflection on the surface of his glasses. It seemed to me one of the images was distorted. "We're talking Jekyll and Hyde."

"Robert Louis Stevenson was a thinker ahead of his time. A psychosis, Mr. Walker, is like a drug. Indulge in it, and your personality changes. Your dress, bearing—even such benchmarks as the set of your features and the timbre of your voice—will be altered nearly beyond recognition. Any estimation you may have formed of Mr. Catalin's abilities and temperament based on information supplied by his wife and friends is useless. He may be smarter, stronger, and more athletic than the person you were hired to find. He will almost certainly be more dangerous."

Five

I LEFT HIM, a pleasant-looking brown man in a green office, and stood on the front doorstep for a minute, replacing the nicotine in my system with the clear sharp sopping air off the lake and wondering what I was going to do with the next six hours and change. I wasn't dressed for strolling on the beach and I didn't care that much about seeing how fudge is made.

"I guess Doc Ashraf didn't find you batty enough to keep."

I turned my head. The flatbed wagon that had brought me there was drawn up down the block, the ponytailed driver in the Regency get-up lounging sideways on the seat with his stovepipe hat on the back of his head and one silver-buckled shoe propped up on the whipsocket. He was munching on a Clark bar.

I said, "I guess that cargo's still gathering barnacles on the dock."

"Zebra mussels, actually. They're getting to be a bitch: choking out all the other marine life, snagging the inlets. We'll get rid of them someday. Then flocks of giant boat-eating seagulls will fly up from Brazil or someplace like that and screw up the fishing. We go from crisis to crisis here. But at least we ain't got Democrats. I'm on a sugar break.

Want some?" He held up the remaining half of the candy bar.

I shook my head, but the suggestion had started my stomach juices going. "Anyplace around here a fellow can get lunch without hocking an heirloom?"

"I could eat too. Hop aboard." He took his foot off the whipsocket.

In a little while he trotted the horses up a hill and drew rein in front of a colonnaded porch the length of the *Queen Mary*. A double row of windows with green shutters and a lookout tower overlooked the straits, where a long hog-nosed ore carrier was grunting its way along the channel from Lake Michigan, bound for the steel-rolling mills in Detroit and Cleveland. Old Glory fluttered from staffs on the porch railing and a hundred or so people in white duck trousers and pastel frocks strolled its red-carpeted length, looking like no more than half a dozen, spread out as they were along that great expanse.

"I said I wanted to hang on to my watch," I said. "This is the Grand Hotel."

"I know. I used to climb on the roof."

They charged you just to step onto the porch; it was the longest in the world, the sign said, and your life wasn't complete until you'd walked it. The fellow who took the money, a distinguished-looking black in his fifties in a red coat and white gloves, glanced at my companion and waved us on through.

"Stab in the dark," I said as we whisked past the line waiting inside for a table. "You're the governor's bastard son."

"Close. Hi, Henry. Snake pit taken?

The man behind the reservation desk, also black and edging into old age in the same uniform, smiled, but only with his eyes. "Hello, Tommy. No, today I'm feeling kindly toward my fellow creatures. Does your friend have any objection to crab cakes?"

I said I didn't. There must have been a bright answer to that one, but I couldn't find it.

Tommy led the way unassisted to a table the size of a corn plaster, jammed between the bandstand and the swinging doors to the kitchen. We were almost behind the backdrop. My view of the entertainment was blocked by an amplifier as big as a refrigerator.

"Nothing to see anyway." My companion took off his hat and stuck it under his chair. "They don't play till dinner, and then you can't hear your fork hit your plate."

"What's the story on the crab cakes?"

"Price of a free meal. You can order anything you like as long as the chef forgot and salted it twice."

"Or dropped it."

He shook his head. It was a good head without the hat, broad across the brow and tanned evenly below the white streak where the band rested. His eyes were blue and clear and smiled at the corners, even when his mouth did not, like the headwaiter's. "Not at the Grand. Gerald Ford dined here when I was twelve."

"What were you at twelve, besides the apple of Henry's eye?"

"Same thing I am now; an island brat. My parents were caretakers of one of the summer houses here. Every Friday night the owners were away, they drank. Every night they drank, I ran away. Here's where I ran. The hotel staff practically adopted me. Did I mention the owners of the summer house were away most of the time?"

"I figured it out." I waited. I wondered how long it would take him to get around to offering to show me the island for a fee. I doubted he just didn't like to eat alone.

A waiter came and went with our drink orders: Chablis

for me, to show I knew what went with shellfish; mineral water with a twist for Tommy. He wouldn't be a drinker.

He got to it. "You said you're not staying at Balfour?"

"No, I shrink my own."

"Checking out the place for a relative?"

"I'm fresh out of those."

When he realized I wasn't going to add anything he sat back. "Good thing it isn't clams. That would make you a cannibal."

"I'm a private cop on a case," I said. "That doesn't mean I don't want to take in any of the sights while I'm here, if the tariff isn't too steep."

He thought about that for a second. Then he rose.

"Enjoy your lunch. I hope you fall off the ferry on your way back." He pushed in his chair and started around the bandstand.

I kicked the chair back out. "Sit down. I said I was a private cop. Invitations to dine in the linen and silver joints don't come my way every day. You look for strings."

He stood with his tongue bulging one cheek. "If that's an apology, I'll consider accepting it."

"When will you know?"

He grinned then and sat down. Our drinks came, and right behind them another waiter unfolded an aluminum stand next to the table and set a tray on it and served the crab cakes and steamed vegetables, arranged artfully on the hotel's simple china plates.

"I wanted to warn you about Balfour, in case you were thinking of putting someone in there," Tommy said when we were alone. "Don't."

The crabs weren't salty at all, just heavy on lemon. They tasted better than anything I'd eaten that year. "The place looked respectable enough."

"The place may be. Naheen isn't. Parks and Recreation

have been trying to shut him down for years. You know Mackinac's a state park."

"The only one in the country where automobiles are prohibited. I picked up a pamphlet when I bought my ticket for the boat."

"Naheen's got a friend or something in Lansing; otherwise he'd be back on the mainland writing self-help books. Did he tell you he videotapes his sessions with patients?"

I said he hadn't. I put down my fork. I didn't want to miss anything under the sound of my own chewing.

"He doesn't even tell them he does it. As far as they know his little spiral pocket notebook is the only record of their relationships with their mothers."

"If he doesn't tell them, who told you?"

"I've been delivering books and equipment there for years. Handymen talk." He shoveled down the last of his crab cakes and chased them with mineral water. There wasn't too much lemon for him either. "What do you figure he does with those tapes?"

"*America's Funniest Home Videos* comes to mind."

"They don't pay enough. Place like that, on an island like this, the patients' average income's got to be up around the president's. Conservative estimate. They're executives, politicians, sons and daughters of captains of industry. People in trouble with money to spend and appearances to maintain."

I drank some wine. "Where'd you go to school?"

"Mackinac Island Post Office. I was too busy running away to graduate the regular way, so I did it by mail later. Also I read a lot. Not much else to do when you spend most of your time waiting for passengers and cargo. You don't need a Ph.D. to guess what Doc Ashraf's got going after hours."

"Blackmail's not the kind of charge you guess about," I said. "What've you got?"

"I got a job and a two-room gatehouse I rent off a lawyer from Alpena who can't bring himself to tear it down. If I had anything more than that, so would the law. I love this place. I don't like to see these downstaters come up here and piss in my lake."

"I'm not investigating Naheen. Sorry."

His face fell, but he caught it. He tipped up his glass, found it empty, and pushed it away. "Well, that's that. I got my hopes up when you said you were a detective. I thought maybe the family of one of the crazies had hired you to turn him upside down and see just what kind of heel he is. I should know by now things don't work out that neat. Just a dumb island hick."

"Not."

His eyes smiled back. "I don't suppose free irregular goods from the kitchen buy me what you *are* working on."

"This one's no secret. I'm looking for a bird named Neil Catalin. His wife wants him back in the cage." I took the posed portrait shot out of my inside breast pocket and handed it to him.

He studied it a moment, then gave it back. "Never saw him. I don't see everybody who comes and goes. We recycle a couple of million tourists a summer."

"It wasn't summer, and he wasn't here to look at the fort. He was at Balfour House in February of last year."

"Not even the governor comes here then. It's colder than a bitch in February. I must have been working on the other side of the island. Winters I shovel out driveways. What's he do?"

"His company produces videos."

After a moment he plucked a roll from the basket on the table and began buttering it elaborately. I had a feeling he didn't want a roll. "That's interesting, considering what I just told you about Naheen."

"Interesting is all it is. If he hamstrung horses on the side, from time to time he might treat a patient who breeds trotters. It doesn't mean there's a connection."

"It would be worth looking into."

"It's worth filing away until I hit a wall. Right now I've got a couple of better leads."

He put down the roll untasted and tugged back one of his lacy cuffs to consult his Casio. "I'd better load some crates. You ought to check out Pontiac's Trail while you're here; it offers the best view of the lake and the Big Mac bridge. Then there's high tea here at the hotel at four. Finger sandwiches and sherry."

"I may give the trail a look. One glass of sherry and I'm wrapping myself in a tablecloth and reciting Marc Antony's speech from *Julius Caesar*."

"Yeah, I believe that. Sure I do." He stood and stuck out his hand. "You never told me your name."

"Amos Walker." I rose. He had a strong grip and didn't feel any need to crush knuckles to prove it.

"Tom Balfour." A slow grin spread over his angular face as he watched it sink in. "That's another reason I want Naheen's wings clipped. Great-Great Grandfather wouldn't take kindly to having the family name taken in vain."

Six

THE EIGHT-FIFTEEN to Detroit took off promptly at nine forty-seven. Ninety minutes earlier, having strapped ourselves in and made our separate peaces with God, fourteen passengers including me were asked to get off and walk back to the terminal when the starboard engine quit on the runway. The wait would be no longer than fifteen minutes. After half an hour of tinkering, the maintenance crew off-loaded the luggage and towed the plane to the nearest Mr. Goodwrench. Much later, over Detroit City Airport, another storm kept our replacement ship circling until the pilot checked the fuel gauge, pushed his cap forward like Errol Flynn, and plunged down a black funnel chased with streaks of lightning, bringing us in at a sixty-degree angle that cracked an axle and shook loose all the overhead oxygen masks. I didn't expect to experience another case of hiccoughs that year.

My telephone was ringing when I got home around midnight.

"Mr. Walker, this is Gay Catalin. I wasn't sure if your phone was working."

"It wasn't this morning. You're my first call. Any sign of your husband?"

"No. I wanted to find out what you've learned."

"I don't like flying; but then I knew that before. I went up and talked with Dr. Naheen today."

"And?"

"He's a clam, like you said. Do you know if he and your husband ever had any business dealings aside from doctor and patient?"

"No. I never heard his name until the police found Neil at Balfour House the last time. Neil wouldn't discuss him with me afterward, or anything else that went on up there. Did Naheen say something?"

"Not about that. Just an island rumor. I'll report when I have something."

"Are you still planning to talk to Vesta?"

"More than ever. Naheen's a clam, but a clam can be opened if you know the trick. It might comfort you to know Neil didn't make it a habit to skip around on you. The Vesta thing bothered him a lot. I want to ask her why."

There was a pause on her end. Then, "I'd like to think it was his conscience."

"So would I. If it wasn't, I've got another haystack to look under."

There was another silence. I wondered if she was sitting in the room full of flowers. "Something else has happened. It might not mean anything, but I feel I should tell you about it. Brian didn't come home last night. I haven't seen him since I sent him to talk to you."

Brian was the brother in the rolling boom box. I'd forgotten he existed. "He told me he was on his way to Cherie's. It's a strip joint in Ypsilanti. He might still be there. Sometimes the help forgets to sweep under the tables."

"He goes there often. I called and spoke to the manager. He was there last night. Nobody saw him leave, and they haven't seen him since. I'm not alarmed. Brian's not like Neil; he stays away days at a time sometimes. He has his own income, from a trust fund our parents set up. Probably he's shacked up with one of his teenage tramps. I just thought you should know, in case you think the disappearances are related."

"Right now I'm not sure how the Marx Brothers are related. So far it's a puzzle without any pieces. If I see Brian I'll shoo him on home."

"Thank you." Her tone lifted. "How'd you find the island?"

"Easy. I just followed the smell of fertilizer."

When we were through talking I dialed Vesta Mannering's number. I didn't get Ma Bell's scratchy apology this time, but on the other hand I didn't get Vesta either. I fixed myself a nightcap and went to bed.

Over coffee and my second cigarette of the day I called Gilda Productions. The same air-conditioned female voice treated me to a medley of Billy Ray Cyrus' greatest hit and then Leo Webb came on. He spoke in clipped, executive-issue tones with no accent at all; he'd been in Michigan a very long time, if he hadn't actually been born here.

"You said you're a detective? I hope you've got something more for me this time than just questions. I'm out better than twenty grand."

"Oh?"

"It's all in your report, for chrissake. Why do you bother to write them up if nobody reads them? Some of that equipment was still in the box."

"Video equipment?"

"Video *and* sound: four cameras, two sound mixers, a seven-channel equalizer, a laser disc player, and eight speakers. Not to mention half a mile of copper wire and I don't know how many gold-plated connectors. All studio quality, none of that Radio Shack shit. Twenty thousand *wholesale*.

I can't tell you what all that's worth on the street. That's
your job."

"Is it?"

He started to say something else, then broke off. When he
spoke again, the guards were up. "Who did you say you
were?"

"Amos Walker."

"My secretary said you were with the police."

"If she's a good secretary, she said I'm a detective. That's
what I told her. Gay Catalin hired me to find her husband. I
understand you're partners."

He came back at me from another channel entirely, cour-
teous and jovial. He had some pretty impressive sound
equipment of his own. "Oh, I wouldn't worry so much about
Neil. He's always been the creative half of our association.
I imagine he's off on one of his intellectual benders.
Probably show up bright and early tomorrow morning,
spewing French phrases and working his hands like an old-
fashioned crank camera."

"His wife says this only happened once before."

"From home, yes. Around here we're used to his missing
meetings and not coming back from lunch. Neil's a dreamer.
I'm not knocking it; it was his dream that started Gilda. I'm
what keeps it going. I do all the scutwork."

"I'd like to come in and talk with you about him. Just in
case he doesn't show up tomorrow morning."

A Rolodex clattered on his end. "I can give you fifteen
minutes at nine-forty-five this morning. I was planning to
use them to go over my notes for a presentation I'm making
tomorrow, but I know it cold. Don't be late."

I started to say I didn't intend to, but I was talking to a dial
tone.

My Mercury didn't want to start. I flooded it, waited five
minutes, then shoved the accelerator to the firewall and

ground it into life. It had been done quicker by others, but I didn't have a hunchbacked assistant. It was time to think about new wheels.

Gilda Productions had a suite on the seventeenth floor of the Michigan Consolidated Gas Company Building on Woodward, a furnace-shaped skyscraper with a lobby out of Cecil B. DeMille, complete with sparkling blue lights mounted under the thirty-foot ceiling and a bronze ballerina pirouetting among exterior pools, looking faintly afraid to be caught downtown without a stun gun and a can of Mace under her tutu. A black security guard in gray twill pants and a white short-sleeved shirt with a gold badge over the breast pocket watched me read the directory and walk to the elevators, one hand resting on the flap of his holster. It was time to think about a new suit as well.

I found the reception area behind a brass-bound door with the outline of an attenuated woman in an evening dress etched Deco-style on the glass. An Asian woman in her late twenties, less attenuated, sat behind a glass desk—not kidney-shaped after all—tapping a set of coral nails against the handset of a slimline telephone, obviously on hold. She had on a champagne-colored silk blouse with a matching floppy bow tie, pink buttons in her ears, and at least three coats of lacquer that turned her face into an ivory mask. Her straight black hair was cut in a page boy that threw off blue haloes.

She lifted a pair of razor-thin eyebrows when I stopped in front of the desk; then just as I opened my mouth, jerked her head down and spoke into the telephone. "Yes. Oh, not long, seven and a half minutes or so. No, my right hand needed the exercise anyway. Well, if he's left for the day, don't you think you might have found that out and told me when I still had circulation in that hand? Yes, I'd be grateful when he checks in if you'd tell him I called. Thank you so much."

She clapped the receiver into its cradle. "Idiot. Are you here to see Mr. Webb?"

I nodded. "Did they make you listen to Country or the Best of Broadway?"

"Sondheim. Do you suppose anyone ever listened to 'Send in the Clowns' voluntarily?"

"You played 'Achy Breaky Heart' for me yesterday."

A nose got wrinkled. "If I had anything to say about it, you'd get Mozart. Are you Mr. Walker?" She had a finger on a leather-bound appointment book lying open before her.

I said I was. She relayed the information through an intercom and sat back, steepling her fingers. "He'll be out in a minute. This is about Mr. Catalin's disappearance?"

"I heard he left pretty abruptly."

"Right in the middle of a meeting. He swept past this desk and right on out without a word."

"Was he in a hurry?"

"I wouldn't say that, exactly. But he was preoccupied. It wasn't like him not to say a word to me in passing. Do you think you can find him?"

"I didn't say I was looking for him."

She was deciding whether to be annoyed by that when Leo Webb came in through a plain glass door behind the desk and shook my hand. He was my height and slender, a year or two older than his partner, although his shaved head and hairless face blurred the distinction. His suit was tailored snugly and there was something about the knot of his silk tie that said he'd given it a jerk and a lift just before his entrance. His eyes were like glass shards, pale and hard.

"How do you do? Sorry about that mix-up over the phone. We had a theft from our studio in Southfield last week. A roomful of equipment walked out an unlocked back door with the alarm turned off. I wanted to strap every employee there to a lie detector but my lawyer says no. I'm shopping for a new lawyer."

"That Bill of Rights is a bitch," I agreed.

He steered me through the door and down a short hallway hung with eight-by-ten portraits of nobody I knew into his office, an enchanted grotto crusted over with Renaissance paintings in heavy carved frames and plaster cherubs teetering on Greek columns. There was a mahogany Empire desk with gold inlay, as big as a bed, and behind it a throne upholstered in wine-colored velvet perched on a swivel.

"Props." Webb palmed the head of a three-foot fountain sculpture in what looked like solid marble of a small curly-haired boy pouring water from an urn and lifted it one-handed. "It's all right if you don't like the place. My first two wives pronounced it hideous."

"It's different."

"That's the diplomatic answer. It's a sure-fire litmus test for detecting phonies. They get all wet over it. One of them asked me for the name of my decorator." He laughed; a short, hard sound, like metal striking concrete.

"If they fail the test, do you refuse to do business?"

"Not really. As a matter of fact, in this business the straight shooters are the hardest to handle. Are you a straight shooter, Mr. Walker?"

"I miss four times out of ten."

"In baseball you'd be batting six hundred. In business—" He shrugged the shrug morticians shrug when the conversation turns to death.

At his invitation, I sat in a wingback chair covered in imitation zebra skin. This put me an inch or two below him when he took his throne. That was okay. I wouldn't recognize equal footing if I had it.

"What can you tell me about the meeting Catalin walked out on?" I asked.

A gilt Diana stood on one foot on a corner of the big desk, notching an arrow into her bow. Webb stroked the point with a fingertip. "It was just Neil and me. I don't remember what we were talking about specifically, just the usual Tuesday bull session: future projects, old business, how to avoid paying Michigan's chickenshit single-business tax and stay out of court. Nothing for either one of us to get our shorts into a wad over."

"That's what you were talking about when he walked out?"

"You've used that phrase twice, 'walked out.' It's a poor fit for someone like Neil. If he were standing on the edge of a cliff and you pushed him, he'd just go ahead and fall. Grabbing your arm would be rude. As I recall he excused himself to get something from his office. When he didn't come back I went looking for him. Ms. Yin said he'd left. I called his home, but Gay said she hadn't seen him since that morning."

"Ms. Yin is the receptionist?"

"Also our secretary. We downsized the staff when the cable companies pulled in their horns."

"Did Catalin take his car?"

"He must have. It wasn't in the lot when I went home later. Last year's LeBaron—gray, naturally. He could afford to drive better, but cars don't mean much to Neil. His sense of style matches his color preference."

"Where does Vesta Mannering fit in that picture?"

The glass shards dulled. It was as if a transparent membrane had slid down over them, like a salamander's. "Well, well. Gay made a clean breast."

"Were you the one who told her about her husband's affair?"

"Christ, no. That would be a violation of the male code."

"You knew about it, then?"

"You can't keep that kind of thing secret in an office. We cast Vesta as the seductress in a PSA about AIDS, and I'm here to tell you there was never a better example of casting according to type. She auditioned here and shot in Southfield. Neil spends a lot of time at the studio, which is his real bent. He was making student films at Michigan, you know, when I was getting my MB. That's where we met."

"I didn't know."

"Oh, yeah. He was Orson Welles to my Bill Gates. I said he was the creative half. Anyway he spent a lot of time on the set, and by the time Vesta came back here to collect her paycheck, those two were striking sparks like a Zippo. Even the kid who delivers sandwiches had to know there was something going on."

"Gay Catalin says she made Neil fire her."

"She may have told him to, and maybe he canceled any plans he had to cast her in other projects. It was a ten-day shoot. She finished and went on her way."

I made a note. "Do you know where Miss Mannering is working? I haven't been able to get her at home."

"I'll ask Judy to look her up in the file." He glanced at a heavy gold watch strapped to his wrist, to show me he'd meant what he said about fifteen minutes.

"How's Neil been acting lately?"

"Same as everyone in this goddamn business, jumpy. The Democrats threaten to shut down television violence, the Republicans threaten to cut public broadcasting subsidies, some little old lady in Taylor complains about her cable bill, and everyone scrambles for a parachute. If it's security you're after, take a civil service exam."

"You wouldn't know that to see this office," I said. "Not everything in here is fake."

He smiled at his reflection in a jade bowl containing erasers and paper clips on the desk. "I admit I'm a sucker for plush things. On top of that I'm supporting two ex-wives and a house in Farmington Hills. It helps to be hungry when you're in charge of financing. God knows Neil isn't. You'll probably find him in a little shit theater someplace, watching *The Seventh Seal* for the thousandth time."

"Can I see his office?"

"I'll have Ms. Yin show you." He reached for his intercom.

When he was through, I thanked him for his time. We shook hands. At the door I said, "Mrs. Catalin's brother is missing, too. His name's Brian Elwood. Do you know him?"

No cloudy membrane now; his eyes would cut paper. "He came to take Neil home once when his car was in the shop. I caught the little punk going through Neil's desk while he was in the john. He said he was looking for cigarettes. I told him if I saw him around here again I'd call the police. I will, too. A thief is worse than a murderer in my book."

I let myself out.

Seven

JUDY YIN WAS WAITING for me in the hallway. She was tall for an Asian, which made her medium height by American standards, the top of her head just clearing my shoulder in three-inch heels. Her smile was cool, as might be expected. Nothing about her would bring water to a boil; around the office, anyway. I'd had some experience with these professional types.

"Mr. Catalin's office is this way, Mr. Walker." She opened an arm and followed it. I followed her. She wore trim-fitting brown stirrup pants with the champagne-colored blouse, and she hadn't anything in the pockets.

Neil Catalin's office was a poor working cousin of his partner's, a third smaller and less demanding on the eye. It had a plain desk and file cabinet and a chipboard table containing a combination TV and VCR with a ten-inch screen and a stack of videotapes in plastic sleeves. A computer terminal on a stand, too, of course, but the hell with that. It wouldn't tell me anything the rest of the office and a kid with glasses in South Bend didn't already know. The only personal items were a smiling picture of Gay Catalin in a silver frame on the desk and a two-by-three-foot movie poster behind glass on one wall: *Gilda*, starring Rita Hayworth and Glenn Ford.

The painting of the red-headed bombshell dancing in a low-cut evening gown was nearly identical to the etching on the glass door leading into the reception area. That explained the name of the outfit.

The receptionist hovered inside the door. I said, "Mr. Webb said you'd look up Vesta Mannering's work number."

"Yes, I'll do that before you leave." She leaned against the door frame and crossed her arms.

I opened the desk drawers and found the usual desk stuff, rubber bands and pencil shavings and unremarkable contraband. The message pad by the telephone was blank. None of the titles hand-lettered on the videotape sleeves on the table meant anything to me. I poked one into the gate and turned on the TV. I watched two minutes of an infomercial for a miraculous new product that turned fresh fruit into compost.

"One of our most successful projects," said Ms. Yin when I turned it off. "Our client sold sixty thousand units in Metropolitan Detroit alone."

I tried the drawers of the file cabinet. They were locked. I made a show of giving up and looked at my watch. "Okay if I call my answering service?"

"If it's local."

The first button on the telephone lit up when I lifted the receiver. I punched Line 2 and dialed the number for Gilda Productions.

The telephone rang in the reception area. Judy Yin stirred and withdrew to answer it. I laid the receiver on the desk and inspected the file cabinet. It was a standard bar lock, as old as the chastity belt. I had it open with my pocket knife in two seconds. Inside I found files. Not one of them was labeled WHERE I WENT.

Disappointed, I closed the drawers, jimmied the lock back the other way, and returned to the desk. Ms. Yin was still telling the telephone hello. I punched the button for Line 1 and hit redial. That was the line Catalin had used last, unless someone else had made a call from his office recently. On the second ring a woman's voice, metal with a serrated edge, answered.

"Musuraca Investigations."

I hung up just as Judy Yin came back. "Did you get your messages?"

I said I got one.

"That puts you one up on me," she said. "There was no one on the other end."

"Kids."

She swung a hard glance around the office that stopped at the file cabinet. She went over to it and tugged at one of the drawers. When it didn't budge she made a noncommittal little noise and turned my way.

"Ziggy's Chop House on Livernois. Miss Mannering's a little hostess there, or was when she left that number." She gave it to me.

I didn't bother to write it down. I knew Ziggy's. I looked at Judy Yin. Her black eyes were bright with something close to anger. I didn't think I was the cause. I said, "I get the impression that when Vesta makes it big, you won't be going to the premiere."

She moved a shoulder. "She's an actress, or fancies herself one on the basis of a couple of cat-food commercials. In her book that puts her above us lowly telephone girls. Even if she does sling hash to keep up her car payments between feminine hygiene spots."

"That's kind of a big chip to still be carrying around two years later. See or hear anything of her since?"

"Not a thing, and neither has Mr. Catalin. For someone who's not looking for him, you seem awfully interested in things he had the use of."

"I didn't say I wasn't looking for him."

She tapped her teeth with a coral nail. They were good teeth, blue-white against ivory skin. "I don't think I'd hire you, Mr. Walker. You have an attitude I wouldn't care for in someone who was working for me."

"It's a handicap. I considered getting help to overcome it."

"What was the decision?"

I shook my head.

She set the lock on Catalin's door and pulled it shut behind us. Back in the reception area I watched her take her seat with a flashy kind of economy of movement she probably wouldn't have used without someone watching. When I made no move to leave she lifted her brows at me.

"That insurance policy between Webb and Catalin," I said. "Were you a witness, or did you just file it?"

"I don't know anything about an insurance policy," she said after a moment. "Is there one?"

"Search me. It was just a gag to get information I didn't want to ask Webb about and make him mad enough to give me the boot. As arrangements go it's standard among long-time partners: When one dies, the other benefits, and the business goes on."

"If you're suggesting something happened to Mr. Catalin and Mr. Webb was responsible, I can't help you. He may not be the ideal employer, but that doesn't make him Klaus von Bülow."

"That kind of information is easy to get."

"How nice for you." She slid her eyes toward the door. I went after them.

My car didn't want to start again. I smoked a cigarette while it got used to the idea, and thought about Musuraca Investigations. I knew Phil Musuraca; not personally or even by sight, but the way a hardworking gardener knows a destructive species of beetle. Where he had gone, no honest investigator could follow without slipping in Phil's greasy footprints. What his number was doing on Neil Catalin's redial was one for Ellery Queen.

Eight

"GOOD MORNING. Ziggy's Chop House."

A low voice for a woman and even some men, with fine grit in it, like a cat's lick. Conversations collided in the background with tinkling flatware and clattering crockery. I could almost smell the carcinogens frying in the kitchen.

"I'm trying to locate Vesta Mannering," I said. "Does she work there?"

"Speaking."

I leaned against the telephone cover. The Penobscot Building across the street shimmied in the August heat ribboning up from the pavement. Parking attendants and Federal Express couriers, their uniforms just beginning to wilt as the Judas cool of the morning burned off, paced themselves like pros as they made their way toward the shrinking shade.

"You're a hard woman to get hold of, Miss Mannering."

"I don't let just anyone get hold of me. Who is this, please?" Her voice had dropped. Not taking personal calls on restaurant time would be among the commandments at Ziggy's. Another would be keeping kitchen secrets.

"My name is Amos Walker. I'm an investigator hired by Gay Catalin to find her husband."

"That again. I told her I haven't seen Neil in over a year."

"Not seeing him doesn't cover telephone calls and letters."

"You left out singing telegrams, which I didn't get either. I lost a valuable career contract because of Catalin. Now this job's all I have, lousy as it is. Do you want me to lose that too?"

There was no reason to play the card, no reason at all, except that I was losing the hand and the Joker was all I had left.

"What about Fat Phil?" I asked. "Heard from him?"

The little silence that followed was like the bank breaking. When she spoke again the background noise was muffled, as if she had inserted her body between it and the telephone. "What do you know about Musuraca?"

"Meet me and we'll swap stories."

"Not here," she said quickly. "Do you know the Castanet Lounge in Iroquois Heights? I'm through here at ten."

"I'll find it."

The Mercury was ready to start finally. Waiting for a hole in traffic, I read the clock on the dash. Eleven hours till Vesta. It was too early for lunch and there was nothing waiting for me back at the office but some bills and a water stain shaped like Mike Tyson. I drove to a garage I knew on the East Side and that the car knew even better, like a tired horse returning to the barn.

OK Towing & Auto Repair worked out of a building that belonged on the National Register of Historic Places, whenever the NRHP got around to recognizing the age of the automobile: one of the dozen or so remaining garages built of white glazed brick still being used for their intended purpose. A Standard gasoline pump, no longer functional and missing its original glass globe (stolen, no doubt, by a collector), rusted out front, its price for Regular Leaded frozen at 29.9 cents, and a cardboard sign depicting the proper firing order of pistons in an eight-cylinder engine slouched in the window, gone the color of mummy wrappings and no longer visible to the people who worked there. The proprietor had declined several offers by the city to buy the building so it could be torn down and replaced by a park named for a felon who had managed to get himself beaten to death by overzealous police officers. Rumor had it the proprietor was waiting for someone from Greenfield Village to take it off his hands and transport it brick by brick to the historical theme park in Dearborn. Meanwhile he papered the wall of his office with citations from the city designed to nickel-and dime him into submission. He had a pit bull for a lawyer and more motions for injunction on the table than a politician has teeth.

I found Ernst Dierdorf seated on a stool at the bench, swamping out a four-barrel carburetor with a toothbrush and a cup of gasoline. The cup was the same one he used for coffee, with his first name lettered on it in gold-leaf Gothic. His Aryan Nation poster-boy features had begun to slip past sixty, the clean chin blurring and the skin growing thick around his chilly blue eyes. The rest of him was the same as always, stunted and misshapen under what had to be the first pair of coveralls he had ever owned, strataed and sub-strataed with layers of black grease.

"I need you to look at my car when you get a minute." I had to shout to make myself heard above the whimpering of air wrenches and the clanging of tire irons.

"I've seen your car." He blew through the carburetor. It made a sound like a flute. Then he went back to scrubbing. It wasn't the note he was looking for.

"You need new material, Ernst."

"You need a new car."

"You say that every time I come in."

"I mean it every time."

"Well, take a look at it."

"I don't need to."

"Why not? Did you find that Nazi gold you buried in forty-five?"

"Go to hell, Amos. I was too young to serve in the Wehrmacht."

"I heard it was the Hitler Youth."

"I don't need to look at your car to know what's wrong. You've got fissures in the block. You had fissures in the block last time. They don't heal."

"Use more epoxy."

"It's ninety percent epoxy now. That's not a car you're driving. It's a rolling advertisement for miracle adhesives." He wiped the carburetor with a rag slightly less filthy than his coveralls, blew through it again. "I got a car for you. Let you have it for a grand."

"You've been trying to sell me a car ever since I bought this one."

"You should've come here instead of buying it hot."

"We're not married, Ernst. I wasn't being unfaithful."

He wiped the carburetor again, with a clean rag this time, and set it on the bench next to the sawed-off Remington shotgun he used to protect himself at night from burglars and the Jewish Defense League. "You want to see it or not? I already got one offer from a collector. Thousand, cash."

"Why didn't you take it?"

"I hate collectors worse than bolsheviks. They treat cars like pussies."

"Show me what you've got."

He climbed down from the stool and hobbled through a back door propped open with the block from a Packard

Eight. He moved painfully, using only the balls of his feet. He had not used the rest since the Russians had got hold of him three hundred feet from the Bunker. All it took to turn Ernst Dierdorf violent was to order a glass of vodka anywhere within his hearing.

Behind the garage was a gravel apron where the hopeless cases were parked, with the occasional work-in-progress mixed in to camouflage it from thieves, should they get over the electrified fence with all their internal organs intact; his lawyer had been trying for years to persuade him to stop cranking the current up to lethal levels. One of the vehicles was covered with a canvas tarpaulin. With no ceremony whatsoever he flipped up the end of the cover and rolled it back over the hood, across the roof, and down the sloping rear window to the trunk.

It was an Oldsmobile Cutlass, twenty-five years old, with a white vinyl pebbled top and a dusty blue battered body. The distance from the nose to the base of the windshield was nearly as long as the rest of the car. A conscientious traffic cop would have been tempted to ticket it for speeding while it was standing still.

"I had one just like this," I said.

"Like hell. You had this one."

"You told me you sold it to a guy for parts two presidents back."

"I did." He stood doubling and redoubling the canvas tarp in his strong hands, as close to bursting as he ever got. He was almost smiling.

I got out a cigarette and speared it between my lips, then decided against lighting it. The ground was soaked as deep as I was tall with gasoline and motor oil.

"It was back in January," he said. "I was on my way to a tow job clear out in Washtenaw County. I passed this pile of junk, up to its knees in weeds in an unplowed field. The farmer's wife was home. She said she was sick of looking at it and I could have it for nothing if I cleared it out before her husband got back from Lansing. I never did get to the tow job. I hitched on and brought it straight here. I almost fell on my face when I read the serial number."

I nodded. Ernst's memory was where old serial numbers went to die. If he ever forgot one you can bet it never existed. He went on.

"Engine and transmission were junk, of course. I had a brand-new four-fifty-five Cadillac V-8 engine I traded a Willys Jeep for to a guy in Dearborn, never used. I found the trans in a salvage yard on Ford Road. I applied for a title based on the serial number of the Caddy. It came through last week. It's as legal as abortion and you don't have to worry about picketers."

"Why just a thousand?"

His face twitched, another memento he carried around from the last good war. "What?"

"Any collector worth the name would give you twenty-five hundred for it as it sits. You don't hate them that much. Where's the string?"

"No string." He twitched again. "Oh, the farmer's wife called me the next day trying to get it back; something about her husband threatening to divorce her. I already had the engine in. I hung up. The farmer has the original title, but that goes to the number on the old engine. I junked that. It would be better if the car weren't here when his lawyer comes around."

"Ernst, that's theft."

His face went stoic. "Thousand's the price."

I undid the latch and threw up the hood. The 455 wasn't anywhere near as clean as an operating table at Johns Hopkins. I slammed the hood shut. "Give me two hundred on the Merc. I'll give you another hundred down and a hundred a month."

"I don't want the Merc. I need half up front. If you're going to pay the rest on time I'm going to have to make it twelve-fifty."

"How's Eric?"

"Eric's good. He's going to be a monsignor." He doubled over the tarp another time, his knuckles whitening. "Give me the Merc and the hundred, cash. I expect the first payment first of next month."

I'd deposited Gay Catalin's retainer check the day before and kept out two hundred for walking around. I gave him five twenties. He laid the rolled canvas across the hood of a Monte Carlo with belts and hoses spilling out like entrails and counted the bills. "Don't you want to take it out for a run first?"

"Anyone else work on it but you?"

"You see anyone walking around here with a broken jaw?"

"Let's go in and swap titles."

He led the way, moving fast on the balls of his feet.

We completed the transaction in his little monoxide-smelling office in the garage. "Come around after this thing goes away and I'll bump out the dings and do you a paint job nobody will know wasn't factory." He handed me a set of keys attached to a washer.

"I like it the way it is."

"You don't put up much of a front."

"Someone would just push it in if I did." I gave him the keys to the Mercury.

Before he went into the Catholic seminary, Ernst's son Eric had been arrested by the Detroit Police on a charge of Grand Theft Auto. As a favor to my mechanic I'd dug up three witnesses who swore Eric was with them at the

Pussycat Theater on Telegraph Road at the time the car was seen barreling out of the dealer's lot at Seven Mile and Dequindre. The cops didn't buy their story any more than I did, but the dealer hadn't wanted to bother with a long trial and withdrew his complaint. And I hadn't paid a penny for a lube and oil change in five years.

Nine

OUR DAILY STORM clouds were in place when I came out on the street after lunch, but they provided no insulation from the heat. Instead they sealed in the temperature and humidity like the lid of a pressure cooker. By the time I found a parking space around the corner from the main branch of the Detroit Public Library, my shirt was shrink-wrapped to my back. The air-conditioned atmosphere inside the building went down inside the back of my collar like an icicle.

I walked past the big globe, passing up the line waiting to play with the computer terminal for the card catalogue section, which since my last visit had moved six feet closer to the back door and oblivion. I'd miss it when it was gone. It would mean allowing an extra ten minutes per trip for the electronic convenience.

The Media section was chock full of information on Neil Catalin's favorite subject. Most were big glossy picture books. There was a file box stuffed with publications targeted at noir buffs, both expensive slicks and amateur jobs photocopied and stapled, part of a shelf devoted to race and gender bias in the genre, and one scholarly tract, *Dark Dreams: Psychosexual Manifestations of Hollywood Crime Movies Circa 1945–1955*, by Asa Portman, Ph.D.

This was a thick volume wrapped in a dead black dust-jacket with its title printed in white capitals like typewriter characters, published that year by the University of Michigan Press.

I lugged the book over to a reading table and waded in. After ten minutes I went to the Reference section and came back with a dictionary. When that didn't help I turned to the author's biography at the back of the film book. Asa Portman, it said, taught courses on psychology and popular culture at Michigan.

I used a telephone on the main floor to call the university switchboard. A series of voices covered with ivy put me in touch with Portman's department, where a student intern laid me down to wait. I had just fed the coin slot a second time when Portman came on. I told him what I was about and he agreed to see me in an hour. I wrote down the location in my notebook.

The German was too modest. In addition to the engine and transmission, he'd replaced the suspension, improving upon the slip-slop system that in 1970 had not progressed beyond the engineering of the family car under Eisenhower. The Cutlass cornered like a Formula I racer and capped the hills as if it were screwed down. On the Edsel Ford expressway west of Romulus, I shot past a state trooper parked on the median, doing eighty, and got nothing from him but a yawn. Those dents and that chalky paint made me invisible.

Ann Arbor, home of the University of Michigan and the five-dollar fine for possession of marijuana, has variously been called the Arcadia of America, the cultural capital of the world, and the last great refuge for artists and philosophers in the age of the music video. It has been called all these things by itself. In fact the city's chief contribution to the twentieth century is the invention of the parking meter.

It has more trees than people—hence the *arbor*—and six traffic lights for every tree. It's a sickly egghead kid with a passion for Tolkien, touchdowns, and tofu; a place where the cop who stops you for running one of its nine million red lights might recommend a book while writing up your ticket; a doddering hippie with a haircut and floral throws over the avocado velour chairs in the den. Every state has one, and each one thinks it's unique.

On campus I negotiated one-way streets, jaywalking students, and a throwback in a tie-dyed shirt hawking copies of an underground newspaper and found a space only a mile or so from my destination. This was an imposing brick hall a city block wide, constructed sometime during the Era of Good Feeling. The chimes in the university tower were just striking three when I threaded my way among a scattering of students sunning themselves on the front steps and heaved open one of the big front doors. Inside I found an acre of veined marble cordoned with Neoclassical pilasters and more steps. Only the discovery of an antique Otis elevator on the next level rescued me from a general strike on the part of my feet.

The room number I'd gotten from Portman belonged to a small auditorium, illuminated solely by the black-and-silver images fluttering on a square screen at the base of the graduated tiers of wooden seats. Fifteen or twenty heads were silhouetted against the screen; in the brief intervals between music and dialogue, fifteen or twenty pens scribbled in notebooks propped on kidney-shaped writing boards attached to the seats. I sat in the vacant top row. The room smelled of varnish and ink and the hot bulb burning in the projector whirring away on a metal desk before and below the screen.

Beyond and above it, where the shaft of white light ended, Robert Mitchum, in fedora and trenchcoat, careered down a dark country road at the wheel of a big car with bug-eye headlamps. Beside him, her shining hair covered by a silk scarf, rode Jane Greer: midnight-eyed, beautiful, corrupt. They were both achingly young. It was 1947.

The music built. As a police roadblock hove into view ahead, Greer's expression turned venomous.

"Dirty double-crossing rat!" She clawed a revolver from her purse and shot Mitchum. The car went into a spin. She fired through the windshield at the officers, who returned fire. After she was killed and the car came to a stop, one of the cops opened the driver's door and Mitchum flopped out, dead.

The lights came up and a small man with a big head and a short beard, half the age I associated with a college professor, turned from the wall switch to address the class.

"Impressions! David?"

A student in his early twenties with the right side of his head tattooed and the left side shaggy to his collar lowered his hand. "Robert Mitchum's—excuse me, Jeff Bailey's— fatal flaw is his affection for Jane Greer. Kathy Moffat. However, according to Aristotle—"

"Aristotle never spent Dime One at the Bijou. Save that for your philosophy instructor. And it's okay to refer to the characters by the names of the actors. What you're saying is Mitchum let his crotch do his thinking when he should have handed Greer over to Kirk Douglas, as he was hired to do in the first place. You can get that much from Leonard Maltin's movie guide. What else? Heather?"

A woman of eighteen or nineteen, in a man's work shirt, with her hair cut short, rose from her seat. "Jane Greer is not the villain of this piece; she's the victim. In a society less dominated by aggressive males, she would not have had to resort to crime to realize her full potential as a human being."

"Bullshit. She's a scheming vixen guilty of triple homicide. How does Mitchum's fate relate to that of the hero in another film we've watched this semester? Yes, Darice?"

Darice was a black woman, older than most of the class, wearing a tailored silk jacket and her hair in rich brown waves. She'd caught Portman's eye with the end of a gold pencil. "What happened to Mitchum is what might have happened to Humphrey Bogart if he'd refused to send Mary Astor over at the end of *The Maltese Falcon*."

"Exactly! We're talking *movie* reality, boys and girls. Not Aristotle's, and certainly not Betty Friedan's. Any resemblance to the world outside Hollywood is purely coincidental. If the script calls for a detective as tough as a forty-minute egg, you go to Bogart, or Lloyd Nolan if Bogie's on loan to Columbia. Mitch is the boy you want for strong-but-squishy. The heavens and the earth were created on the first day of the shooting schedule, and Central Casting is God. Go now into the sunshine, and don't forget your papers are due Tuesday."

The students climbed the steps toward the exit, talking among themselves. David and Heather looked perturbed. Darice, sliding her notebook and gold pencil into a calfskin portfolio slung from her shoulder, looked like someone whose paper was already written.

Portman reversed the projector, rewinding the reel while he shoveled books from the metal desk into an old briefcase. They were not textbooks, but dilapidated paperbacks with covers in tarnished primaries showing beetle-browed pugs in dirty trench coats watching blondes undress: two-bit potboilers from the heyday of the drugstore press. Teachers under Eisenhower had confiscated them by the case from students who smuggled them into class behind *Understanding Trigonometry*. Now they were study guides.

"The real thing!" Portman put down his briefcase to

shake my hand. "I wish you'd come earlier. I could have filled the class period comparing your experiences with those of the private eyes of fiction. Tell me, do you pack a rod?" His teeth shone in his beard. Up close he was older than he looked from the back of the room.

"Every time I go fishing. Are all your classes this intimate?"

"You mean small. Summer sessions are always tiny, but I never pack the place the way this type of course did in the sixties and seventies, when colleges were turning out Coppolas and Scorseses by the dozen. You know Lawrence Kasdan studied here."

I said I didn't know.

"That was the film school generation. They worshiped at the shrine of Welles and Godard and Kurosawa and Fellini. This new batch would rather clear a million on a splatter-fest, and don't even talk to them about black-and-white. They'd colorize Whistler's Mother."

"The man I'm looking for would probably agree with you." I sketched out the case. He listened, staring at the blank screen in front of the blackboard as if the story were playing up there.

"So his wife thinks he's run off to play cops and robbers for real," he said when I'd finished. "Not unusual, considering the medium. The cinema is the most visceral of all the arts. It passes through the cornea directly into the brain."

"A psychiatrist I spoke to said pure cases aren't common."

He made a noise beneath the dignity of an educator. "Psychiatrists are frustrated plastic surgeons. By the time they find out they can't stomach the sight of blood and bone splinters, they've spent too much on their education to back out. That's when they opt for the couch and the bust of Jung. During the Depression, when most Americans couldn't afford to buy bread, they laid down their nickels by the millions to see a movie once a week. Nikos Kazantzakis' *Last Temptation of Christ* was in libraries and bookstores for years without a peep from the religious Right; Scorsese puts it on film and they pour out to protest it like nothing since the Great Schism. That's the power of celluloid and safety stock. You can't get to the heart of it lying on your back bitching about your poor toilet training."

I felt for a cigarette. "I must have one of those faces. Everyone's giving me lectures."

"It *is* a lecture hall." But he smiled apologetically. "What do you need?"

"I dipped a toe in *Dark Dreams* at the library. Most books on noir are for buffs. The man I'm looking for went beyond that somewhere around the fifteenth time he saw *Pitfall.* Yours is the only book I found that takes on the psychology of the form. I thought you might translate the Latin."

He switched off the projector and removed the take-up reel. "It's a simple enough fantasy, on the surface; which is as far as any film goes, whether the director is an *auteur* or a studio hack. It's a two-dimensional medium after all. In many ways that's its appeal, but we'll get to that. We've always identified with gods and heroes. The allure of the noir protagonist to modern man is he's more approachable than Beowulf or Sherlock Holmes. It takes a Superman to slash away at Grendl or to match intellects with Professor Moriarty, but this guy is an ordinary slob with tall troubles who usually comes out on top, even if it does kill him sometimes."

"Stiff price to pay for victory."

"But a price we feel the need to pay. Years ago we died for God and country, but we've stopped believing in the one and no longer trust the other. So instead we throw it up for points."

"We're a tangled mess, all right," I said. "Tangled enough anyway to make me wonder why anyone would throw it over for something as complex as the noir world."

"Actually it's simplistic. I said it was two-dimensional. You've got your good guy, your heavy, your good girl, and your tramp. Upon examination the noir landscape makes more sense than ours. I don't wonder that an obsessive like your client's husband would prefer it to his own snarled affairs. His wife, whom he perceives as the good girl, represents the crushing responsibilities that landed him in therapy the first time. The girlfriend, whose situation might have come out of any crime movie of the forties—*Pitfall* is an excellent example—promises adventure and uninhibited sex and a respite from his oppressive routine. The whole thing might have been made to order for a man with his fixation."

"Even the danger?"

"*Especially* the danger."

I watched him place the reel in a flat can labeled OUT OF THE PAST and seal the lid. "What would it take to shake him out of it?"

"The shock of reality might do it, if he isn't too far gone."

"The third dimension."

He nodded. "The world we live in has more twists than any screenplay. Villains turn out to be just guys trying to get along. Bad girls are just good girls in trouble. Angels turn into whores while you're looking at them. If that doesn't bring your man around, neither will electrodes."

I thanked him. He tucked the film can under one arm and shook my hand again. "This is stale stuff," he said. "There's a classic film festival taking place next week at the DIA. You can catch the originals there, the way they were meant to be seen."

"You think he might show up?"

"That's only part of it. The festival is connected with a VIP reception next Friday night at the Fox Theater, when Austin Alt's new picture premieres. He's one of our greatest living directors. He apprenticed under Fritz Lang and Billy Wilder, and survived the blacklist. He's expected to attend."

"Tell me, does shilling pay better than teaching?"

He smiled again, this time without apology. "Alt is the man you want to talk to. Your man will, if you don't. Otherwise his wife might as well have him declared legally dead."

I drove back to the office and put in the time till quitting opening my mail and wondering if a complete set of the 100 Greatest Books Ever Written, bound in genuine leather and stamped in fourteen-karat gold, would do anything for the office. At length I concluded I would have to redecorate the place around them and decided instead to replace the dead plant in the waiting room. My service reported that Gay Catalin had called three times without leaving a message, but when I called her number no one answered. I was reaching for the telephone to try again when it rang and I picked it up and it was her.

"I still haven't heard from Brian, Mr. Walker. It's been two days. I'm worried."

She sounded calm. I pictured her in the room filled with flowers, drawing from their drowsy serenity.

"Did you call the police?"

"No. I thought I'd talk to you first."

"Call them. That's what you pay taxes for. I'll let you know if I come across anything on this end."

"Should I tell them about Neil?"

"Sure. They'll bawl you out for not going to them first,

but even they won't be listening. File a report on Neil while you're at it. Make sure they put out a BOL on his car."

"BOL?"

"It stands for Be On the Lookout. It's like an All-Points Bulletin, only without Broderick Crawford. People have been known to vanish, but a car has to be parked somewhere."

"Do you think Brian's being gone has anything to do with Neil?"

"Maybe not. Coincidences happen, although I wouldn't try to sell that to the cops. You'll know something when I know."

She thanked me and hung up. That was the five o'clock whistle. I bought supper at a drive-through and went on home to rest up for Vesta.

A bright green Camaro was parked across the street when I pulled into my garage. It didn't mean anything. It didn't mean anything either that someone was sitting inside. What did mean something, or maybe not, was the fact that he was sitting on the passenger's side. That was an old trick. The street was residential on both sides, made up mostly of retired people waiting for their children to visit or inflation to eat up their Social Security. There was no reason for anyone to leave a passenger waiting while he ran a quick errand.

It could have been nothing. Just to prove it was nothing, I called the downtown branch of the Secretary of State's office to give the license number to someone I knew there. A recording told me the office was closed until 9:00 A.M. tomorrow.

After ten minutes the man slid under the wheel, started the motor, and drove away. I couldn't see him well enough through the window to recognize him again. I was sure it was a man.

It was probably nothing. But before I left the house I took my spare gun from the top shelf of the bedroom closet and cleaned and oiled and loaded it. I could feel my pulse where the butt pressed my right kidney when the holster was in place.

Ten

FROM TWO O'CLOCK Sunday morning until five o'clock Friday night, Iroquois Heights slumbered seven miles north of Detroit and a thousand miles outside its consciousness. In the memories of the citizens of this sprawling eighty-percent-black metropolis, the Heights was the place where a generation ago an angry mob dumped over a school bus full of children to protest cross-district busing for the purposes of racial integration; and there was still a bigoted message to be read in its aggressive advertising campaign warning lawbreakers to steer clear of its city limits.

All that changed after quitting time Friday. With Detroit's night life in its twentieth year of catatonia, city folk in search of colored lights, loud music, and sparkling liquid motored up Telegraph Road and shrapneled out into half a dozen nightspots along the main stem, offering themes from 1940s Retro to head-banging, ring-in-the-nose Heavy Metal.

No amplifiers needed apply at the Castanet Lounge. A foyer paved with blue-and-white Mexican tiles opened between a pair of wicked-looking six-foot mescal cacti into a big room covered in *faux*-adobe. Here were tables, a long Bakelite bar under blue lights, a hardwood dance floor, and a stand holding up a mariachi band in sombreros and pink ruffled shirts. A honey-skinned Hispanic host in a white jacket conducted me to a table in a corner, where I ordered Scotch and soda from a waitress wearing a sarong and a pile of fruit on her head.

"Carmen Miranda, eh?" I said, when she returned with my drink.

"Huh?"

"Well, then, Bette Midler." I indicated her headgear.

"Sorry, sir. If you were looking for either of those people, you should have asked the host."

The band hurled itself into "Cielito Lindo," drowning out any further conversation. I smiled at her and she left, clomping in her cork sandals like a mule on a wooden trestle. All around me people were drinking from glasses the size of cuspidors. The breeze off the heaps of crushed ice gave me frostbite.

Ten o'clock came and went, followed by ten-thirty, and still no Vesta. A few couples danced, the band finished its set, rested, and started another. They were playing requests, but everything sounded like the little Spanish flea. The clientele was strictly silver-haired graduates of Arthur Murray and Generation X-ers who had discovered Tony Bennett—nothing in between; sequined gowns and ripped jeans. I felt like Jane Goodall, crouched in the bush with binoculars. Time clicked past on flamenco heels. I nursed the first drink. What I did with the second and third was more like CPR. I was sure I'd been stood up.

Just before eleven she came in. I knew it was her, although I'd never seen a picture or been given a description, and my opinion of Neil Catalin went up a notch. Coming in from the cold white glare of the floodlit parking lot she was just a silhouette, square shoulders and a narrow waist and long legs in a dress of the last shade of indigo this side of black and a bonnetlike hat tied under her chin with a ribbon, but it was clear she was the most interesting thing to happen to the place all night. As she stepped under the inside lights and paused to look around I saw eyes slanted just shy of Oriental, soft, untanned cheeks flushed a little from the day's heat, red lips, a strong round chin. If like Neil you were thinking of kicking over the traces, you could wait years for a better reason. When her gaze got to me I stood. She came over. Her heels made no more noise on the tiles than a panther's paws.

"Mr. Walker?" Her voice had even more husk on it in person than it had over the telephone.

I said I was Mr. Walker. She nodded slightly. She offered neither her hand nor an apology for being late. I came around and pulled out the other chair for her, holding it while she coiled herself into it. She laid a blue patent-leather handbag the size of a pocket pistol on the table, took off her hat, and shook loose a fall of glistening blue-black hair. By that time Carmen Miranda was there. Vesta traded her the hat for a whiskey sour.

When we were alone she said, "You don't look like someone who'd be working with Phil Musuraca."

"What would someone who'd be working with Phil Musuraca look like?"

She glanced toward the ceiling, lost in the darkness above a canopy of tobacco smoke. The whites of her eyes were as clear as the Milky Way. "Dirty nails, bad teeth, cheap necktie, soup stains on his lapels. Smelling of Old Spice. Reeking of it."

"I don't pay a lot for my neckties."

"But you know how to tie one. No dimple."

"That sounds like a description of Fat Phil."

"So you are working with him."

"Never met him."

"Did Neil tell you he was following me?"

"Who hired him?"

She seemed to realize she'd tipped something. She took a cigarette out of her handbag and tapped it on the table, fumbling for a light. I struck a match and leaned over. I didn't smell onions. Whatever she had on made me think of pale blossoms under a full moon. She blew a jet at my shoulder. "You haven't talked to Neil."

"Me and the rest of the human race." I shook out the match and dropped it into an ashtray with writing on the bottom welcoming me to Cabo San Lucas. "Tell me about Musuraca."

"First tell me why you're asking."

"I found his number on Catalin's redial. Did Catalin hire him?"

She leaned back, scissoring her cigarette between long fingers. The nails were enameled scarlet, as hard as Kevlar. She took a puff, blew a plume at the ceiling, and crushed out the cigarette in the ashtray. "I suppose if you're any sort of detective you'll find out anyway. Musuraca's working for my ex-husband. His name's Ted Silvera."

The name thumped a rusty bell wrapped in old newspapers. I waited for more.

"He pushed over a bunch of video stores downriver three years ago," she said. "The papers and the TV news called him the Shotgun Bandit."

"I remember the trial. The prosecution offered him a deal to rat out his accomplices and tell where he'd stashed the money."

"Ninety-two thousand dollars, can you believe it? I keep telling Ziggy he should get out of the restaurant business and rent tapes instead. Anyway, Ted told them what they could do with their deal and he's doing seven to twelve in Jackson. The police followed me around for a while, but when they got the idea I didn't know what Ted did with the money they laid off."

"But not Musuraca."

She sipped at her whiskey sour. "Ted's the jealous type. It's one of the reasons I divorced him, although he thinks it's because he's in prison and I can't wait. He got wind somehow about Neil and had his lawyer retain Musuraca to follow me. Then Neil's wife found out and my acting career dried up because Gilda Productions wouldn't hire me for any more jobs. Musuraca gave up after that. Then yesterday someone opened the door at Ziggy's while I was standing at the reservation desk and there he was, standing out front. He tried to duck, but he wasn't fast enough. I'd know that fat tub of lard in the dark."

"What makes you think he's working for Silvera this time?"

"I went to Ted's lawyer and he said no, but who trusts lawyers? Who else but Ted would care what I do and who I see?"

"Silvera had accomplices: a wheel man, and maybe a fence to launder the money. Maybe he didn't tell them where he hid it either."

"I wouldn't know their names. Ted never discussed his work. Do you think I'd be growing bunions in a chop house if I knew where I could lay my hands on ninety-two grand?"

I lit a cigarette for myself. "It's only been three years. Not a long time to keep Dr. Scholl in business while you wait for the coast to clear."

She thought about that for a minute and decided to get

mad. "Thanks for the drink, mister." She picked up her handbag.

"You haven't drunk it yet," I said. "I don't care if you've got the money sewed in your brassiere. I'm looking for Neil Catalin."

"I don't have the money. I don't know where the money is. I don't know how many other ways I can say it."

"Don't bother. I believe you."

She was still clutching the bag in both hands. Women and their purses. "Why?"

"In my business, if you get to not believing any of the answers—and sometimes you do—you might as well stop asking the questions. If you stop asking the questions you starve. I like to eat. Anyway you wouldn't have come here tonight if you knew where the money is. I got up your curiosity with that crack about Fat Phil."

She put down the bag then. "I don't know where Neil is either."

"What was he doing calling Musuraca?"

"Why don't you ask Musuraca?"

"I'd rather ask you. You smell better."

Carmen drifted over and I ordered another round. Our glasses were less than half empty but it was that kind of night. The band took off its sombreros and started something slow with a calypso beat that after a while I recognized: "Ain't No Use." That winnowed the dancing couples down to the over-fifty set. They were the only ones who didn't have to look down at their feet when the tempo let up.

Vesta said, "I don't know why Neil would be calling him. I told him about Ted and Musuraca—well, before. That was a mistake."

"After that you couldn't get rid of him. He thought he was protecting you."

That confused her for just a second. "I forgot you're a detective. For a moment there I thought we were just two people talking."

I didn't nibble at that one. "Did you know Catalin has a screw loose?"

"My father died when I was little," she said. "I married Ted when I was sixteen to get out of the house. I didn't see much future in dropping my pants for my stepfather every time he came home with a snootful. When Ted got sent up I saved every penny I made waiting tables to pay for my acting classes. Gilda Productions was my ticket out of places like Ziggy's. Mister, I've been tripping over loose screws since I was six."

"So you hedged your bet by cozying up to the boss."

She watched me over her drink. "You can't cozy up to a rock. There has to be some give." She swallowed and thumped down the glass. "Oh, hell. I'm not actor enough to carry off that hardboiled pose. My motives weren't pure, but neither were Neil's. And he was so clumsy and sweet about the way he moved in. I knew by the second day of shooting he wasn't hanging around the studio just because he liked playing C. B. DeMille. When you've heard all the lines it's a relief just to meet somebody who couldn't deliver one with a crib sheet. It was fun for a while. Then it got weird. That's when I dumped him."

"His wife says she made him dump you."

"He may have let her think that. All I know is Gilda didn't call me back, and I *know* I shot the best feature it ever made."

"Catlin's got an old-movie complex, his wife says. Your situation comes right off a Hollywood back lot. If he's gone bugs again he might look up you or Musuraca to write himself in as the hero."

"Well, he hasn't looked me up."

I put out my cigarette. "Catalin's brother-in-law is missing too. His name is Brian Elwood. Did you ever meet him?"

"The little creep was always sneaking around the studio, looking for something to steal. He caught Neil and me behind the scenery once. We weren't doing much, but it was pretty clear he wasn't coaching my acting. The creep told Neil if he gave him a thousand dollars he wouldn't tell his sister."

"What did Neil say?"

"He told me to go home. I finished the job the next morning and left before he showed up. When he called me that night I told him it would be better if we didn't see each other and asked him not to call me again unless it had to do with work. Well, he didn't, and neither did anyone else at Gilda. So I guess we can figure out what Neil told Brian."

"Not necessarily. Catalin couldn't have been feeling very charitable toward you with your heelprint in his heart."

"You don't know Neil. He had his faults. Being vindictive wasn't one of them. When he wouldn't come through on the extortion, Brian made good on his threat and ratted him out. Neil's wife put her foot down, and here I am juggling menus."

"Leo Webb told me it was obvious you two were keeping company outside the studio. If that's true anyone at Gilda could have blown the whistle."

"Leo." She smiled without enjoyment. "If sweetening the job were all I was after, I'd have taken up with him instead of his partner. There wouldn't have been as many complications. God knows I had enough chances. My stepfather was subtle compared to Leo."

"Gay Catalin wouldn't say how she found out," I said. "It would make sense that Brian told her. She may have suspected her kid brother was capable of blackmail. No sense hanging out all the dirty linen."

She flagged our waitress and asked for her hat. "I just put in twelve hours," she said. "I only agreed to see you to find out why Musuraca's following me again, but I don't know any more than I knew when I came in here, while you know everything."

"Does Musuraca drive a green Camaro?"

"He couldn't get behind the wheel of a Camaro, green or otherwise. Why?"

"No reason." I hadn't seen it since it had pulled away from my house. The gun butt against my kidney told me I had a persecution complex. The old bullet wound in my ribs told me I was entitled to one.

Her hat came. She stood. "I usually get taken home from this place."

I took out my wallet and held up a fifty-dollar bill. "That ought to cover gas."

"I'm not a whore."

"You're an actress who seats customers in a restaurant. Put it toward a ticket to Hollywood."

"What are you going to do?"

"Get a look at Fat Phil."

"Believe me, it's not worth fifty." But she took the bill and left, trailing her hat by its ribbons, along with every male eye in the place. I put down money for the drinks and went out behind her.

In front of the canopy the parking attendant, wearing a buff-and-blue uniform from the Mexican War, held the door of a red Triumph for her and she gave him a dollar and drove away. A moment later a pair of headlamps came on and a black 1960 Buick Invicta with one white fender pulled out of the line of spaces across the street and bur-bled after her. By that time I was sliding under the wheel of the Cutlass six spaces over. I waited until the big car turned left onto the main stem, then swung out and did the same. Phil Musuraca and I had one thing in common: We never used valet parking.

of the Chene-street station, when I waited until the windshield was in front of them that it was not one of the sedans that posted a small army of touts to enhance the workload while parking.

Eleven

IT WAS A SHAME I knew where he was going, because I could have tailed the big Buick through a black hole. Since the Invicta had rolled off the line, Detroit had filled the highways with cars that could parallel park in the space between its taillights. On top of that its shock absorbers were shot, probably from having had to carry Fat Phil for so long: every time the car hit a bump the red lights kept bouncing for a block. Just watching them made me seasick.

Not having to concentrate too hard on the tail job allowed me more time to look in the rearview mirror. I was watching when a green Camaro turned into a side street behind me and cruised under the corner lamp.

It must have followed me from home. It was Friday night, and the traffic of restless day-laborers out for a good time had been heavy enough in that comparatively early hour to swallow it up. I'd been watching, but the guy was good. He didn't seem to care about being good now. I didn't like that by half.

The motorcade slowed down near a painted brick house on a hilly street. When the house was built, sometime in the thirties, it had been intended to shelter one well-off family by Depression standards, possibly belonging to an executive at Ford or GM. Since then it had been converted into apartments. Vesta's Triumph pulled into a parking lot the size of a placemat and stopped next to a Dumpster. She got out and let herself in the back door with a key. After a minute a light went on upstairs.

The big Buick coasted to a stop against the curb. I drove on past and parked around the corner. The Camaro kept on going when I turned. I wondered where it would park. I locked up, checked the load in the bulky Luger for the second time that night in the light from a window, and trotted back around the corner. The Invicta was still there with its lights off. I got in on the passenger's side.

Fat men are often fast. This one sprang his gun from its underarm clip with an economy that would have impressed Wild Bill. But Hickok knew better than to try to pull the trigger on a man whose gun was already drawn. He let his hand fall into his lap with the pistol in it.

"You should lock your doors," I said. "This isn't Kokomo."

"Who the hell are you?"

It was a light voice for so much man. In the glow from the corner he had on a dark suit that could have been used for a dropcloth and a light-colored porkpie hat whose narrow brim made his face seem more bloated than it was. Actually his face was in proportion with the rest of him. He would run three hundred stripped. It was a picture I got out of my head as quickly as it came in. He had one eyebrow straight across and a blue jaw. It would always be blue, even when it was still wet from shaving. The smell of Old Spice in the car was thick enough to float the boat on the bottle.

I waggled the Luger. "Give me the cannon and I'll tell you my name."

"That ain't no trade."

"I'll sweeten it. Give me the cannon and I won't blow your spleen through your back."

"Who gave you that piece, Colonel Klink?" But he gave me his. It was one of those Sig-Sauer automatics the cops are so hot on, nine millimeters in a shiny chrome case with black composition grips. I put it on the dashboard out of his reach and lowered mine.

"So much gun for one girl," I said. "The name's Walker. You wouldn't know it."

"Don't bet on it. Detroit ain't as big as it used to be. What's the play?"

"Who's paying you to tail the Mannering woman?"

"Never heard of her."

"What are you doing parked in front of her house?"

"I stopped to take a leak."

"They arrest you for that here."

"This is Iroquois Heights. They arrest you for breathing without a permit."

"How about Neil Catalin, ever hear of him?"

"Uh-uh."

"Your number was on his office redial."

"So what? I'm running a small business. I ain't so swamped I'm unlisted. Listen, I got a sour gut. There's a bottle of Pepto in the glove compartment."

I opened it. The second my eyes flicked away his hand went up to the sun visor on the driver's side. I swung the Luger, cracking the barrel against the knob of his elbow. He yelped and brought down the arm. With my free hand I reached up and slid a two-shot .22 out of an eyeglass case clipped to the visor.

"For a guy that knows nothing from nothing you've got plenty of ordnance," I said. "What's Vesta Mannering to you?"

"Why should I tell you?" He rubbed his elbow.

"I have three guns and you have none. Also I'm asking polite. You don't want to be around me when my manners start to slip."

"Shit. I heard about you. Mr. Integrity. You wouldn't stomp a cockroach."

I reversed ends on the Luger and smashed his nose with the butt. They knew how to cast steel at Krupp. He shrieked and covered the bottom half of his face with his hand. Blood slid out between the fingers. I shook open my handkerchief and gave it to him.

"Lean your head back. Press hard and breathe through your mouth. That part should come easy. That's the boy. What's Vesta Mannering to you?"

"Jesus, you busted my nose." He sounded like Arnold Stang.

"It was too small for your face anyhow. Vesta Mannering. What's she to you?"

"Didydoogad."

"Say again?"

"Ninety-two grand." He leaned on each syllable. He was looking up at the roof of the car with his head tipped all the way back and the handkerchief bunched up against his nostrils, turning dark. "She's got that pony stashed someplace. She can't stay away from it forever."

"Even the cops gave up on that. What makes you smarter than the cops?"

"Cops ain't smart. That's why I quit and went private. Ted Silvera didn't have no safe deposit box and he didn't trust his friends. Where'd he put it if he didn't give it to her?"

"Too thin, Phil. This town's rotten with divorce work. You're not the kind of dick to throw it over on a hunch. What's your source?"

"Idodadode."

"Say again."

He swallowed blood and mucus. "I got a note. In my inside pocket, left side."

"Fish it out. If it's more iron I'll shoot you in the head. It's not much of a head but it'd be a shame to spoil that hat. The state fair souvenir stand doesn't open for three weeks."

He lowered his head and changed hands on the handkerchief. The note came out slowly. I laid the Luger in my lap, took it, and unfolded it, an 8½ x 11 sheet of heavy Xerox paper with two words printed on it in block capitals:

VESTA KNOWS

"Who sent it?"

He shook his head. The bleeding had slowed. He wiped his nose. It didn't look as bad as it would once the swelling started. Right now there was a wide white welt across the bridge. "It was a fax. I got it Wednesday. That's all there was."

"You'd throw out the clutch and take off after her on the strength of an anonymous note?"

"For ninety-two thousand I can afford to look like a chump."

I put the note in my pocket. My hand brushed something there. I brought out Neil Catalin's picture and turned it toward the light so he could see it.

His eyebrow rippled. "Sure, he was sniffing around the Mannering broad two years back. I ran his plate through the Secretary of State's office but he wasn't nobody. I guess Catalin could of been the name."

"You need a memory course, Phil. He's the reason Silvera hired you, to find out if his wife was running around on him while he was in the tank."

"I was hired to find out who she was seeing and where she

was going. Silvera wanted to make sure she didn't skip with the cash."

"He told you that?"

"I never talked to him. His mouthpiece did the hiring. He didn't say it in so many words but I figured it out."

"Did you ever get a good look at Vesta?"

"Nice-looking piece. You can buy a couple of nice-looking pieces for a lot less than ninety K."

"Could be he loved her. Some guys are strange that way. A King of England threw over his throne for that reason."

"Not lately." He blew his nose into the handkerchief and inspected the carnage. "What's with this bug Catalin? He on the lam?"

"Maybe. His wife wants him back. Seen him around?"

"I might have. If the price fits."

I shifted my weight on the seat. He sucked in air and covered his face with both hands. Grinning, I broke the little .22 and shook out the shells. I took the shiny automatic from the dash, kicked out the clip, and put it in my pocket. I ejected the shell from the chamber onto the floor on the passenger's side. Then I shut both guns in the glove compartment and holstered the Luger. I opened the door.

"Go back to wiring motel rooms, Phil. You're not a money player. You don't even have what it takes to be a good grifter. Bottom-feeders can't fly."

"I don't see no Rolex on your wrist, pal." He blew his nose one last time and flipped the gory linen over the back of the seat.

"Nice car. You ought to take better care of it."

He lifted his lip. "Repo. Bank went bust and I took it in place of my fee. Fucking savings and loan."

"Know anybody who drives a green Camaro?"

His eyes went right and left. "I might."

"Yeah, yeah. If the price fits."

I got out, slammed the door, and walked back up the street. The storms had let up for once. There was no moon, but the stars were as big as eggs. I didn't see the Camaro. I didn't have to; it was there. The light had gone out in Vesta's window. The femme fatale was in bed, asleep. The streets belonged to the plucky hero, the heavy, and Mr. X.

Fadeout.

It was past midnight when I entered my street. I hadn't spotted the Camaro, which meant exactly nothing. I didn't bother with any circus tricks to throw it off. There didn't seem to be much point to it. The driver knew where I lived.

Just as I swung into the short driveway I caught an orange arc in the darkness in front of the garage that could only belong to a cigarette being flipped to the ground. My first instinct was to throw the Cutlass into reverse and clear the hell out of there. My second instinct told me I wouldn't get any answers that way. My third instinct was to go with my first, but by then it was too late. I coasted to a stop and set the brake. The metallic blue of a Detroit Police Tactical Mobile Unit shone in the beam of my headlamps.

"Mr. Walker?" A five hundred-candlepower flashlight shaft caught me full in the face. The officer behind it was a large indistinct hulk in a thin leather Windbreaker whose shiny surface gleamed softly in the backglow.

"If this is about that rented VCR, I've been too busy to return it," I said.

If he found that amusing at all he didn't tip it. "Would you come with us, please?" I had an impression of a broad face with blue-black skin, a heavy bar of moustache, and behind that of another uniformed figure in the darkness. "What's the ruckus?"

"Would you come with us, please?"

"Is this a pinch or can I follow you in my crate?"

He seemed to consider that. "We're going to the southeast side. Don't get lost."

"What street?"

"Ferry Park."

"With or without air support?"

"Please keep up with us, sir. We wouldn't want to have to double back and look for you."

The flashlight snapped off and a pair of broad hips with a creaking gun belt strapped around them turned and started back toward the cruiser. His partner waited until he was inside the car on the driver's side, then went around and got in beside him.

There is something about the way a cop in uniform says "please" and "sir" that is like the way an animal trainer says "sit" and "roll over." I backed out of the driveway and waited obediently for the city car to take the lead.

Twelve

THE ADDRESS on Ferry Park was ten minutes and two worlds away from my cozy Hamtramck neighborhood, a crumbling monument to the last city administration, whose mayor hadn't owned any property there and so left it undeveloped: Grass speared up through buckles in the asphalt out front, pheasants nested in the weeds of the empty lots on both sides, and every time a long-haul semi thundered down the nearby interstate, shingles showered down from the roof like dandruff. It was a squat house with all the paint rubbed off the boards and a patch of burnt lawn wormy with mole tunnels. The bars on the windows were the only improvement it had seen in forty years.

Against this frayed backdrop, the yellow police tape encircling the lot looked garish, the throbbing red and blue strobes of the parked police cruisers as frivolous as Christmas lights at a vigil for the dead. I parked at the curb behind the Tactical Mobile Unit and got out. The big black sergeant who had shone the flashlight in my face asked me to wait there and ducked under the tape. A small group of local residents in fuzzy bathrobes and knee-length football jerseys had gathered on the sidewalk in front, staring at the house and at the officers quartering the yard with flashlights, not looking as if they expected much in the way of entertainment. Police activity in that neighborhood would be almost a nightly event.

The sergeant's partner, a lean cob with a withered-looking face, leaned back against the cruiser, arms folded, daring the crowd with his bitter little eyes to make some move that would give him the opportunity to dazzle them with his fast draw. I saw videotape in his future.

The sergeant leaned his big head out the front door and beckoned to me with his arm. I felt a dozen pairs of eyes on me during the trip up the cracked front walk.

"The lieutenant will see you now," said the sergeant.

"Which lieutenant?"

"Thaler."

That was good news, aesthetically speaking. I found Mary Ann Thaler in the tiny living room, conversing in a group that included a pair of officers in uniform, one of them female, and a young Asian male in a snappy white turtleneck and a corduroy sportcoat with leather patches on the elbows. The lieutenant was a trim 115 pounds or so wearing a red blazer over a silver blouse, black miniskirt, black hose, and moderate heels. She wore her hair longer these days, tumbling in rich light brown waves to her shoulders, and glasses with large frames in a color that matched her hair. The plastic police ID she had clipped to her handkerchief pocket was a fashion don't, but she carried it off. The room was just a room with some furniture in it. It needed cleaning, but then so did mine.

"You look like the tattered end of a long day," she said by way of greeting.

I said, "You look like spring blossoms. Nobody else in Armed Robbery does justice to a miniskirt."

"It's Felony Homicide now, and watch your unenlightened mouth. This is Albert Chung from the coroner's office. Amos Walker."

The Asian shook my hand. "CID?"

"P.I.," I said. "Who's dead?"

He opened his mouth to reply, but Thaler cut him off. She had her notebook out, a nifty slimline pad with imitation alligator covers. "You're working for a Mrs. Neil Catalin in West Bloomfield?"

My inner stem wound itself a notch tighter. "It's Catalin?"

"Missing Persons took a report from her this afternoon. I'm starting to like our new computer system; it cross-references complaints. Mrs. Catalin's maid says she's out for the evening. Sergeant Binder and Officer Wise burned twenty-four dollars in city money waiting for you at your place. You dating clients now?"

I shook my head. "I'm not putting them on electronic tethers, either. Who am I here to identify?"

"These officers were cruising the block when they heard shots." She indicated the Adam-and-Eve team. "They couldn't tell which house the shots came from, so they started pounding on doors. This one was open. It looks like the perp exited out the back. If he had a car it wasn't parked on this street. Two hits?" She lifted her eyebrows at Chung.

He nodded. "Maybe three, but I'm betting one's an exit wound. I'll know more when I get inside."

"The officers heard six shots," she said. "We found three holes in the walls and a freshly broken window, broken from the inside. If it was a professional hit, the pro was either in a hurry or blind or trying to make it look homemade. I vote for genuine homemade. A buy went bad."

"Drugs?"

"Hot merch. Let's take a look."

I followed her through an open door into a kitchen the same size as the living room, that hadn't been done over since Nixon. The cabinets and countertops were avocado to match the refrigerator and four-burner stove. A flycatcher of an imitation Tiffany ceiling fixture shed greasy light onto worn linoleum, stacks of electronic equipment, and Brian Elwood, Gay Catalin's kid brother.

He lay half on his back on the linoleum with his knees drawn into his stomach and his head resting on a baseboard, staring up through the ceiling, the rafters above that, and beyond them the roof, trying hard for the stars. Three of the four bulbs in the fixture weren't working; the one remaining cast shadows from the leading between the panes, etching a spiderweb pattern across the gray bloodless face. There was an angry red hole in his tank top where the pectorals met, frozen pink bubbles on his lips.

"Lung shot," Mary Ann Thaler said. "Drowned in his own blood, probably. You can see he tried to crawl through the side door. Left a track like a snail. His black Jeep's parked next to the door; that's where we got his name, from the registration in the glove compartment. He was trying to get to his wheels."

I bent over him, keeping my lips tight. His shaved head was as gray as a stone. There was blood clotted in his goatee. I tried to make eye contact and gave up. He was seeing something the rest of us would have to wait for.

Straightening, I turned and looked at the equipment piled in the corner. I identified four large video cameras, a laser disc player, a rectangular black box that might have been a seven-channel equalizer, and several thirty-six-inch speakers encased in ebony. There were coils of copper wire and a number of fiberboard cartons with stenciling on them I didn't bother to read.

Thaler said, "We're checking the hot sheets now. There must be ten, fifteen thousand bucks' worth of toys here."

"Twenty," I said. "Wholesale."

"Really. I thought you were still listening to eight-track tapes."

The room smelled of old meals and something much more acrid that didn't belong in a kitchen. "When?"

"Squad car team heard the shots a little after ten. They were another fifteen minutes locating the source; time enough for Little Brother to give up the ghost. He was still plenty warm. The hatch is open on the Cherokee. Either he'd just finished unloading the stuff or he was getting set to cart it away. A few shots wouldn't have drawn much interest in this neighborhood. It was the perp's bad luck the cops were within earshot."

"If he was planning to cap him anyway, why didn't he do it when the stuff was still in the Jeep? He could've just driven it away."

"Maybe the perp wasn't buying. Maybe he was selling, and decided to keep the cash *and* the merch."

"Then he should've waited until it was loaded."

"It could have been spur-of-the-moment. He wasn't used to it or he wouldn't have missed four times. Then he heard the officers banging on doors and bugged out."

"Maybe he didn't care about the merchandise or the money. Maybe he just wanted Brian dead. The whole idea of the buy could have been a set-up."

She hooked a thumb inside her belt, exposing the butt of the service revolver holstered under her blazer. "This was a crack house last year. Before that it was a house of prostitution. I suppose there was a time when it was just a house, but that was when the Irish were still in control. I'd have to check the zoning regulations, but using it to engineer a hit for the sake of a hit is probably a violation. This guy could be in a lot of trouble with the Planning Commission."

"Well, now you're just being facetious."

"I wish I knew what *you* were being."

I looked at her. She was all cop. There was a time, back when women began joining the department, when it was thought they would change it, but the system has been around nearly as long as women, and unlike them it hasn't changed that whole time. It's rock-scissors-paper, and you can cut paper and break scissors, but when you wrap paper around a rock it's still a rock. I said nothing.

"I just came on this one," she said. "You've been on it a couple of days. If there's a connection between Catalin's disappearance and his brother-in-law's death, you don't want to wait till morning to lay it out for us. If this is a plain old kill and not a murder in the commission of a felony, it's not mine anymore. Then it's Homicide's, and you don't want to drag your feet with them. They lack the woman's touch."

I moved my shoulders. "I've got a couple of hunches. They don't make a lot of sense."

"Try me."

"You'll get this off the hot sheets anyway. Neil Catalin's partner at Gilda Productions is a man named Leo Webb. When I spoke to Webb yesterday he thought I was a police detective investigating a theft at Gilda's studio in Southfield. He said someone walked out with twenty thousand in video and sound equipment the night before."

"Anything else?"

"Brian Elwood's name came up during our conversation. He said he caught him once going through Catalin's desk."

"You think Elwood boosted the equipment and Webb shot him for it?"

"Webb's no Boy Scout. Killing a couple of zeroes in the company ledger is more his speed."

"Catalin then. It would explain his taking a powder. He is a mental case."

"Even mental cases have motives for what they do, or convince themselves they have them. Simple theft doesn't seem strong enough, even for someone with problems of his own."

"It's thin," she agreed.

"I said it didn't make a lot of sense."

"Anything else?"

Suddenly I tasted Scotch and soda. Heard a mariachi band playing "Ain't No Use" in slow reggae. Saw a woman in an indigo dress. Telling me something about Brian Elwood. *The little creep.*

I shook my head.

The lieutenant gave it another beat, watching me. Then she unhooked her thumb from her belt and looked down at the corpse. "So do we have a positive ID?"

"It's Brian all right. I only met him once, but he left an impression."

"You can't always tell by appearances. My older sister's boy wears a ring in his nose. He starts Princeton next month."

"I hope he stays clear of places like this."

"If he doesn't, I'll shoot the little son of a bitch myself."

I knew a curtain line when I heard one. I asked if she needed anything else. She said nothing I was willing to give her and that I might think about letting her know if I had any business that took me out of the area. Like I said, nothing's changed.

I fired up the Cutlass and cut every short I knew between Ferry Park and West Bloomfield, which were a good deal closer than the quality of life suggested. I didn't bother looking for the green Camaro. I couldn't afford the time it would take to shake it. I wanted to be standing on Gay Catalin's doorstep when she came back from wherever she'd been all evening.

I was too late. The maid, looking less accommodating than usual in a quilted housecoat with her eyebrows scrubbed off, asked me to wait, then came back after a minute to say her mistress would see me.

She conducted me to the sun porch, where my client sat in a wicker chair surrounded by flowering shrubs in troughs and potted dahlias, mums, geraniums, and a dozen or so varieties outside my knowledge of botany—looking, with nothing but darkness beyond the glass door walls, like a selection of prom dates for the last-minute shopper. Tonight the dress was cream-colored, the lady's face ashen. One hand rested atop a yellow telephone on a lattice table.

"The police just called," she said. "Brian—"

"I know. I just came from there."

"Oh, God." She put her fist in her mouth and started to rock to and fro.

I turned to the maid. "Is there any liquor in the house?"

Her expression turned inward, plumbing the depths of her English. I brought my cupped hand up to my lips. She nodded then and scuffed out in pink slippers. When she returned with a glass of something that smelled like bourbon, I took it and handed it to Mrs. Catalin, who sat hugging herself and made no move to lift it.

I said, "It only works if you drink it."

She drank then, cupping the glass in both hands. She coughed shallowly and tried to put it on the table, but I put my hand around hers and made her lift it again. She was starting to get some color now.

"Now I know why people drink." She tried to smile.

"Alcohol's like war. If it didn't have some good points we'd have figured out a way to get rid of it before this."

"Thank you, Angelina. Go to bed now."

The woman in the housecoat hesitated, then withdrew, drawing shut the doorwall that separated the porch from the living room.

"Was it horrible?" Mrs. Catalin's eyes were on me, as steady as the eyes in a painting.

"It was all over pretty quickly," I said.

"What was he doing in that neighborhood?"

"Your brother was into some things he shouldn't have been. You must have suspected it. Most older sisters have sensors for that kind of thing built in."

"We were born twenty years apart. Our mother was very young when she had me. Brian was a surprise late in life. In many ways, culturally, we were as distant as a parent and her child. I did worry, though. He never stayed with a job more than a few months, but he always seemed to have money to make the payments on his Cherokee, and to buy speakers and things. I wasn't a very good sister. I didn't ask the questions I didn't want to know the answers to."

"That puts you in good company."

"They want me to identify the— to identify Brian. Will you take me? I don't think I can drive."

"Who'd you talk to?"

"A Sergeant Somebody at police headquarters."

"That was old business. I took care of it. They might want you to go to the morgue tomorrow, but there's no reason to visit the murder scene. They'll be around to ask you questions."

"Murder scene." She looked down, rediscovered her drink. She raised it and swallowed.

"One of the questions they'll ask is where you were tonight," I said.

She started. "I forgot. Neil called."

I was stripping the cellophane off a pack of Winstons. I paused, then went on. "When?"

"I didn't look at the clock. It must have been after nine. He wanted me to meet him. He was out of breath. He sounded as if he'd been running."

"Where'd you meet him?"

"I didn't. He asked me to come to the old Michigan Theater."

"The one in Ann Arbor?"

"No. The one in downtown Detroit. It isn't a theater anymore. They gutted it twenty years ago and turned it into a parking garage. He said he used to see movies there when he was in college."

"Why didn't you meet him?"

"He never showed up. I stood in front for two hours. I didn't feel safe waiting any longer; the streets were empty. My car was parked inside. When I went back I found this under my windshield wiper."

She fished a rectangle of pale pink cardboard out of a pocket of her skirt and handed it to me. It was a ticket to Monday night's motion picture screening in the auditorium of the Detroit Institute of Arts. The feature to be shown was *Pitfall*.

Thirteen

I'D LIT THE CIGARETTE, but after the day I'd had I needed both hands to hold the ticket steady, so I tilted my head back to keep the smoke out of my eyes. It didn't do much good. If the etching of the statue of the Spirit of Detroit in the corner tipped me a wink, I'd missed it.

"How sure are you Neil put it on your windshield?" I asked his wife.

"Who else would? He's always been a great supporter of the film series at the DIA. He once rescheduled an important meeting to attend a showing of *Citizen Kane*, a film he already had on tape. I looked at the cars parked nearby, just in case the ticket was part of a promotion of some kind, but mine was the only one that had it. What do you think it means?"

"Could be he thought someone was watching you and decided to change venues. Did you mention hiring me when he called?"

"He didn't give me time. He said, 'Remember my telling you about the Michigan? I'll see you there.' That was it. He hung up before I could ask him any questions."

"You're sure it was him?"

"Yes. It was Neil's voice."

"No 'Hi, honey'? Or darling or poopsy or slugger?"

"No. If there'd been anything like that I'd have known for sure it wasn't Neil. He's not much for endearments."

"Who picked up the telephone. Angelina?"

"She was upstairs, ironing. I answered." She started to set her glass on the lattice table, missed it, and had to look to make contact. Then she twisted her hands in her lap and looked at me. "Do you think he's in trouble? Real trouble, not the kind he'd make up to fit the plot of some movie?"

"I don't know. I don't like that he didn't show. At least not between a quarter to ten and ten-thirty."

Her lips formed a *W*, but the question didn't come out. A curtain slid down behind her face. "That was when Brian was—there. In that place. When he was killed. Wasn't it? You can't suspect Neil."

"The night you hired me and told me about your husband's affair, you wouldn't say how you found out. It was Brian, right? He told you."

"You don't know my husband if you think he'd kill him for that."

"I met Vesta Mannering tonight. She said your brother offered to keep their affair secret from you if Neil came across with a thousand bucks."

"What makes you think you can believe anything that harlot says?" Her cheeks were hot. The pallor had fled.

"If Brian's the one who told you, it means at least half her story is true."

"My brother wasn't a blackmailer."

"Five minutes ago you as good as told me you suspected he was a crook."

"There's a difference between petty thievery and extortion."

"For Brian, that difference was about twenty thousand."

"What's that mean?"

I pinched out my butt and dropped it into a terra-cotta pot containing a purple blossom as big as my hand. "When I talked to Leo Webb, he was complaining that someone had just spirited away that much in electronic equipment from Gilda's studio in Southfield without breaking so much as a window. Tonight the cops found your brother's body in a kitchen that looked like the back room at Radio Shack. When the cops trace the stuff back to Southfield, they're going to ask the same question I'm asking now: Who gave Brian a key?"

"It could have been anyone. Someone might have left a door open accidentally."

"Someone might have. It might even have happened on the same night your brother decided to see what he could boost there. Vesta might have made up the story about the touch. All of this might even have taken place within twenty-four hours of Neil's disappearance. Coincidences happen all the time. Try and sell that to the cops when they put out a warrant for your husband for first-degree murder."

She looked up quickly. "How much did you tell them?"

"Webb told me he caught Brian going through Neil's desk once. I gave them that. They like it when you give them something. I didn't tell them about Vesta Mannering."

"Neither did I, when I reported Neil and Brian missing. I didn't think it was important. I have an idea you didn't tell them because you thought it was."

"At this point I don't know what's important, only what makes me curious. I didn't want to trip over any more cops than I had to satisfying my curiosity. I hope it doesn't come back and bite me on the neck. But it's my neck."

"What do you think happened, Mr. Walker?"

I looked at my reflection in the dark glass enclosing the porch. I saw a tired face on an exhausted body in a suit that needed pressing. "I think your brother had something on your husband; something more serious than an extramarital affair. He approached him with the same deal he did two years ago, only this time the price for his silence was higher. Twenty times higher. All Catalin had to do was throw back a bolt and look the other way. Brian would know where to fence the equipment, and Neil knew from before that he wasn't bluffing when he threatened to tell what he'd dug up."

"What could it have been?"

"I've got a guess or two, but they need running out. One has to do with ninety-two thousand in stolen cash hidden somewhere by Vesta's ex-husband, and a fellow named Musuraca who's looking for it. You told me Neil had money trouble." I rubbed my eyes. They burned as if I'd been watching movies all night. "Whatever it was, it was bad enough to make Neil decide to drop out of the picture for a while."

"Then you don't think it had anything to do with his obsession?"

"It might have had everything to do with it. Those films are the only reality he knows, or accepts. We do what we do from instinct and learning. If your teachers were Humphrey Bogart and Dick Powell and Alan Ladd and Orson Welles, you handle things the way they did. It doesn't matter that it was some hack screenwriter's idea of how to satisfy the requirements of entertainment, studio policy, and the Hays Office, or that the people you're dealing with may not have read the script. He wouldn't think of the fact that in real life there are no retakes. That when the bodies are through falling they don't get back up when the director yells cut."

"What do you propose to do?"

"To begin with, I need to borrow a few more movies from your husband's collection. It would help if you can pick out the ones he watched most often. Not every case gives you a peek at the missing party's shooting script."

"I'm afraid I can't give you many titles. I hadn't been watching with him for quite some time, so I can only describe what I happened to see on the screen whenever I looked in on him."

I grinned. "This is where my wasted youth comes in handy. I overslept through most of high school after staying up with the Late Show."

"What about the DIA?"

I gave her the ticket. She took it without looking at it. "You want me to go in alone?"

"He'll be looking for it. I'll be there early. If Catalin shows, I'll talk to him."

She stood and smoothed her cream-colored skirt. I stepped back to give her room, but she took a step toward me. Even through the competing perfume of the flowers that surrounded us I could smell the euphoric scent she wore. "Is there anything else I can do?" Her eyes were planets of mystery and promise.

"Not unless you know someone who drives a green Camaro."

Disappointment caved in her face. "I—I don't notice people's cars. One is pretty much like all the others. Does it bear on the—case?"

"Maybe not. Most things don't. That's another difference between our world and Neil's."

"Do you really think he killed Brian?"

"I'll let you know what I think when I'm no longer just thinking," I said. "It's not impossible. Up on Mackinac Island, Dr. Naheen told me the Neil Catalin I'm looking for may not be the Neil Catalin you knew."

"Naheen." She hugged herself. "I don't like that man.

Even over the telephone I felt something unclean about him."

"You're not alone. He's one of those guesses I want to run out."

She turned then, and we went to the basement to pick out some movies. She moved carefully on the stairs, like a guest in an unfamiliar house.

Fourteen

I AWOKE WITH THE SUN in my face and some optimism for a bright summer Saturday. By the time I was shaved and dressed the hole in the clouds had closed up along with my hopes. Some hysteric at the radio station I listened to over toast and coffee actually dusted off the emergency signal to warn all of southeastern Michigan it was under a severe thunderstorm watch. God forbid we should all get wet.

I broke out the belted raincoat, drove to the store where I'd rented the VCR, and threw some money at the clerk to keep the video police off my back. On the way home I stopped at Kroger's for some grocery items and got out forty-five minutes later behind a line of local residents laying in for a long siege. Flashlight batteries and canned goods were the order of the day.

Back home I wasted no time. I scooped a videotape at random from the sack Gay Catalin had given me and poked it into the machine, trying to see as much as I could before the blackout. I got through *Detour* and then *Double Indemnity*, but just as John Garfield was about to bash in Cecil Kellaway's skull in *The Postman Always Rings Twice*, a bolt struck nearby with a noise like a forklift truck falling off the kitchen table. The signal snapped and the screen went black.

I jerked all the plugs and sat in my one comfortable chair smoking cigarettes in the leaden gloom, thinking while the rain slapped the siding and the wind rocked the house. Some of Hollywood's best and grimmest were still in the sack, waiting their turn to live again in the cramped confines of my nineteen-inch Motorola: *Gun Crazy*, *Kiss Me Deadly*, *Cape Fear*, *Dead Reckoning*, *D.O.A.*, more I couldn't remember. The titles alone played like a dirge, with a police siren for a minor key. I knew them all, by reputation if not by experience. Like those I had watched already that day, they all had to do with ordinary, not-too-bright characters who plunged or were shoved in up to their necks in dirty money, poisonous women, demented villains, and their own self-devouring angst. When it came to role models, Neil Catalin had set his sights low enough to score a bullseye first shot out of the box. The whole business lined up like Rubik's Cube. It was such a perfect pretty thing I hated to twist it apart.

Hating to do something isn't the same as not doing it. I picked up the telephone, found it was working, and dialed Barry Stackpole's number at the cable station in Southfield where he worked. The female voice that answered said he wasn't in, but she took my name and promised to pass on a message. Fifteen minutes later the bell rang.

"Amos. I thought you were watching Rocky and Bullwinkle this time of a Saturday." He sounded as if he were shouting through an electric fan.

"I might if I could get my set to operate on kerosene," I said. "Don't tell me you popped for a car phone. You always said the three places you most didn't want to be reached were the bathroom, your car, and work."

"The station put it in my contract. They didn't say I had to turn the damn thing on. I mostly use it to order pizza. What's the skinny? Who'd you kill?"

"This isn't for broadcast. I need a favor."

"What? You're breaking up, pal."

"Barry, that's beneath you."

"No, I mean I'm really losing you. Fucking hills. Listen, I'm only about twenty minutes from your dump. Got any beer?"

"It might not be cold by the time you get here."

"That's okay. I'm the bastard son of an English barmaid. See you anon." The connection crackled away.

The lights were still out when he knocked on the door. I opened it to find him drenched. His white-blonde hair, thinning now, was plastered to his scalp, exposing the oblong outline of the metal plate underneath. His shirt was transparent. The harness that held his Fiberglas leg in place stood out beneath the soaked flannel of his slacks. Despite these impediments to exercise he was as trim as ever. His grip would crack hickory.

"You know, owning an umbrella is not an admission of weakness," I said.

"This is Detroit. We drive to the mailbox. Who needs umbrellas? There was talk of warm beer."

"I thought you were AA."

"Oh, I quit that crowd. What good's listening to people's hard-luck stories if you can't publish them?" He glanced around the living room. "Nice. You ought to have power failures more often. It's cheaper than redecorating."

I told him where the towels were and went into the kitchen. When I came back with the beers he was looking at one of the tapes from the sack. His hair stood straight out from his scalp and he had a towel draped across his shoulders. "*Cry of the City*," he read. "Don't you get enough of this kind of thing at work without taking it home?"

"That *is* work." I tossed him one of the beers. He caught it one-handed, put down the videotape, and popped the top on the can with his left hand, the one that was missing two fingers. He'd left them on Livernois some years back, along with his leg and a piece of his cranium. In those days he wrote a crime column for the Detroit *News*, and the people he offended weren't the kind who wrote letters to the editor. Now he chaired a weekly segment on cable entitled "Meet Your Neighbors," and his ratings share and the quality of his contacts had promoted him above the victim line. I let him have the easy chair, found the end of the couch with the most springs, and asked him what he was working on.

"The Russian godfathers are hawking their wares in our hemisphere," he said. "Clear violation of the Monroe Doctrine. I tapped the phone of a hardware dealer in Highland Park who claims to be a Ukrainian, but for a guy who sells hammers and extension cords he spends a lot of time reminiscing about air-lifting Simonov carbines across the Chinese border during the Korean War. I think he's negotiating a trade with the old Matador mob downtown: a carload of Kalashnikova AK-47s for a tanker full of Colombian cocaine."

"Can you use any of it?"

"The station's lawyers say no. But through his brother-in-law the station owner's got title to three more network affiliates than the FCC allows, and I've got affidavits to back it up. I've been saving them for just this situation." He drank off half his can at a gulp.

"Did you ever think of doing one of those call-in gardening programs?"

"With my luck I'd get a call from some clown who dug up Jimmy Hoffa with his flowering hibiscus. What's the favor?"

"I didn't want to have to haul you all the way over here, Barry. I just need a name to go with the number on a license plate."

He drained the can and squashed it with his incomplete hand. "That's it? You can get that from the Secretary of State's office."

"It's closed weekends. I thought if anyone had access outside the regular channels it'd be you. I'd have asked you over the telephone if those damn cellulars worked better than two cans and a string."

"Tell me about the case."

"It wouldn't interest you. There isn't a Sicilian or a Russian in sight."

"Someone said the same thing about the hardware dealer. Then a UPS dispatcher whose kid I helped put through college sent a box to his store containing twelve volumes of Tolstoy in the original."

I took a sip and put my can down on the coffee table and left it there. Warm domestic beer has the consistency of saliva. "You can't use it until I give you the green light."

"Hell, Amos. You think I'd have told you about Highland Park if I thought it'd end up in the Sunday magazine?"

I told him then, leaving out Dr. Ashraf Naheen and Balfour House. I wasn't sure where they fit in myself. When I finished he frowned and ran his fingers through his hair, smoothing it back from the widow's peak.

"I sat in on the Silvera trial," he said. "Two of the video store managers owed money to the same shylock in Taylor, and it looked like the robberies might have been set up to arrange a payback. But there was no connection with the others and everything about Silvera screamed independent. The Ferry Park murder's nothing. Back on the *News* we'd have buried it with the horoscopes."

"I said there wasn't anything in it for you."

"Now tell it to me again, and this time put back in what you took out."

"That's the kit."

He smiled slowly, the way he had when a state liquor control commissioner insisted on the air he'd awarded Sam Lucy a license to sell alcoholic beverages without knowing Frank Costello had given the bride away at Lucy's wedding. "This is Barry. The guy you fell on in a shell hole in Da Nang, remember? The only guy in Southeast Asia who was a better liar than you."

I lit a cigarette and pushed the match through the hole in my beer can. It spat when it touched liquid. "Catalin fell off once before, a year and a half ago. He landed in a *casa del loco* on Mackinac Island. One of the natives there told me he suspects the shrink in charge of taping his sessions with well-heeled patients and selling the tapes back to them later." I gave him the shrink's name.

"Naheen. Don't know it. That grift's as old as Freud's couch. Video or audio?"

"Video."

"Anything to it?"

"Your guess is as good as mine. Resort island like that, a laugh-house honcho's got to be about as popular as sharks offshore. Stories are going to be made up. Even if this one is true, I can't see how it ties in."

"Maybe you haven't watched enough movies."

"*There's* a line I never thought I'd hear from anyone," I said.

"Seriously, everything about this one has to do with videotape. Gilda Productions, Catalin's obsession, the shotgun robberies, the shrink. I'm guessing you played with that."

"We're living in the age of the couch potato. Everything has to do with videotape. Even the cops look to make sure there's a blank tape in the minicam before they check the loads in their revolvers. That's no handle."

"What about the Camaro?"

"Search me. That's why I called you. Sometimes it's there, sometimes it's not. It's there too often to be coincidence but not often enough to draw a lot of attention. That means he's done it before. It might not even connect to the Catalin case. Not everything has to."

"Be nice if it did, though. Life's snarled enough as it is. No wonder your boy prefers Hollywood."

"That's what everyone says. Hell, it's not even a town. Just a street that never really existed."

"That's the draw." He craned an arm and scooped the telephone from its table into his lap. "What's the plate number?"

I gave it to him. He dialed from memory, waited, began talking. He knew whoever was on the other end fairly well. I was pretty sure it was a woman. A man's tones usually soften when that's the case, regardless of what he thinks of her. He made no notes. Barry Stackpole's memory for names, dates, figures, and details had been known to reduce more than one trial lawyer to frustrated splutters in the middle of a cross-examination.

He thanked her and hung up. His eyes were bright, even for him. I recognized the mood. He was going to let me dangle for a while.

I had time. It was the weekend, after all. I took a drag and flicked ash into the beer can. "Who'd you talk to?"

"Secretary of State."

"I guessed that much."

"No, you didn't." His expression was deadpan.

I looked at him. Realization wore through with a pace like erosion. "How'd you come to know the Michigan Secretary of State?"

"I didn't. She came to know me. She's the one needs the good will of the media." He moved his shoulders. "Okay. I slap the handball around sometimes with her husband at the Detroit Athletic Club. I got him the exit-poll results in the last election, two hours before they were announced. It gave her a head start on her acceptance speech."

"Talk about your backhand."

"With what's been happening to the First Amendment, I need all the help I can steal. Anyway her personal computer is wired into the mainframe in Lansing. Don't you want to know what it coughed up?"

"I figured you'd tell me when I'd twisted long enough."

"Trouble is you don't twist. The Camaro's registered to Orvis Robinette, Sherman Hotel, Detroit." He spelled the name.

Not having Barry's memory I got up and wrote it on the telephone pad. "What's the gag? The city condemned the Sherman five years ago. They needed another empty lot."

"It's still operating, a very exclusive address. You can't register without a record as long as Pete's feet. Every lammister, sneak thief, kneecapper, crumb bum, and congressman who's anyone has hung his brass knuckles at the Sherman at one time or another."

"I wonder which one of those things Orvis Robinette is."

"You mean you really don't know? How do you make a living at this?"

"I don't. I'm only doing it to keep busy until the presidential nominating committee calls." I waited.

"You'd better say yes. I don't know what he's been up to lately, but three years ago the cops downriver arrested him for suspicion of complicity in the shotgun robberies. Orvis covered Ted Silvera's back."

REEL TWO
Cross-Fade

Fifteen

I WAS RUNNING down a dark narrow alley, darker than you'll find in the era of twenty-four-hour security lights and narrower than they make them in this country; I couldn't see my hands but I could touch one to each wall merely by spreading my arms. The bricks felt springy. I could have pushed my fists through them without much effort. They were painted canvas.

What illumination there was reached me by ricochet, the green-and-pink phosphorescence of a neon advertising sign mounted on some high roof reflecting off the chemical slime with which the false bricks were sprayed. I knew it was green and pink, but I couldn't see the colors. Everything was black and white and a sinister grade of silver, like nitrate splinters in film manufactured before the invention of safety stock. The celluloid was volatile. It could burst into flames any second if the bulb in the projector got too hot. Meanwhile, the silver continued to oxidize steadily, dissolving the walls and sky and shining pavement with the inevitability of human mortality, curling up and turning brown at the edges, collapsing upon itself like plastic melting. Existence itself was ephemeral, and mine was only a matter of the immediate present. Death was behind me. In front of me there was only darkness, interrupted by scratches and splices and age-cracks through which edged that silver light, serving only to make the blacks seem blacker.

I ran and ran. My side ached and my breath sawed in my throat. My own footsteps clattered back at me. I couldn't separate them from those of Death. I ran around a sharp corner, and suddenly I was no longer in an alley. Now I was running down the midway of a deserted amusement park. No one rode the merry-go-round, no lines waited to enter the arcade, the lighted Ferris wheel turned at a mournful pace against a starless vault with its gondolas swinging empty. I heard the echoes of the day's merriment, hollow and drawn and forlorn, like the cries of the ghost riders in the old song. The warped soundtrack popped and sizzled.

I ran, stumbled, and ran faster to catch myself before I fell. The scenery whirled, became a smear of painted horses and wicked-looking clown faces and Uncle Sam on stilts and barkers in straw hats and stripes with faces like skulls. Other images, having nothing to do with the sights and sounds of an amusement park, bled in from offscreen: cars slamming into light poles, stacks of poker chips telescoping to the sky, exploding storefronts, chattering submachine guns, bodies rolling into gutters. I was trapped in a montage from an old Warner Brothers gangster film.

At length I spotted the Tunnel of Love and dived into it. A boat shaped like a dragon was waiting. I handed a coin to the gondolier standing in the bow and climbed onto a seat. He pushed off, singing the theme to *Laura* in a high, ethereal voice that reminded me of the doomed street singer in *The Body Snatcher*. I interrupted him to warn him to look out for Boris Karloff. He turned, and I saw that he was Brian Elwood, complete with bullet holes in his torso, a fleck of congealed blood on his lips, and that vacant stare that none living could intercept.

My eyes sprang open. I was clutching the sides of my mattress with both hands, as if I were trying to push myself out of a boat. The sheets were soaked through with my sweat and the muscles of my jaw ached from clenching.

I snapped on the lamp and looked at the wind-up alarm clock on the nightstand. It was ten after three Sunday morning. The street in front of the house was quiet, as it never was any other hour of the week. The storm had long since passed. The power had come back on sometime during the night.

I got up, threw on my robe, and padded into the kitchen to pour myself a glass of milk. I needed the nutrients. Barry and I had progressed from beer to gin, killing off a bottle with a picture of Queen Victoria on the label I found in the cupboard over the sink and listening to the Tigers lose to Seattle on my portable radio. I'd poured him into a cab sometime around 7:00 P.M. Now my head was whanging and my tongue felt as thick as a sofa cushion.

I finished the glass sitting at the table in the breakfast nook, smoked half a cigarette, and put it out when it started to taste like stale gin. Then I went back to bed and the nightmares I was more accustomed to: Vietnam and my marriage.

In the morning I swung out of my way to stop at the video store, waited ten minutes for it to open, and pulled three tapes off the shelves. The kid behind the counter, eighteen and forty pounds overweight in a NO FEAR T-shirt with Clearasil stains on the neckband, was watching a pair of Asians kicking the sushi out of each other on the monitor. Reluctantly I turned away to process my selections.

"*Singin' in the Rain, The Mating Game, Tammy and the Bachelor*." He demagnetized them and handed them back. "Debbie Reynolds fan?"

"Not especially. But nobody ever gets killed in her pictures."

"Except for *How the West Was Won*."

I pointed at the monitor. "What do you get out of those?"

He hunched his round shoulders. "I watch 'em and then I don't go home and stomp the shit out of my old man."

"If it's that bad, why don't you move out?"

"Then I wouldn't have nobody to stomp the shit out of but me." He let his shoulders fall. "Your life's so great you got to go out and monkey around with other people's?"

"If my life were that great I wouldn't need Debbie Reynolds."

I pushed on the door. As it drifted shut behind me the kid's voice floated out: "Attaboy, Bruce. Kick his nuts up between his ears."

I often leave the door to my waiting room unlocked, for those customers who don't mind waiting and reading about pet rocks and disco in the magazines on the coffee table. I'd had a visitor that morning. There were ashes in the tin tray and the air was sticky with a scorched smell that made me wonder at first if I were having a flashback. Marijuana smoking's less common in public places now that no one cares. I didn't poke through the ashes to determine the grade, or inspect the pile carpet for footprints. Sherlock Holmes had more time on his hands and no living to make.

I unlocked the door to the Fortress of Solitude, scooped up the mail under the slot, and carried it to the desk. I checked my service, but there were no messages. I dialed Gay Catalin's number to ask if she'd heard anything more from Neil. Angelina told me her mistress was at Detroit Police Headquarters, making arrangements for the release of her brother's body. Next I called headquarters and asked for Mary Ann Thaler. The sergeant I spoke to said she was away from her desk. I left my name and number and asked him to have Lieutenant Thaler call me when she showed up.

"This police business?"

"It's about the Brian Elwood murder."

"That isn't Thaler's now. It's been booted over to Homicide."

My chair creaked when I sat up. "What happened?"

"You'll have to talk to the inspector about that."

"Inspector who?"

"Alderdyce."

"So there is a God."

"Huh?"

"Nothing. Put me through to the inspector, can you?"

"This isn't your lucky day, mister. He's out too."

"If it was, it'd be my first. Please have him call me when he gets in."

I opened my mail, filed the bills under the blotter and a check for a credit job in my inside pocket, then unholstered the Luger and swapped it for the .38 Smith & Wesson revolver I kept in the top drawer of the desk. I'd never liked the Luger and only carried it when the Smith wasn't handy. My father had traded a '48 Hudson for the German automatic, which a friend had swiped off a headless corpse at Bastogne and never got around to registering. It was as comfortable to hold as a printing press and once you'd squeezed the trigger the action had to take a slow boat to Stuttgart and back to complete the firing chain. It worked on the same principle as a pocket lighter and was about as reliable.

The revolver needed cleaning. I took it apart and broke the kit out of the file cabinet. I wasn't at loose ends. I needed the mindless repetitive task to keep my hands busy while my brain gnawed at the latest bone to be thrown my way.

If the Elwood killing had been taken out of Thaler's hands and given to Alderdyce, it was no longer considered a homicide committed during the course of a lesser felony. It was a case of someone being made dead merely for the sake of having him dead. That meant that between Friday night and Monday morning something had happened to redirect the progress of a criminal investigation system that normally conducted itself as if Truman were still in the White House. It promoted Gay Catalin's kid brother from spear carrier, if not to a spot on the bill, to at least a part with a bigger spear. I wondered how much it all had to do with Neil Catalin's vanishing act; or, if it hadn't, how much longer this straight pass of coincidences would go on until it came up snake eyes.

I was rearranging all this heavy philosophical furniture when a visitor who made no noise at all on the balls of his feet came in from the waiting room. He was holding a gun, and unlike mine his was all in one piece.

Sixteen

HE WAS TOO SHORT for a basketball center, but that was the only thing he'd ever be too short for. At six-five he ducked his head from long habit to clear the top of the door frame. He had a swimmer's build, slender and smoothly muscled under a green silk sport shirt and mottled jeans secured with a braided leather belt just under his solar plexus. His feet were small for his size, cased in spotless Nikes whose heels lit up when he placed his weight on them. He had a diamond in one earlobe and his short coiled hair was dyed a bright tangerine orange. His skin was the deep rich brown of a walnut gunstock.

The pistol, a nine-millimeter Beretta, blue-black with an orange front sight to match his hair, rode in his right hand like an extension of his palm.

He shut the door behind him and stepped aside from it, increasing his field of fire to include the doorway and the desk where I sat. It was a professional move, smoothly choreographed from much repetition. At this point I was pretty sure who he was, but I let him start the discussion.

"I guess I'll have you keep your hands there where I can see them." His voice was as deep and rich as his coloring. When he'd found out there was already one Lou Rawls, the disappointment had driven him to a life of crime. "You're

Walker. You ought to spruce up that Cutlass. It's a cherry machine."

"I told someone else the same thing last week, about his Buick," I said. "You keep up that Camaro pretty good."

"It ain't nothing. I drove a black Jag for a while, a real cherry, but I had to get rid of it. It's a cop magnet."

"So's the hair. It's part of the profile of a dope dealer. They know you can't be Dennis Rodman since he left the Pistons."

"Rodman stole it from me. Tell *him* to change. You know who I am, huh."

"I didn't for sure, until the Camaro gag. You're Orvis Robinette. You helped Ted Silvera push in a row of video stores downriver three years ago."

"That's what the cops said. The eyewitnesses didn't agree. You know how them suspects in police sketches are always wearing knitted caps? They all look alike."

"I guess the dye job throws them off at lineup."

"Got the idea all by myself. See, everybody up there tries not to be noticed. They scrunch theirselves down, keep their eyes on the floor. Me, I raise my chin and look straight out like I can see 'em right through that one-way glass. Guy like that, orange hair, they just know he can't be the one. It's like being fucking invisible. Where's Catalin?"

The sudden shift from patter to business caught me without words. He thought I was stalling. He extended the arm with the gun, sighting down it to a point between my eyes.

I fought the urge to spread my hands. Berettas have hair triggers. "If I knew that, I wouldn't be here now. I'd be down at the Frank Murphy Hall of Justice hunting up another job."

"Where was you this morning? I waited here for you twenty minutes after I lost you on Telegraph."

I hadn't spotted him this time. That made me mad enough

to tell him the truth. "I went to a video store and rented three Debbie Reynolds movies."

His smile was broad and bright and died a mile short of his eyes. "Man, you arc so dead."

"I want Catalin because his wife wants him and she's paying me to bring him back. Why do you want him?"

"Why should I answer anything a dead man asks me?"

"Cut the crap, Robinette. If I weren't worth more to you alive, you'd have plugged me on principle the second you came through the door. You've been following me all over greater Detroit, hoping to find out what I find out as soon as I find it out. I figure I picked you up at Catalin's place in West Bloomfield. What's your interest in Catalin? Why'd you stake out his house? Tell me something and maybe I'll tell you something back. You can put all the holes in my head you want to, but it's not going to spill out."

He held the bead. I had an itch between my eyes worse than any I'd known.

"Shit." He relaxed his arm. Without taking his eyes off me he hooked an ankle around a leg of the customer's chair and tried to pull it around to the corner of the desk. When it wouldn't budge he glanced down at the floor. I thought about the Luger in the top drawer. That was as far as I got, the thought, when he looked back at me. "It's bolted down. How come?"

"I like to breathe oxygen, not onions. Don't worry, it's not wired."

He gave the door a quick look, considered, then sat down and laid the pistol on the corner of the desk nearest him and farthest from me. From his shirt pocket he brought out a slim plastic case like the ones the cigarette companies used to give away and pulled it apart. The bottom half contained three twists of brown paper. He stuck one between his lips, set fire to it with a disposable butane lighter, and returned the case and the lighter to his pocket. "I'd offer you one, but these days a nickel bag costs a quarter. Gummint's got to do something about this here inflation, you know what I'm saying?" His vocal cords were strained. That sticky scorched smell began to fill the office.

"I'll write my congressman. Okay if I smoke tobacco?" I used my knee to nudge open the drawer a crack.

"Rather you didn't. Bad for your ticker." He sat back and crossed his legs, resting a hand on the ankle nearest the Beretta. He wasn't wearing socks. "I had some poor luck after Ted went in. I went to Chicago to shop. Illinois state cops stopped me on the way back with a couple of MacIntoshes and a laser printer in my trunk, still in the box. I done twenny-six months on a one-to-five in Joliet. Man, it was hot there. When I got out last month I thought I'd catch a breeze up here. Shit, it's as hot as Biloxi. What the fuck you folks go and do to the weather whilst I was gone?"

"It's all caught up with the Fall of Russia; we're still trying to figure it out. You muck around a lot with stolen electronic equipment?" My tone was as casual as lunch at the drive-through.

"Diversification, that's the key to success in bidness." He grinned. "See, I only ducks and shuffles when I wants to. Well, it was a bad call. When I get bored I do stuff I shouldn't. I'm bored now."

"Damn straight it was a bad call. Especially with ninety-two grand of your own hard-stolen money out there just waiting for you to dig it up."

He uncrossed his legs and scooped up the gun. "If you know about that, you talked to Catalin. Where the hell is he?"

"Don't be modest. Your little string of heists made the papers. Silvera pulled down a heavy sentence for refusing to tell what he did with the money or who helped him get it."

"Ted's stand-up. That's why I threw in with him to start. My last partner had a big mouth, so I went with one that had no mouth at all. He didn't even tell *me*."

"Wasn't it a little careless to leave the whole bundle to him?"

"Would've been more careless not to. I had a record as long as Woodward when we hooked up. Whenever anything goes down in this town, the cops throw out a loop and I'm always in it. I couldn't risk getting snagged with even half that money on me. The cops didn't know about Ted. He could carry the cash down the street in a basket and they'd just think he was on his way to the Laundromat. I figured, what the hell, I can always pry it away from him if he decides to get cute. I *didn't* expect him to get picked up before he had the chance."

I was getting a handle on Orvis Robinette. I was just there to keep him from justifying himself to himself. He was gesturing with the hand holding the gun as if he'd forgotten it was there. I nudged the drawer open another couple of inches.

"They had Ted in the can so quick I was sure they got the money too," he said. "That's when I made my little trip west, to tide me over till another sweet thing come along like the video stores. By the time I found out the cops in Detroit didn't know any more about where the cash was than I did, I had troubles of my own. Not no more, though." He stood, pointing the Beretta.

I hoisted my eyebrows. "You think *I* know where it is?"

"If you did you wouldn't be sitting around no grubby office in no hot city. You be out on some cool cruise, sniffing that salt air and dipping into them single women out fishing for rich guys. Catalin's the one knows where the money is.

It's right there in his hip pocket, and you got a line on where he and his hip pocket are keeping theirselves."

"What makes you think Catalin knows?"

He had an infectious smile, if you didn't look at the top half of his face while he was wearing it. "You ain't too good at this. The guy with the wand's the one gets to axe the questions. Stand up. You're taking me to Catalin."

I rose, bracing my hands on the edge of the desk. I slipped one inside the drawer and pointed the Luger at his midsection, what there was of it.

The smile set like concrete. "Now, what's this?" he said. "One guy with a piece, that's cool. Two guys without pieces is okay. But two guys both with pieces is just stupid." He fired the Beretta.

I was clinically dead. As a pro he knew it, and that was where he threw it away. He thought he had all the time in the world. While he was using it, watching the scene like a disinterested third party, I pulled up on the edge of the desk, getting my left hip under it. The top of the desk collided with his pistol just as he squeezed the trigger. Later I found a hole in the heating return pipe running up from the furnace that had come down the river with Father Marquette.

He had good reflexes. He backpedaled to keep from falling over backward, where the desk would have crushed him, but neglected to consider the bolted-down chair. His face showed its first sign of panic when the backs of his knees came into contact with the edge of the seat. By then my right hand was in motion. The barrel of the Luger struck the left side of his head along the cheekstrap with a noise like a Lou Whitaker double and he dropped below my line of vision. When he opened his eyes he was sitting in the chair with the desk tilted across the tops of his thighs, pinching off his circulation, with me leaning against it on one hand with the Luger in the other, tickling the strip of flesh between his nostrils with the muzzle. His own gun lay on the rug near the connecting door to the outer office, mixed up with the scattered parts of my dismantled revolver.

I was beginning to develop a grudging respect for the German automatic.

He struggled, realized his forearms were trapped between his thighs and the desk, and gave up with a general subsidence of his long tubular frame that might have broken my heart if he hadn't tried to kill me fifteen seconds before.

"Well, hell," he said. "Things just ain't been working out for me outside."

"You're rusty." I tickled his nostrils with the Luger. "Wand. What makes you think Neil Catalin knows what happened to the ninety-two thousand?"

"You could let up a little. I got no feeling in my toes."

"That's how gangrene starts." I leaned harder, repeating the question.

He grimaced. "I figured if Ted told anybody he told his wife, so I axed her."

"You talked to Vesta?"

His skin had lost its sheen. I let up a notch. He exhaled. "I walked in on her in her dump the day after I got out," he said. "I'd of done it the day before but it took me twelve hours to find out where she moved after she divorced Ted. I batted her around some, not too hard. I like Vesta. She said the night before he got busted Ted sent her to bed while he talked in the kitchen with someone named Ernie, she didn't know what about. That'd be Ernie Fishman. We used to fence stuff through his junk shop in Flatrock, equipment we boosted from places where there wasn't much cash in the till. Ernie dealt everything: coins, tape decks, hot rocks. I figured Ted invested the cash with him."

"Invested how?"

"Well, you got to know Ted. He was always going on about how the smart guys were the guys who made money off the dumb guys who took all the risks stealing it. Said if me and him had any brains we'd quit the heist jobs when we had a nice round figure and let it ride with Ernie. I says, 'Yeah, but what if Ernie don't pay it back?' He says, 'Then we just steal it back from Ernie.' That was the beauty of it, see, we had the experience."

"So you went to see Ernie."

"You need a spiritualist to see Ernie. Ernie died last year. His landlord sold off the inventory to pay off the lease. City bought the building and knocked it down for a parking lot."

"Then the money's gone."

"That's what I thought, but I don't give up that easy. I went back to see Vesta just to see if she was funning me about Ernie coming to visit. That's when I seen this guy Catalin coming out of her dump."

"You saw Catalin when?"

Bullets of sweat popped out of a crease in his forehead. I realized I was leaning all my weight on the desk. I straightened, tipping it back onto four legs. The edge had left a furrow across Robinette's forearms. He started to pull himself out of his slouch, couldn't get a grip on the sides of the chair, and sat working his fingers. As circulation returned he glanced up at me, but the calculation fled his face when he saw the Luger still trained on him. He rubbed his thighs.

"Last week sometime," he said. "Tuesday, I think. It was late."

That was the day Catalin had walked out in the middle of a business meeting. His wife hired me the next day. "How'd you know it was Catalin?"

"I didn't. I got curious and followed him. He drove clear to Detroit and parked in back of the Alamo Hotel down there on Jefferson and went into one of the rooms. When he didn't come right back out I checked the registration in his glove compartment."

"Where'd he go from there?"

"I didn't hang around to see. I had his name and address so I figured I could find him if I needed to. See, I didn't know him from Sam's cat. I went back to Vesta's and axed her about him. I didn't need to bat her around this time; she remembered how it was before. She told me she and Catalin wrinkled the sheets a couple of times after Ted went into the can but this was the first time she seen him in a couple of years. She said he told her he thought he knew where the money was. He wouldn't say where, but if he was right he'd be back to split it with her."

"You believed her?"

"I believed her enough to go back and axe Catalin. Only he wasn't there. Clerk at the Alamo told me he checked out around one A.M. I drove out to his place in West Bloomfield, but his car wasn't in the garage. I staked the place out. Nobody came or went in the next fifteen hours except this kid in a Grand Cherokee, and he sure wasn't Catalin. Then you showed."

"You're pretty handy with a car door lock," I said. "I may have to find another place to keep my registration."

"Don't bother. I know all the places. When I looked you up and found out you was a private cop, I decided to adopt you. You almost threw me off when you switched cars. I thought you was on to me."

"Not then. You're pretty handy all around." I put away the pistol and showed him the picture of Neil Catalin.

"Could be him. It was dark, and he had a hat on. You figure his old lady knows about the ninety-two large? I can't think of any other reason why she'd want him back."

"You never know with these quiet ones." I walked

around the desk and picked up the Beretta. "What about the kid in the Grand Cherokee?"

"What about him? I thought he was peddling subscriptions to *Rolling Stone*."

"He was Catalin's brother-in-law. The Detroit cops body-bagged him out of a house on Ferry Park Friday night. Somebody pumped three bullets into him." I sniffed the barrel. If it had been fired recently, it had been cleaned since.

"So that's where you went with the cops. I split when I seen 'em. They're bad luck for me."

"Care to tell me where you were around ten P.M. Friday?"

"Looking for a way to sit on my front seat that didn't hurt my hemorrhoids while you was listening to spick music with Vesta in the Castanet Lounge."

"You could have gone off to do the brother-in-law and been back before we left."

"Could of. Didn't. I ain't in the habit of doing folks I ain't met. What you think I am, one of them Cheerio killers?"

"You don't mind if I hang on to your piece, just in case the cops aren't as reasonable as I am."

"I don't guess I'll have much to say about it in the can."

"I'm not turning you in. If I started reporting people for criminal stupidity, there wouldn't be anyone left to pay taxes. That will change if I catch you tailing me again."

"You won't catch me." He stood up.

"I don't suppose it would do any good to advise you to give up on that money."

He shook his orange head. His confidence was returning. It would never be absent for long. "Ted's in the can, I can't touch him. Your guy's on the street. I hunt the street. Ask anybody."

He walked out past me.

I found all the parts of the revolver except one small screw. That meant a trip to a gun shop, and life with the Luger until then. I picked up the telephone and replaced the receiver. Just then the bell rang, and it was John Alderdyce. They're never around when you need them.

Seventeen

Seventeen

I'D VISITED John Alderdyce's office only once before since he made inspector. It hadn't changed, not the requisite Academy class picture in a metal frame on the wall or the shots of his wife and two children in their younger years on the desk or the expired flies in the bowl fixture suspended by chains from the ceiling. He had, though; he'd aged visibly. Some of it was good: the gray in his short hair softened the brutal Masai-warrior cast of his face, making it look less like the rock against which a thousand alibis had been smashed. Some of it was less beneficial: the weight he'd gained since he'd stopped going to crime scenes had settled in for the duration, forming jowls, a serious paunch, and a roll around his chest that messed up the lines of his custom shirt. It was getting hard to believe that we were almost the same age. Or I hoped it was.

"What did you call me about?" he said when I came in and pushed the door shut behind me.

"That's it?" I asked. "No, 'Hey, Amos, how's the boy'?"

"Your color's good and you've got that same cocky son-of-a-bitch look you had on your face the time you shot me in the ass with a Daisy rifle. I can guess how the boy is."

"It was a Red Ryder. And we were playing *Sands of Iwo Jima.* I was John Wayne."

"John Wayne waited for the Japs to turn around before he shot them."

"The Japs didn't outweigh John Wayne by fifteen pounds." I spun a chair and straddled it, folding my arms across the back. "Anyway, you called me."

"I was returning your call." He closed the folder on the arrest report he'd been reading and rested his hands on top of it, looking as impassive as igneous.

"I heard the Elwood shooting got bumped to Homicide. I wondered why."

"I traded Lieutenant Thaler two drive-bys and a domestic murder for it. I needed the change of pace."

"Hey, that's my schtick. You're supposed to throw me through that partition when I ask too many questions."

"You're bigger than you were at the time of the Red Ryder incident." After a short silence he opened his desk drawer and skidded a glassine bag across the top. It contained a video rental card with Neil Catalin's name embossed across it. "Forensics found that at the crime scene. We figure either it fell out of Catalin's pocket when he was bending over the body or the pocket got torn when Elwood put up a fight and it fell out then. That takes it out of the category of a homicide connected to a lesser felony. Catalin traced the equipment that was stolen from his production company to his brother-in-law and shot him. That makes it a revenge killing."

"Anybody could make up a card with Catalin's name on it. It could be a plant."

"Getting his prints on it is a little harder. They check against a set we had on file from a gun registration Catalin made two years ago. His wife can't find the gun, by the way. It's a nine-millimeter S-and-W semi-automatic. Care to guess what caliber slug Dr. Chung dug out of Elwood at the morgue?"

"Nine millimeter's the Chevy of guns. I've got a Beretta in that caliber sitting in my safe I'll send over later. You might want to check it out."

"Why might we?"

"I'll tell you if it matches up. If it doesn't it won't much matter, except it'll be one less gun on the street. Any other prints?"

"Should there be?"

"If Catalin used the card there should be at least one other set, belonging to the clerk in the store where he used it the last time he rented a video. The turnover in that business is worse than McDonald's; unless the clerk's been printed for some reason in the past you probably won't match it. But there should be another set."

"Not if he obliterated it when he handled it last. He had to put the card away after the clerk returned it."

"Anyway, that answers my question."

"Who belongs to the Beretta you're sitting on?"

I'd already thought about that. Having Orvis Robinette picked up for questioning in the Elwood homicide would get him off my neck for a while, probably for years considering the rules against possession of a handgun while on parole, but it would pull Vesta Mannering into the police investigation, and I had a couple of questions I wanted to put to her myself before the cops started in. I hung on to Brian's attempted blackmail of Catalin for the same reason. I'd gotten that from Vesta.

"I found it in an empty lot," I said.

"What empty lot?"

"I can't remember. You can't cut through a vacant block in this town without tripping over ordnance."

"I can tank you as a material witness."

"Can you? I sure can use the rest."

He pointed at the door. "If that gun isn't on my desk by

five o'clock I'll get a warrant and toss your office. I'll dump your case files on the reading table in the employee lounge downstairs. That ought to do plenty for your reputation as a confidential agent."

"Well, it beats threatening my license. I was getting tired of that."

"Just send over the piece. And call if you find Catalin. He's more than a missing person now. He's the prime suspect in a murder investigation."

"Not exactly an exclusive group in this town."

He pointed. I went.

It was lunchtime. I set the Cutlass west on Michigan and followed it to Livernois, checking the mirror from time to time for Orvis Robinette's Camaro, which didn't make an appearance. I had a taste for the cuisine at Ziggy's Chop House.

The Power Lunch was a Ziggy's specialty. The restaurant's low ceilings and Mission Oak tables and chairs did little to absorb the clatter of flatware on crockery and buzzle of masculine voices, folding every variety of corporate thimble-rigging inside the din of Cro-Magnons feasting on saber-tooth steaks and medallions of mastodon. The only females in evidence were the help. Women weren't barred; they just didn't like the place. The current record belonged to a distaff member of the design team at Chrysler, who had endured five consecutive lunches among the rep ties, white-on-white shirts, and gold cufflinks flashing over bloody T-bones and bowls of black bean soup and remains of butchered competitors, then conducted an orderly retreat to the Olive Garden and a more genteel brand of carnage. Ziggy's continued to operate as it had since the Irish ran Detroit, not in defiance of the sexual revolution so much as it seemed unaware of it.

"Have you a—"

Vesta broke off when she recognized me. She looked a little less ethereal standing behind the reservation desk than she had among the shadows of the Castanet Lounge, but no more undesirable. She had on a multicolored silk blouse that wrapped around her waist without a button and an ankle-length black skirt with a row of jet snaps along the slit that allowed her to be as daring as she chose. Today she had dared as far as the knee. Her feet were arched in black patent-leather heels with silver clips shaped like Art Deco butterflies. She wore her black hair up, exposing onyx buttons in her ears.

"No reservation," I said. "I'll take the table for two by the kitchen where the personnel break."

Her dark glance darted past my shoulder to the customers waiting behind, then back to me. "Smoking or non?"

"That depends on whether you need a cigarette. You're joining me."

"I can't." She whispered it.

"Sure you can. I had a visit from Orvis Robinette this morning."

She surprised me by turning pale. I'd had her pegged for a better poker player than that. She touched the arm of a passing waitress. "Linda, can you hold down the desk for a little while?"

"All I've got is a party of undertakers and a guy reading the *Wall Street Journal.* They won't even notice I'm gone."

I followed Vesta all the way through the dining room and out a fire exit leading to a row of parking spaces reserved for employees. The temperature change from the air conditioning inside was a shock, but not as harsh as the waves of heat crawling beyond the building's shade.

I said, "I guess this means we don't eat."

"I've waited tables in a lot of places. You can't have a private conversation in a restaurant." Producing a set of keys from her skirt pocket, she unlocked the driver's door of her red Triumph, got in, and leaned across to pop up the button on the passenger's side. The black leather seat was warm against my back.

"There's a fresh carton in the glove compartment," she said. "Break out a pack for me, will you?"

She smoked Kools. I lit one for her and a Winston for myself. "Start with Robinette," I said. "You told me you didn't know who your husband's partner was in the video store robberies."

"I told the police the same thing. I was telling the truth then. If you went to them with another story, they'd think I lied and that I knew everything, including what Ted did with the money. They'd be all over me."

"How much do you know?"

She looked at me. There sitting behind the wheel of her own car she was no longer pale. "Ted never told me anything. I didn't lie about that. I never heard of Robinette before last month, when he broke in on me in my apartment and started slapping me around, asking me where the money was.

"I've been hurt before," she said. "I can stand pain. I can't afford to have my face messed up permanently. I know I'm not the world's greatest actress; I need these looks."

"You told him about Ted's meeting with Ernie Fishman. Their fence."

"I heard Ted call him Ernie. I didn't hear any other name and Ted didn't tell me who he was. Do you believe me?"

"Robinette believed you. He had a lot more to gain by not believing you."

"I guess some people still say crime doesn't pay. I don't know about that, but I sure know being married to a criminal doesn't pay. The only thing Ted ever gave me was this car, and he bought that secondhand, on time, with money he earned stacking cartons at Kroger's. He was afraid to spend the money he got from stealing because it might draw too much attention. So what was the point?"

"He had to have done something with the money. He didn't burn it."

She took a deep drag, spat out smoke, and snapped her butt out the window on her side. She got the least amount of good out of a cigarette of anyone I'd seen in a long time. "So that's what this is about," she said. "The money. I needed another Fat Phil Musuraca on my case. That's the only thing I was missing."

"I like money as much as the next guy, if the next guy isn't Orvis Robinette. That's the difference between him and me, apart from our colorists. I'm all practiced up on poverty. It'd be a shame to get rich all of a piece and see that go to waste. I'm looking for Neil Catalin. When I find him I collect my five hundred per diem plus the cost of cigarettes and whiskey and gasoline and get my start on my first million. Where's Neil?"

"I haven't the slightest idea since two years ago the first of this month."

"That isn't what you told Robinette."

That bothered her a lot. She reached up, tilted the rearview mirror, and smoothed her lipstick with a fingertip. "I was wondering when you'd get to that."

"It seems to have slipped your mind Friday night when I asked you for the second time when was the last time you saw Neil. I mean about his coming to see you Tuesday night."

"That's because he didn't." She flicked something away from her left eyebrow.

"Orvis robs people at gunpoint and beats up women. If

you tell me he's a liar to boot I'm going to give up all my faith in human nature."

"I wouldn't want to be responsible for that. When Robinette forced his way in on me a second time I thought I was in for another beating. I had an audition Thursday. Even if I hadn't I wasn't looking forward to swallowing teeth. When he seemed to think I'd just had a visit from Neil I saw a way out. If he thought Neil knew where the money was he might leave me alone."

"So you sicced him on Catalin's wife."

"Why not? The bitch cost me a good gig at Gilda."

"I can't think why. All you did was steal her husband."

She turned my way. Her eyes glittered in the depths of the shade. "No woman ever stole a man. He had to meet her at least halfway, and to do that he had to have a reason. She should have looked closer to home before she yanked my living out from under me. The only difference between me and her is she saw Neil first. If once she'd landed him she thought she could relax, I shouldn't be the only one to pay for that mistake."

When I said nothing she sat back, directing her gaze to the blank brick wall in front of the windshield. "If I thought she was in any real danger from Robinette I might have come up with something else. When you read in the paper that a woman was raped or beaten in her own home and it turns out that home was a house in West Bloomfield, you're reading the front page. When it's an apartment in Iroquois Heights, you're reading the police column in the third section. That's because that kind of thing doesn't happen in West Bloomfield. There, even the thugs mind their manners. The worst she'd get was followed. I know what that's like, and it beats a broken jaw."

"Robinette saw Catalin coming out of your place late.

Catalin's car was parked out front with his registration in the glove compartment."

"I don't know about the car, but it wasn't Neil he saw coming out of my apartment. He saw Leo Webb. Neil's partner." She shook a cigarette out of her pack. "It was after two A.M. You're the detective. You figure it out."

Eighteen

WHILE WE WERE SITTING there a waitress came out the side door, fishing cigarettes and a lighter out of her apron pocket, spotted us, and moved farther down the line of parked cars to lean against the building and light up. The smokeless society has convened a new counterculture in America's alleys.

I let Vesta fire hers up from the dashboard lighter. Gallantry was getting old. "You and Webb?"

"My mother made Judy Garland's mother look like June Cleaver," she said. "On my third birthday she signed me up for tap dancing lessons at Arthur Murray. At six I played Little Nell in *The Old Curiosity Shop* in a children's theater group production in Garden City. I did a Crest commercial and sang the Oscar Mayer song when I was eleven. Dramatic scholarship at Wayne State. I got my SAG card when other girls my age went shopping for training bras. If there were any other choices I never saw them. I don't want to schlep menus when I'm forty."

"So it's business."

"What else would it be? Half of Gilda Productions belongs to that cueball, and he doesn't have a wife to foul the nest. When it comes to recreational sex I like a full head of hair to get a grip on. I like your hair," she added.

"Don't flirt. How long have you and Webb been keeping company?"

"What's this, Monday? Tomorrow will be a week."

"Tuesday night was the start?"

"He called me that day at Ziggy's. I told him where I lived. He brought flowers and a script. The shooting's next week. I play Christina Ford in a docudrama about Henry the Deuce."

"All this slipped your mind when we spoke Friday."

"You asked if I'd seen Neil. You didn't ask about Leo."

"If I had, would you have come clean?"

She gestured with her cigarette. "If I didn't think it was your business I'd have refused to answer. I only act when I'm paid."

"Why was Webb driving Catalin's car?"

"I don't know. I didn't know he was until you told me just now. Robinette didn't say why he thought Leo was Neil. Maybe he borrowed it."

"If Catalin loaned it to him, it means they saw each other after Catalin went missing. I asked Webb about his partner's car specifically. He said it wasn't in the company lot. He didn't say he's the one who drove it away from there."

"I hope he's got a good explanation when you ask him about it. I need the work." When I said nothing, she looked at me. "What are you staring at? In your line you must meet a lot of determined survivors."

"So that's what you call it."

"I don't have to justify myself to anyone," she snarled. "Talent's the smallest part of the equation in my business. The rest is luck. I can't make luck, but if it's out there groping around in the dark I can damn well turn on a light."

I snapped my filter end at the handicapped symbol stenciled on the wall of the building, scoring a bull's-eye in the center of the wheel of the wheelchair. "I wonder if you're as hardboiled as you like to make out. And if you are, I wonder why Catalin didn't run to you first thing after he hopped the fence this time. You're made to order for the scenario he's looking for: the femme fatale, cold as a polar cap and tougher than old deviled eggs."

"What can I say? If he did I wouldn't need to keep time with Leo. At least Neil has a heart. Whatever his partner's using for one is due back at the prop department at Gilda."

"You're sure it's you he wants?"

"Thanks for the compliment."

"Beautiful women need compliments like Scrooge McDuck needs a bank loan. Two years after you left Gilda, Webb comes to you with a script in one hand and his hormones in the other. Why now, just after his partner disappeared? He didn't by any chance, say, in a moment of passion, ask you about the ninety-two thousand?"

She opened her door. "Break's over. I'm sick of hearing about that damn money. If I knew where it was I'd turn it over to the cops just to get everyone off my back."

I stayed where I was. "Don't go back and take it out on the customers. The question had to be asked."

"Well, he didn't say anything about the money, or anything else I didn't already tell you. Not counting what I *won't* tell you. I may bed anything that moves for a leg up, but I don't discuss the details."

"You'll never get anywhere with that attitude. What will you tell your ghost writer at memoir time?"

After a pause she decided to smile. I grinned back. She let go of the door handle and slid closer.

"So you think I'm beautiful?"

"It was a statement. Not a pickup line."

"I've got a bump on my nose." She touched it. "I hit a curb and took a flyer over the handlebars when I was ten. My mother was furious. She thought I'd ruined any chance

I ever had at a career. I made an appointment once to have it fixed, but I chickened out."

"Anyone can order a nose from the catalogue. Garbo had big feet."

She touched the more obvious bump on my nose. "What happened to yours?"

"I asked a detective a personal question."

She drew back in a hurry. "Excuse, please. I didn't realize I was trying to seduce an apostle."

"Is that what you were trying to do?"

She stabbed out her cigarette in the dashboard tray. "Well, I didn't put my weight behind it."

"I don't have a script to offer."

"I don't work on the career all the time." She got out. "Lock it up when you leave, okay? This car's third on the thieves' list this year."

"You ought to get the Club."

"What I ought to do is trade it in on something more quiet. But I agreed to hang on to it so Ted wouldn't contest the divorce. He wants to buy it from me when he gets out."

I said, "I ran into a left jab."

She had turned to slam the door. Now she turned back and leaned down to look in at me. "What?"

"It was my fifteenth fight in college. He feinted with a right cross, then nailed me with his left. When I came out of the anesthetic I decided not to go into boxing."

She smiled again and pushed the door shut.

I smoked another Winston. Then I got out and walked down the line of cars to where Phil Musuraca was sitting behind the wheel of his big Buick Invicta. The motor was running. The loose compressor belt on the air conditioner squealed like rats in an Osterizer. When he looked at me over his *USA Today* I made a rotating motion with my right hand. He folded the paper and cranked down the window on

his side. The cloud of Old Spice that puffed out on the rush
of cold air nearly knocked me over.

"What." His big face all but filled the opening. His nose
was all over the place, but there hadn't been much swelling.

"I'm curious," I said. "What do you do when your blad-
der's full?"

"I got me a wide-mouth jar. What do you?"

"Coffee can. How much do you know about a fence in
Flatrock named Ernie Fishman?"

"I know he's dead."

"I could get that from the obits. What else?"

"Why should I tell you?"

"Right. Like you're any closer to that ninety-two grand
than you were three days ago."

His eyes slid right and left under the shelf of his single
brow like the bubble in a carpenter's level. "You talking
partners?"

"This case is breaking. If it breaks off in two directions
I'm going to need a leg man. I'm guessing you've seen
enough of parking lots and brick walls for a while."

"Fifty-fifty?"

"Sure."

His eyes fixed in the center. "You agreed to that mighty
quick."

I leaned against his doorpost. I could feel the heat of the
metal through my suitcoat. "You don't trust anyone, do you,
Phil?"

"The last person I trusted was my mother. She left me
with an IRS debt. It took me ten years to pay it off."

"Meanwhile, not trusting anybody has got you your own
detective agency, a company car, and state-of-the-art sani-
tary facilities."

"What've *you* got, Rockefeller?"

"Oh, but I'm honest. That's a whole different set of delusions. What have you got to lose? If I get to the money first you can always swipe it."

I could hear his brain running as easily as the big engine under the hood. After a moment he turned off the key. "I sold Fishman some stuff from time to time," he said. "Clients got a way of being broke when you hand them your bill. Sometimes you have to take it out in merchandise."

"What did he deal in?"

"What didn't he? Radios, coins, toaster ovens, luggage, rocks—"

"Diamonds?"

"Sure, diamonds. What other kind of rocks is there?"

I got out a cigarette, then thought better of it and put it back. The smoke from the last was still scraping the walls of my empty stomach. "Phil, do you ever read anything besides that cheesy newspaper?"

"You mean like *Sports Illustrated*?"

"No. Books."

He shook his head. "They ain't big enough to duck behind when your tail turns around."

"You might give one a hard look sometime when you're not working. Edgar Allan Poe has a lot to say to guys in our profession."

"How many people is that?"

"Just one." I straightened up and slapped the roof of the car. "I'll be in touch."

"Bring that guy Poe. He sounds like he's smarter than you."

Judy Yin clittered her coral nails on the glazed top of her reception desk, which was as much agitation as she would ever show within the confines of Gilda Productions. Today she wore a cranberry silk blazer over a green jumpsuit, but the ivory mask was the same as on my first visit. Her page boy gleamed like polished anthracite.

"As I told you over the telephone, Mr. Webb left for Los Angeles this morning," she said. "I don't expect him back before Thursday."

"That was last week's excuse. Tell him it's about Vesta Mannering."

"That's what it was about last week."

"Then it was about Vesta and Neil Catalin. Now it's about Vesta and Leo Webb. You know, like *Bewitched*: same Samantha, different Darrin. Are you going to buzz him, or do I walk in and catch him fighting with Endora?"

"I'm going to buzz Security if you aren't out in the hall in thirty seconds."

"Security frightens the hell out of me in this town," I said. "I've seen what they'll take in the police department. What they won't take I wouldn't send out for a pizza. Buzz them, by all means. Leo and I will be waiting for them in his office."

"You can't—"

I didn't wait for the rest. It wasn't as if I didn't know where she was going. I swept down the interior corridor, found Webb's door unlocked, and went in. It took me a second to realize he wasn't there. He could have been hiding behind the bric-a-brac.

"*Now* will you go?" said Judy Yin from the doorway.

I turned around faster than she expected, before she had time to close her Asian features. She was as surprised as I was to find the room unoccupied.

Nineteen

THE AUDITORIUM at the Detroit Institute of Arts belonged to the new addition behind the original building, whose marble Italian Renaissance façade went with the blank gray granite of the upstart section like a carved cherub on the wall of a penitentiary. I parked on John R a good hour before the feature was scheduled to run, bought a ticket for one of the cheap seats located in the next county, and admired the glassed posters in the lobby, selected from among Austin Alt's best films and those of his mentors from the old Hollywood in honor of the world premiere of Alt's new picture next Friday at the Fox Theater. Here among the faux marble walls and hollow plaster columns, George Raft rubbed shoulders with Kevin Costner, Veronica Lake glared through her peek-a-boo bang at Kim Basinger, and John Wayne reached back to hurl a hand grenade across the concession stand at Sony International. The advertising for the newer films looked mechanical and cheerless against the old; but then I'd been brought up on fresh-popped corn served with real butter in motion-picture palaces dripping with gargoyles and red velvet, not greasy bits of Styrofoam scooped from plastic trash bags in the concrete bunker at the end of the mall: a dinosaur at forty-three.

For the first twenty minutes I had the place all to myself except for the ticket-taker, a pair of ushers, male and female, in crimson blazers, and a security guard who looked like a steelworker in a rented tuxedo, eyeing me as if I might walk off with one of the wall sconces. Then customers began to file in, longtime patrons in couples wearing suits and dresses, movie buffs in singles in jeans and suspenders, and film students in gaggles dressed for the Bleeding Eardrums Tour of the Screaming Graceless Zombies; you could tell the orchestra seats from the bleachers at a glance. Nobody who looked like Neil Catalin turned up in the first wave. At ten minutes to showtime, Gay Catalin came in, had her ticket torn in half, and glanced my way long enough to see me shake my head, then went on through the double doors into the auditorium. She had on a yellow cocktail dress, white shoes and purse, and amber beads on a string around her neck.

"I see you took my advice."

A second went by before I placed the bearded face above the T-shirt and worn sportcoat. It seemed as if a lot more than eighty hours had passed since I'd discussed the psychology of film noir with Asa Portman in the chalky air of a lecture hall at the University of Michigan. He was the one who had first told me about the DIA film festival and upcoming reception to celebrate the Alt premiere at the Fox.

"I always take advice when it means going to the movies." I shook his hand. "Are you working?"

"I'm strictly here as a fan. Any sign of your missing man?"

"Not yet."

"If he misses this series he's no buff. Are you sure he's still in this area?"

"He may have committed a murder here in town over the weekend."

He stroked his beard. Men who wore them could never let them alone. "That's out of character for a noir hero. Unless it was self-defense?"

"Doesn't look like it." I bent a little to peer under the floppy brim of a passing hat. The face belonged to an old woman.

"As a rule identity cases become violent when their delusion is threatened. If someone calls them by their true name they'll just ignore it, but if they're barraged with questions that challenge their logic, anything can happen."

"You said reality could shake him out of it."

"The transition is never smooth. Having to be born all over again into a world he's already rejected as unsatisfactory is painful as hell. He might strike out just to preserve the status quo."

"This one struck out five times with a pistol."

He stopped fooling with his whiskers. "That's a serious case."

"I figured that out and I don't even have a Ph.D."

"I don't mean it that way. I mean if he's that deep into his persona, the movies are no longer his escape; quite the opposite. Whatever's left of what he was will avoid them just to keep from asking himself why those actors on the screen are imitating him. From there it's a short hop to asking himself why *he's* imitating *them*. If he's willing to commit murder to duck that one, you couldn't drag him into this building with a rope."

"So this noir character he's become didn't kill anyone. Walter Mitty did, to protect Don Quixote."

"One of the most dangerous animals in the world is a rabbit in a corner."

The last straggler had gone in. I looked at my watch. One minute to showtime. "This rabbit made an appointment to meet his wife at the old Michigan Theater the night of the murder. When she gave up waiting and went back to her car, she found a ticket to this screening clipped to her windshield. Why would he do that if he has no intention of showing up?"

"You're a detective," Portman said. "You've seen your share of these films. When A arranges to meet B at a certain place and time and A doesn't show, what's obvious?"

"A knows where B is at that time."

He spread his hands.

"The last time he stood her up, someone got killed," I said. "If he suspected she'd hired a detective to look for him, he might have thought I'd go with her to the meet. She said she tried to call me, but I was in Iroquois Heights, interviewing her husband's mistress. Now all I have to work out is who he's planning to kill this time while I'm out of the way."

The lights went off and on three times. It was Portman's turn to check his watch. "Well, you've got two and a half hours to do it. The picture's only ninety minutes, but they've stuck in an intermission followed by a short feature to bring the event closer to one of Austin Alt's bladder-bursting epics."

"I'll stay out here, in case he shows up after all."

"You can see the whole auditorium from my seat. It's a cheapie; I'm just a poor educator. There are bound to be plenty of vacancies in the section. You might as well enjoy the show while you're waiting."

"I saw it last week on video."

"Then you didn't see it at all. Come on."

The room was already dark, lit only by the countdown taking place on the big screen at the far end. We groped our way to a pair of seats in the rear corner. The room smelled of popcorn and orange soda, just like the theaters of old.

Portman was right: I hadn't seen *Pitfall*. On a full-size

screen, before an audience, the film unfolded like a sinister flower that had been preserved between the pages of a book neglected for nearly fifty years. The crisp black-and-white images shimmered with a silvery sheen, the dialogue crackled, the orchestral score throbbed beneath the suspense scenes like an escalating pulse and soared over the action like exploding rockets, just as it must have when postwar crowds bought out the showings in 1948. Dick Powell, tight-jawed, with jaded eyes and lips incapable of curving into a smile, might have been any one of thousands of disillusioned American GIs trying to accustom themselves to civilian clothes and peaceful ways in the wake of Hiroshima and the Fall of Berlin. Pretty, level-headed Jane Wyatt, a decade before her similar turn as the female half of the nuclear parents on *Father Knows Best,* represented all the faithful, nurturing women of the Home Front. Lizabeth Scott, husky-voiced and slinky, stood for the danger that tempted all those returning veterans away from the predictable and sedate. Hulking, villainous Raymond Burr was the epitome of the Great Evil they thought they had destroyed after four bloody years in Europe and the South Pacific, only to find it waiting for them at home, draped in a thousand guises, each far more subtle and malevolent than anything in jackboots and a Tiger tank. The narrative spoke to the world after Watergate and Vietnam, sunk in the dreary morass of political correctness and trapped in a society divided along lines racial, sexual, philosophical, dogmatic, and religious, exactly as it had spoken to a world suddenly deprived of an obvious, conveniently foreign enemy and forced to look to itself for a substitute; and if the audience with whom I shared the experience snickered at the cornball wisecracks and outmoded fashions, they flinched when Burr sucker-punched Powell in the shadow of Powell's own suburban garage and gasped when Powell shot a man dead for the first time in his life, crossing the line into Burr's world, just as that earlier audience had under Truman.

At first glance it was just another sordid love triangle: bored, married insurance agent, seductive model, unscrupulous private eye. At second glance it was about the death of our collective colonial innocence. Although it ended with the bad guy subdued and the good guy still standing, it did not end happily, but uncertainly, and with the nagging conviction that things would never again be as they had been. When the lights came up, so did the applause.

"Great flick," said Portman as we stood near the exit watching the moviegoers trickle past in search of rest rooms and refreshments. Some used the auxiliary exit at the opposite end of the auditorium, and I craned my neck, wondering if I would recognize Catalin from the back had he managed to slip in unnoticed. "Good noir. Better than *Out of the Past,* which is muddled by too many flashbacks, and much better than *Detour,* whose hero is a moron. The critics love those. They wouldn't know a good storyline if it rolled over their feet. I'm sure you caught the sexual connotation when Dick Powell took the controls of Lizabeth Scott's speedboat, the only gift from her boyfriend he let her keep when his company confiscated everything else for the insurance. It was like the first honest-to-Christ climax he'd had in years. Then later, when Raymond Burr forces him to turn it in, the theme of self-castration is hard to miss."

"I thought it was just a boat."

"Could be it was. Occupational hazard." He smiled. "How about when Powell asks his boss what it's like to be a respectable married man? There's a moment just as poignant in *Sudden Fear,* when Joan Crawford—"

Gay Catalin emerged into the lobby. I excused myself and followed her.

Portman called after me. "You don't want to miss the assortment of vintage movie trailers they're showing next."

"I know. If I haven't seen them on the big screen, I haven't seen them at all."

"Well, no. They sucked as big then as they do now."

I caught up with her at the water fountain. She straightened up and dabbed at the corners of her mouth with a lace handkerchief. Her face was flushed, as if she'd been running. "Mr. Walker, what kind of game is Neil playing? Does he blame me for his colorless life? Is that why he's tormenting me?"

"I'll ask him as soon as I find him. Have you thought any more about what I told you about Webb?" I'd called her at her home before leaving for the auditorium.

"I can't think of any answers. He doesn't pick up his phone. Do you think they're in on this together? And what is *this*? What does it have to do with what happened to poor Brian?"

"I don't know. Webb's being tight enough with Neil to borrow his car when you and everyone else thought Neil was long gone could mean Webb knew about your brother's murder, and that's why he panicked and ran. Another way of looking at it would be that Webb killed Brian—he was mad enough about the equipment theft from Gilda's studio to track him down and extract some old-fashioned vigilante justice—and framed Neil by dropping his video rental card at the scene."

"I'd believe that before I'd believe Neil was capable of murder," she said. "There was always something slippery about Leo I didn't like."

"Slippery is right. Orvis Robinette assumed your husband was the man who visited Vesta Mannering Tuesday night because he read Neil's name on the registration in the car parked out front. Say Webb knew she was being watched. He chose a night visit because it was dark enough so anyone who had the place staked out wouldn't be able to tell it wasn't Neil going in and coming out. He even wore a hat just to make it more difficult. So now Neil's connected both with Brian's murder and—"

I swore.

"And what? What's wrong?"

"Neil didn't leave that ticket on your windshield," I said. "Webb did. And I know why." I swung toward the street exit, almost knocking down an older couple in evening clothes.

"Where are you going?" Gay Catalin's voice was fading behind me.

I was too busy running to answer. Webb had already had a ninety-minute head start, and that had been long enough for the director of *Pitfall* to commit two murders.

Twenty

A LIGHT RAIN had been falling since early evening, but it had let up by the time I reached the Iroquois Heights city limits. The Cutlass's tires swished on the wet pavement as I swept all the mirrors for red flashers; the local police had not invented the concept of the speed trap, but they had been practicing it long enough and with sufficient consistency to apply for a patent.

If Webb had killed Brian Elwood and left Neil Catalin's video rental card at the scene to hook him up with the murder, he had driven Catalin's car to Vesta Mannering's apartment for the same general purpose, to establish a connection between the two that hadn't existed for two years. Her telling me about Webb, and my attempt to confront him, had made it more important than ever that she be gagged permanently. The L.A. dodge his receptionist had handed me had been meant to alibi him for the time I was busy at the DIA, preparing for a nonexistent meeting with Catalin.

That sign familiar to all who entered the Heights, SPEED LIMIT 35: 36 MPH MEANS $36 FINE, swept by so fast I couldn't have read it if I didn't already have it memorized.

I shot up the incline to the house where Vesta lived and was out the door, Luger in hand, while the car was still rocking on its springs. The red Triumph wasn't in the little parking area. That relieved me, but not for long. It could have broken down and she'd caught a ride home. I racked a shell into the Luger's chamber.

The door to the ground floor was unlocked. The cramped foyer contained a rubber mat, a cheap metal coat rack, and a painting in an oval frame of a sour-faced harridan with a cameo at her throat and grapes on her hat. A twenty-five-watt bulb at the top of the narrow stairwell cast more shadows than light. I started climbing the edge of the steps with my back to the wall. I still made too much noise. The house smelled of lemon wax and old wood.

A new shadow joined the pattern, slowly enough that I wouldn't have noticed it except I'd committed the others to memory. I ducked just as something rammed the wall where my head had been, showering me with plaster. The echo of the report filled the well. I fired back. I couldn't see what I was shooting at. I was just clearing the way.

Footsteps slapped the second floor. I took the rest of the stairs two at a lunge, then paused again at the top, flattening against the other wall this time. I counted to two, then pivoted, landing on both feet in the upstairs hallway with the pistol in front of me in two hands. At the far end by an open door, a tall silhouette spun on its heel and leveled an arm straight at me.

I fired. I couldn't tell if I hit anything. The figure pitched shoulder-first through the open door. Something inside fell over with a crash. There was a pause, then a bigger crash. I sprinted down the hallway, stopped this side of the door to assume the position, and pivoted on through, letting the weight of the Luger do the work.

An empty living room yawned in my face.

A lamp burned in a corner, shedding light over a lot of blonde furniture, white carpet, and the twisted frame of an automobile windshield pretending to be art over the false fireplace. The remains of another lamp lay in pieces on the carpet near an overturned table. Opposite the door, a pair of filmy curtains stirred on both sides of a broken window. I circled the room in that direction and edged my face past the wooden frame. There was a twelve-foot drop to the tiny parking lot. As I was doing the arithmetic, a big engine started nearby with a blat of twin pipes. Tires yelped, gears crunched, the engine wowed and went away.

The house was coming to life beneath my feet. A door banged, voices started up. I didn't have much time alone. I went back to the door, kicked it shut, and snapped the lock. Then I started on the apartment.

The kitchen was four feet of linoleum with the standard fixtures and some cupboards. I covered it in a glance. Likewise the bathroom, just big enough to do what was required there. The bedroom took a little longer. It was the second largest room in the apartment and held a double bed with a headboard upholstered in pink satin, a walnut bookcase, a dressing table and mirror, and a slipper chair drawn up to the table and upholstered to match the bed. The drawer of the table had been pulled out and flung to the floor amidst a litter of jars and bottles that had been swept from the top. The bedding lay in heaps at the foot of the bed, torn from the mattress in a single motion. Half the books that had stood in the walnut case had been taken from their shelves and scattered across the carpet; even their dustjackets had been removed.

It was an uncomfortable clutter to have to stretch out on, and the position of the man who lay atop it—fingers clenched, knees drawn into his chest—showed it. He wore a light waterproof topcoat over his suit, still damp from the rain, and one of those floppy canvas hats like Woody Allen wore to conceal his features and make sure everybody knew it was him. It had slid forward over his face when he fell. I lifted it. It wasn't Woody.

I felt for the thick artery below his left ear. His flesh was warm, but that was just a question of time. I took hold of his lapels and dragged him over onto his back to see where the bullet had gone in. There was a bright stain the size of a dinner plate on his blue shirtfront.

I looked for his weapon, but it could have been anywhere in that mess and I decided to let the cops have some of the fun. I looked to Leo Webb for answers, but his eyes were squeezed shut, as if the light hurt them. His bald dome glistened softly under the lamp.

Something else glistened and I bent down and picked up an extracted shell. The embossing on the brass base told me it belonged to a nine-millimeter. That was the caliber of the slug the coroner in Detroit had dug out of Brian Elwood. I rolled it between my palm and the leg of my trousers and let it fall. There would be at least one more at the top of the stairs.

The air stank of sulfur and saltpeter and the coppery odor of blood. I went out of the room to breathe.

The house was all the way awake now. Slippered feet scuffed the floor outside the room, voices murmured. I heard the word "police"—hushed, like "doctor." No one wanted to knock. That wouldn't last.

I went back into the kitchen and searched the cupboards until I found a bottle of Cutty Sark two-thirds full. I filled a thick-bottomed glass and sat on the sofa in the living room to drink and wait for the first polite knock of Iroquois Heights' finest.

Twenty-one

THEY HAD REPAINTED the squad rooms since the last city administration, covering the tough old government green with a not entirely unpleasant shade of eggshell, but they had overdone it. The walls, baseboards, ceiling, and even the switchplates in the interrogation room were all the same color. After two hours I wondered when I was expected to hatch.

I was sitting on a steel folding chair drawn up to a yellow oak table freckled with old cigarette burns, initials, and one brave attempt to carve PROUST SUCKS, aborted just after the U, probably by some civil servant with a fist the size of a hog. Not that the perps in Iroquois Heights were especially literary; Mark Proust had been the local chief of police until his involvement in a scheme to pit incarcerated suspects against one another in wrestling matches (gambling encouraged) removed him from office. I had had something to do with his exposure, but no one there had gone out of his way to express gratitude to me this night.

First I had been questioned by a pair of detectives I remembered vaguely from the Proust years, one of whom wanted to adopt me. The other indicated that his appetite wouldn't have suffered if I hemorrhaged farm machinery.

That was the drill in every police department since Byzantium, but in Iroquois Heights they did it with feeling, especially the hemorrhaging part. Then a watch captain named Malloy, small and neat with brushed hair, French cuffs, and a gold collar pin under the knot of his club tie, had come in and sat down on the other side of the table and stared at me for ten minutes. I admit it, I blinked. I had spent most of the last seventeen hours on my feet and my eyes grated like rusty doorknobs when I moved them. Satisfied, he got up and left without having said a word. For the next half hour I was left alone while the squad observed me through the two-way glass in the door for subversive behavior. I felt like the new puppy in the house.

Then the cavalry came.

John Alderdyce walked through the door and used up all the space in the room, leaving only the doorway for Mary Ann Thaler to stand in. The inspector wore a lightweight blue summer suit, single-breasted to accommodate his underarm rig. The lieutenant from Felony Homicide had on a turquoise silk jacket, gabardine slacks, and open-toed shoes with heels low enough for running through alleys after fleeing suspects. In her hairband and glasses she could have passed for a coed. She carried her small clasp purse in her left hand, with the latch open. I wouldn't have bet which one of them would win in a fast-draw contest.

It struck me then that I had never seen both of them in the same room at the same time.

"This shoots my theory to pieces," I said. "I'd have sworn you were one and the same person."

Alderdyce crossed his arms and leaned his broad back against the wall. He looked as casual as a halftrack. "Generous folks here in the Heights. Always ready to boot a homicide over to Detroit when it hooks up to something outside the city limits."

"That's a small town for you. They don't cotton to us urban sophisticates coming in here and hiking up the crime statistics."

Thaler said, "Where'd they cast this town, Black Rock? Ever since John and I walked in they've been looking at us like *Guess Who's Coming to Dinner.*"

"White flight to the suburbs," said the inspector. "Like rats fly." He went on looking at me. "Tell it."

So I told it all again, from Brian Elwood to Leo Webb. They listened without interrupting, a relief. I'd had to loop back every time one of the local cops asked a question, repeating myself so often that it had come out sounding as flat as a wooden hubcap.

"So you figure Webb killed Elwood for ripping off the studio and left his partner's video card behind to pin it on him," Alderdyce said. "Why'd he drive Catalin's car to the Mannering woman's apartment? What did he have to gain by making anyone who happened to be watching think she and Catalin were still together?"

"He needed a strong motive to finger Catalin for the Elwood killing. When Catalin refused to pay up the first time, Elwood ran straight to his sister and told her about the affair with Vesta. Making it look like they were still seeing each other would explain how Elwood got a key—Catalin gave it to him, to keep his mouth shut—and why Catalin tracked him to the house on Ferry Park and shut it for good. Webb couldn't care less about the brother-in-law or the stolen equipment. It would be insured. He just wanted a body so he could frame his partner for murder and take control of a business on its way back from bankruptcy. Webb liked nice things." I fished an empty pack out of my shirt pocket and crumpled it.

Alderdyce produced a box of Marlboros. I lifted my eyebrows; he'd quit smoking last I'd heard. He shrugged. I took one, found a match, and lit it. "When Webb found out I knew it wasn't Catalin who went to see Vesta, he took a powder. She was the only person who could definitely identify her visitor the night his partner disappeared. He'd already arranged to send me on a wild goose chase that night, just as he had the night he killed Brian Elwood. He ducked me to avoid having to answer my embarrassing questions until the thing was done."

"The locals combed the building," Thaler said. "They didn't find a weapon."

"That's because whoever killed Webb and shot at me took it with him when he went out the window. Webb walked in while he was tossing the place. That was a surprise, and before Webb could get over it he had his gun taken away. Maybe he was shot during the struggle. I'm betting that slug in the staircase wall and the one in Webb matches up with the one your man dug out of Baby Brother Brian."

Alderdyce played with a Marlboro. "So who's the shooter?"

"B-and-E's happen all the time." As I said it I felt my argument going away. When you hold back a key brick you can't expect anyone to move into the house you built.

"Try this," he said. "Catalin's the shooter. The Mannering woman lied when she told you Webb came to see her in Catalin's car. Whether she knew what he had in mind or just wanted to protect her lover man is something we'll get out of her when the car I sent for her brings her back from Ziggy's. She's working late tonight, or didn't you know?"

"I didn't know. Webb could've been shooting her full of holes while I was calling to find out."

He wasn't listening. "It was Catalin all the time. He fell off his rails once over this Vesta cunt—Sorry, Lieutenant."

Thaler flipped him a forgiving finger.

"Here's the option. Either seeing her again triggers another breakdown, or he takes up with her just to draw out his brother-in-law. He pretends to cave to the blackmail, then offs him in that rotten neighborhood so it looks like he tripped over one of his perp friends. Okay, so it sounds like something from a crummy old crime picture. He's a nut on them, you said."

"Even the crummy ones tend to make sense," I put in. "What about Webb?"

"She was seeing them both, and Webb walked in while Catalin was there waiting for her. Then Catalin tossed the place to make it look like a homicide in the commission of a burglary. You said yourself you didn't get a good look at the shooter."

"You said Vesta lied about seeing Webb."

"So she didn't. I'm as flexible as the next guy. Webb had a key to the apartment in his pocket. She'll tell us who gave it to him. Meanwhile, if those slugs match up, it means Catalin's carrying the same gun, and we've got a swell chance of catching him with it still in his possession. A pro would've thrown it away after the first killing, but it's a little harder for a private citizen to score a replacement without leaving tracks. That Beretta you sent over tested negative, by the way: no match. I don't suppose you'd care to tell me now who you got it from."

I shook my head. "For a private citizen, I attract guns like lint."

"Who told you you're a citizen? Citizens don't pull a pair of star detectives out of a nice warm squad room in Detroit in the middle of the night and plunk them down in a stink-hole like Iroquois Heights at the peak of the riot season."

"A little louder, Inspector," Thaler said. "I don't think they heard you downstairs."

"The hell with them. And while I'm at it, the hell with

you, too. You're only here out of professional courtesy. This hasn't been your case since that card turned up."

"And may I take this opportunity to thank you. The snot-nose uniforms at Thirteen Hundred don't undress me with their eyes nearly enough. Up here I get to inspire wet dreams for an entirely different class of scum."

I made the "time out" sign with my hands. "Can I walk? I'm in the cross fire here."

Alderdyce blinked at me as if he'd forgotten I was in the room. "You got wheels?"

"Back at Vesta's. I'll hoof it."

Thaler said, "I'll give you a lift. I've got my personal car. We came separately."

"Sorry to hear it. I'm still broken up over Sonny and Cher."

"Just let's go."

I stood. "How married are you to that theory?" I asked Alderdyce.

"Enough to go to bed with it. The ring comes later. It fits the facts."

"Not all of them. Did the locals turn Webb's car?"

"Blue Taurus, this year's model. Registration's his. They found it around the corner. Did you expect him to try that gag with Catalin's car?"

"He was dumb. Dumb enough anyway to try to jazz up a simple murder. He wasn't nuts. The car wasn't on every Detroit cop's pullover sheet the first time. If he was there just to see Vesta, why didn't he park in the apartment house lot like any other honest lecher? Why take pains to park it out of sight unless he didn't want whoever might be watching to identify the car as his?"

"Don't tangle this up with one of Catalin's old movies, no matter how much it may look like one. Not everything ties up at the end with a granny knot. Maybe there are pigeons on the roof and he didn't want to have to stop at a car wash after midnight."

"Maybe," I said. "And maybe Catalin grew six inches since he went underground. That's how much taller the guy I swapped lead with was than the description Gay Catalin gave me of her husband."

"Too bad you aren't a better shot. If he'd bled some DNA we wouldn't be having this conversation."

"That's the kind of thinking that's going to make you chief."

The skin of his face, already the deep blue-black of a Masai warrior, darkened further with congested blood. "Get him the fuck out of here before I smear him all over the walls," he told the lieutenant.

Thaler and I left.

On the ground floor I asked about my Luger. The desk sergeant, forty pounds overweight with broken vessels in his cheeks, consulted his property sheet and told me they were holding it for a registration check. That meant I'd seen the last of it until it turned up as evidence in my trial for possession of an unregistered handgun.

Thaler drove a three-quarter–ton black Bronco, a surprise. I'd expected something small and fuel-injected. She drove with both hands on the wheel, but she wasn't afraid of it. She worked the clutch as if her stroller had been equipped with four on the floor.

"That wasn't the best thing you could have said, about making chief," she said. "John had a shot at commander when the city administration changed. He was in line five years ago, but he and the old chief hated each other's guts. Now the new chief thinks he was the old chief's pet, along with all the others who were up for promotion. There's talk of bumping him over to Auto Recovery. Climbing any higher than sergeant in this department is a forty-hour pain in the butt."

"Maybe the change isn't such a bad idea. It's hard to make a carjacking look like bike theft."

"I thought you two were friends."

"I was friendly with a detective lieutenant. I don't know the inspector from Richard Nixon."

"What makes your theory any better than his?"

"They're both full of holes. The difference is I'm concerned about plugging up mine."

The Bronco wanted to hydroplane on a puddle between two flooded storm drains. Thaler turned into the skid and had it straight in a second. "Last time I looked there were sixteen open homicides on the platter downtown. How many are you working on, Columbo?"

"Homicide's your job. I'm just looking for Neil Catalin."

"So are we."

She let me off at the apartment house, where a uniform guarding the yellow police tape demanded to see identification, checked it against his notebook, and let me get into my car and drive away. Like a lot of the cops there he was ten years too old for his officer's rank: The IHPD was where you went when the department you worked for busted you out for splitting one skull too many in interrogation, with your pension five years off.

Dull gray steel had begun to wear through the black velour over metropolitan Detroit. The 4:00 A.M. shift at the auto plants was starting to pull in traffic from the suburbs; I had to wait for a break before turning into the street. While I was waiting I noticed a rectangular patch of dry pavement next to the curb, where a car had parked before the rain and pulled out after it stopped. If it had been there earlier I hadn't noticed it, coming in hard in darkness, looking for Leo Webb. It wasn't the car I'd heard roaring away after the shooting. That had been parked on the other side of the block.

I thought about it, and when I swung out of the driveway I knew I wasn't going to bed, not yet.

Twenty-two

ACCORDING TO THE DIRECTORY I kept in the car, Phil Musuraca operated out of an address on Furlough Street, a healthy hike from Iroquois Heights' major tax base. There was no home listing, so I expected a long wait before he reported to work. I figured I could toss his files for entertainment.

The number belonged to a twenty-four-hour Chinese restaurant with a plaster pagoda over the entrance. A hand-lettered sign taped to the glass door read RING AFTER 12 P.M. The time mistake was common enough to Occidentals, so I forgave them. The button I pushed, with exposed wires disappearing through the crack between the door and the frame, gave back a phlegmy buzz. Well before the end of the Year of the Pig an ancient Chinese crept up to the door, peered, threw a dead bolt, and backed away, leaving me to open the door for myself.

The old man did not belong to the same world as Albert Chung, the doctor from the Wayne County Coroner's office who had examined Brian Elwood's corpse, or Judy Yin, the receptionist at Gilda Productions. Less than five feet tall, he had white hair like streaks of chalk on a scalp the color and texture of an old scroll and a wisp of transparent beard that stirred in the slight current of air. He wore a black pullover shirt outside loose white slacks and linen slippers with crepe soles; he wouldn't have looked out of place in a pigtail and mandarin's cap.

He waited for me to speak. He would have gone on waiting, without moving or changing expressions, while dust layered his stooped shoulders and the candles on the tables behind him guttered and died and grew as cold as jade.

"Musuraca." I traced a broad circle in front of me with my index fingers.

"In back, taking a snooze."

His accent was pure Great Lakes. I crossed the room and pushed through a swinging door into a small kitchen smelling of hot grease and soy sauce, where a Buddha in a stained white apron and a paper chef's hat sat on a stool reading a Chinese newspaper. He looked up and jerked his chins in the direction of a door in back. I went through that and found myself in a room not much larger than the kitchen, with a metal-shaded bulb hanging straight down from the naked rafters and a gray steel desk shoved up against the only wall that wasn't covered by steel utility shelves to the ceiling. A fax machine shared the desk with overflow from the shelves, cardboard cartons and food cans the size of wastebaskets. While I was standing there, something snapped in a dark corner, followed by a frenzied squealing and then silence. I hoped that wasn't tomorrow's special.

The place looked uninhabited, but the old Chinese was too picturesque to be a liar. A partition consisting of four black-painted metal file cabinets, not quite old enough to qualify as antiques, isolated the corner nearest the desk. I walked around it into the middle of a rank humid odor, as in a kennel at the pound, if the animals used Old Spice. The source of it sprawled in all his two hundred sixty pounds across a rollaway bed that had come over with Leif the Lucky. Leif had inherited it from Eric the Red, who had won it in a crap game from Pepin the Short. He was fully clothed; even his tie was knotted as tight as packing cord. His porkpie hat rested on his nose.

There was a long moment during which I thought I'd found another corpse. Then his mouth dumped open and a ratcheting snore made the big cans vibrate on their shelves. I hadn't improved things when I'd flattened his nose. This went on for a while. When he paused again, the quiet hurt my ears.

It was a cozy enough corner for a fat bachelor. He had commandeered a set of shelves for his toiletries: a squashed tube of Ultrabrite, toothbrush in a moldy glass, disposable razor, can of Barbasol, an assortment of suppositories still in the foil like nasty little Hershey's Kisses. Hemorrhoids would be a fact of life for a fixture like Phil. No deodorant or mouthwash, but the six cases of his favorite aftershave covered that. It took a tough breed of odor-causing bacteria to swim upstream through the fumes.

One of the file cabinets would hold his shorts and socks and underwear. He would wash and relieve himself in the restaurant men's room, and he could live on what came back from the tables. The pay telephone near the entrance was as good as any for conducting business, as long as his quarters held out. All the comforts of a mansion in Grosse Pointe and an office in Birmingham, and none of the overhead, except whatever he slipped the owner for the space and maybe the local zoning inspector to look the other way.

No wonder he preferred to spend most of his time in his car.

The black composition butt of his shiny automatic stuck out from under the pillow where his head lay. I slid it out slowly, removed the clip from the handle, worked the slide to empty the chamber, and sprang the cartridges from the clip. Then I put it back together and returned it. He let out a fetid gust then, and took in a draft with a noise like a kid dragging a stick along the iron spikes in a cemetery fence. I waited until the next pause, then reached into an open case for one of the squat white bottles with a schooner printed on it. I pulled the stopper, sniffed, and recoiled from the citrus-and-alcohol stench.

Perfect.

Just then he exhaled. I leaned across the bed and held the bottle to his nose as he breathed in.

He snorted, choked, sputtered, and jackknifed into a sitting position, nearly knocking the bottle from my grip. His hat slid off his face and he swiveled his head, eyes bulging, mouth working. When he realized he wasn't alone he snatched up his hat and plopped it on top of his bald head, then went for the automatic under his pillow. His reflexes were more than respectable, but I questioned the order.

"Don't shoot," I said. "I may have saved your life."

"What?" His gaze flicked down to the bottle in my hand, clouded slightly. He'd expected something else. He squinted back up at my face through a network of swollen veins. That checked with the stink of sour mash that clung to his clothes. "Who the fuck are you?"

"Amos Walker. We met before. You probably just didn't recognize me without your hat on."

"Oh, yeah." The gun stayed on me. "What's this horseshit about saving my life?"

"That sleep apnea can kill you. One of these times you'll stop breathing and forget to start back up."

"Oh, that. Horseshit. My wife used to hook me up to this electronic gizmo that set off a bell every time I quit breathing."

"What happened?"

"I gave it to her in the settlement. What time is it?"

"Why, you don't want to miss your favorite show on the TV you don't have? Let's talk about what happened last night at Vesta's."

"Go to hell."

"How come you were staked out in front of her place when she was at work?"

"Fuck you."

"Who'd you see come barreling out her apartment window after the shooting stopped?"

His face bunched up like bubble wrap. He wasn't pretending he didn't know what I was talking about; he had simply run out of sophisticated rejoinders. After a moment he came up with a dandy.

"Go to hell."

I raised my brows. "You mean this isn't it?"

"I can shoot you right now for busting into my place."

"You'll need these." I opened my left hand. The cartridges fell to the floor and scattered like peanuts in the shell.

He scowled, pointed the Sig-Sauer at a can of water chestnuts big enough to feed Beijing, and snapped the hammer on the empty chamber. "Aw, shit." He flipped it onto the tangled bedcovers.

I put down the bottle of aftershave and looked around. "Nice hole. Southwest exposure and all the moo goo gai pan you can eat. Where's the secretary I talked to when I dialed your number on the telephone in Neil Catalin's office?"

"I pay—*paid* a high school girl to answer the phone during business hours. She quit yesterday. Some horseshit about minimum wage."

"Enough small talk. How come you were staked out in front of Vesta's place when she was at work?"

"Jesus Christ." He patted his pockets.

I let out some air. "Phil, don't make me take away that

twenty-two again. This time it'll be the jaw. You'll be sucking your Crab Rangoon through a glass straw."

"I ain't got it on me. I'm looking for Pepto tablets. I told you before I got a sour gut."

"Things are tough all over. I haven't been to bed since Sunday. Let's skip the next part. You know: I ask you again why you were watching Vesta's apartment instead of Vesta, you say you weren't within a mile of the place, I kick out your teeth and start all over. I saw your car," I lied. "I know it was yours. *American Graffiti* isn't in town."

"I went to the library yesterday. I borrowed a book."

"How come hell froze over and nobody told me?"

"Huh?"

"Nothing. What book?"

"A bunch of stories and poims by that Poe guy you told me about."

"Did you read it?"

"Part of it. Weird shit. What was this guy on, anyway?"

"Just about everything, from what I heard. Did you get to 'The Purloined Letter'?"

"Yeah. That's just about the only one I liked, except for the one where that guy bricked up this major pain in the ass in his basement. The letter story's the one you were talking about, right? All those guys running around looking for this thing that was right there in front of them the whole time."

"That's the one." I waited. I was a patient teacher waiting for the student at the bottom of the curve to see the dawn. I realized I liked Phil Musuraca in a distant-relative kind of way, like Dr. Leakey and Zinjanthropus.

"I figured what you meant was I been wasting my time following the Mannering broad all around, like she's going to lead me to that ninety-two large when she knows I'm right behind her. I mean, you got something valuable, where do you hide it? You can't trust your friends, and if you bury it someplace public, sooner or later somebody's going to dig it up putting in a sewer or a duck pond or something. So you hide it at home, right?"

"Makes sense."

"Sure it does. So I hightail it over to her joint figuring to frisk it while she's at work. I mean, I didn't expect to find the cash laying around in a great big sack with a dollar sign on it, like the cartoons. I'm thinking maybe there's a map or a key to a bus locker or something like that. Even if I come up empty it beats sitting around growing cobwebs on my dick."

"You were the one who tossed the place?"

"Hell, no. I'm parked out front getting the lay when someone goes in ahead of me. I'm thinking it's another tenant or maybe the janitor, but then a light goes on in the broad's apartment. So I wait. I mean, if he comes out carrying a TV set it's cool, just another B-and-E; they happen. If not I brace him."

"Who was it?"

"It was dark. I didn't get a good look, except I'm thinking he's black. From the way he moved."

"What'd he do, tap-dance across the parking lot?"

"Shit, what do you think I am, some redneck racist? You know what I mean, that street swagger." He demonstrated, swaying his shoulders while sitting on the bed. He looked like Oliver Hardy doing the Lambada. "Plus he's tall enough to shoot hoops for a living. Anyway I'm sitting there going over my options when another guest arrives at the party."

"Leo Webb."

He blinked. "Leo Webb. How come I know that name?"

"He was Neil Catalin's business partner."

"Okay. Well, I never saw him when I was working the Silvera case so I wouldn't know him this time."

"You saw him when you were working this case. He

drove Catalin's car to her place last Tuesday night and stayed a couple of hours. You weren't the only one staking her out that night. Somebody else saw him too."

He blinked again. Crusts of dried matter clung to his eyelashes like stalactites. "I was in Toledo Tuesday, working a divorce case. I didn't get that VESTA KNOWS fax till Wednesday."

I filed that. "Go on. Another guest arrived."

"This one had on a hat and a raincoat. It was drizzling then, but I got a better look at him on account of he walked down from the corner under the lamp, right past my car. He was white, but I didn't know him. The other one came in from the other side."

"Neither one looked like Neil Catalin?"

"Shit, no. Even if I'm wrong about the first one being black, he was way too tall, and the second one just wasn't him. Anyway this one lets himself in the same door. I'm outnumbered now, so I decide to stay put and see what shakes down. Play it by ear. Then I hear a shot."

"Hold on. How long between the time the light went on in the apartment and the second man went in?"

"Two-three minutes."

"When did the shooting start?"

"Just one shot. Say, thirty seconds after the second guy went in. I got my piece out now. I'm figuring to brace whoever comes out that door. My hand's on my door handle when that Cutlass of yours comes slamming around the corner. You almost clipped me turning into the driveway."

"Sorry. Did you get a better look at the first man when he dived out the apartment window?"

"I don't know nothing about nobody jumping through no windows. I left after you came. That was one too many for me."

The door opened and the man in the apron and chef's hat

waddled in. Without glancing our way he went up on his toes, embraced a cardboard carton shelved at eye level, and backed out lugging it, pushing through the door with his hip pockets. When we were alone I said, "Phil, you need to learn meat cutting at home. You're not a good enough liar for this line of work."

"Hey, I didn't have to tell you squat."

"Sure you did. No one likes the taste of his own teeth. I saw the bedroom. It takes more than two or three minutes to turn a room inside out; I know, because I've done it, and so have you."

"Maybe the shooter frisked the place afterwards."

"That's what the cops think, because it checks with their theory that Catalin killed Webb and tore the room apart to make it look like a burglary. Either way it takes too much time. You said you heard the shot thirty seconds after Webb got there, then I showed up before you could get out of your car."

"My watch don't light up. Maybe it was longer." A whining note had crept into his voice. It hadn't been musical to begin with.

"Which time? Don't bother, I'll choose. At least fifteen minutes went by between the time the first man went in and Webb came along. That's how long it would take for you to hotfoot it over to the next block where the first man walked in from, get the number off his license plate or read the name on his registration, and be back in your car in time to see Webb. You were still there when I went up and traded shots with the first man and he left through the window. Maybe you got a good look at him then, maybe not. It wouldn't matter, because you already had a line on who he was. It was Orvis Robinette."

"I don't know that name."

"You aren't getting any better at this. If you knew about

the ninety-two grand Silvera got from the video store robberies, you knew Robinette was his accomplice. Robinette
went to Vesta's place for the same reason you did, to search
for some clue to where the money was hidden. Webb walked
in on the middle of it and wound up getting shot with the
gun he was going to use on Vesta." I ran a hand down the
rumpled front of his coat, then smelled the whiskey on my
fingers. "What's the celebration, Phil? Is Robinette going to
show his gratitude for keeping your mouth zipped about
Webb's murder by cutting you in on his future heists?"

The left side of his face slid up in a lopsided leer. I discovered I didn't like him after all.

"What's the matter, you sore on account of you didn't
think of it first?"

Twenty-three

"HAVE YOU MET Robinette?" I asked Musuraca.

"He's living in a hotel. I called him. We're meeting later."

"Planning to hand him that old dodge about leaving the information with someone who'll take it to the cops if anything happens to you?"

"I ain't stupid."

I wasn't sure if that meant yes or no. I opted for the Brotherhood of Man. "Neither is Robinette. Even a bad lawyer can get a written statement thrown out of court without a witness or his body to back it up. They won't find your body."

"I guess I got this far alive."

"That's because you weren't worth killing. Congratulations. Your stock just went up."

He took that as a compliment. "Guess you underestimated Fat Phil, huh? Guess everybody did. Well, that time's past. If you find that ninety grand, you can keep it. I'm investing in futures. No more peephole jobs. No more sitting on my piles in my car outside crummy motels. No more cold squid. Next time you want to see me you can call my secretary and make an appointment. I'll be heading up my own agency on Main Street, hiring grunts to stake out joints while I practice my putting."

"Bye-bye, Phil," I said. "You think I hope it doesn't work out, but you're wrong. I'd like to see a little grifter make a big score for a change. The big chains are taking too much of the market."

He straightened his tie and slung a finger along the brim of his hat. "Pick yourself up some cashew chicken on your way out. It's the most expensive item on the menu. Tell 'em Phil's buying."

I left him there amid the rat droppings and MSG, a little fat man with dreams too big for his belt, and drove home through the rusty rays of dawn over Windsor, smuggling themselves in under the black shelf of yet another storm-front. I was swimming against glue. I could feel my own foulness under my arms and in the bends of my elbows, and my chin rasped against my collar when I turned my head at intersections. When I pulled into the garage and jerked the key from the ignition, the weight of the ring was like dumb-bells.

I crossed through the kitchen and living room with flatirons strapped to my feet and threw myself across the bed without undressing. Nothing separated me from Phil Musuraca now except seventy pounds and hope for the future.

FADE IN: EXTERIOR CITYSCAPE—NIGHT
BOGART: So many guns around town, and so few brains.
INTERIOR BAR
CAGNEY: Top o' the world, Ma.
INTERIOR CAR—IN MOTION
LADD: So long, baby.
EXTERIOR WHARF—NIGHT
POWELL: Let's call it a retainer.
INTERIOR HOTEL ROOM
LANCASTER: Once I did something wrong.

INTERIOR NIGHTCLUB

STANWYCK: You and me, Walter—straight down the line.

EXTERIOR POLICE HEADQUARTERS—NIGHT

MITCHUM: Someone's trying to put me in a frame. I'm going up to get a look at the picture.

EXTERIOR ALLEY—NIGHT

GARFIELD: So long, baby.

INTERIOR STAIRCASE

BACALL: If you want me, just whistle.

EXTERIOR CARNIVAL—NIGHT

WELLES: When I set out to make a fool of myself, there's very little that can stop me.

INTERIOR OFFICE

HOLDEN: Poor dope. He always wanted a pool.

EXTERIOR BEACH—NIGHT

GRAHAME: We're sisters under the mink.

INTERIOR GARAGE

RAFT: So long, baby.

SCOTT: So long, baby.

CRAWFORD: So long, baby.

FADE OUT

It wasn't a dream, exactly. Dreams come with a plotline, whether or not it hangs together in the compassionless glare of the sun. It was more like a scattering of fragments of brain pictures that had slipped their sprockets, stuttering at demented angles in front of the bulb: Grubby walk-up offices lit by slats of moonglow through venetian blinds, city skylines dusted with glitter, carnival midways tilted forty-five degrees, their merry-go-rounds and Ferris wheels turning perpendicularly like huge gears, fans attached to nightclub ceilings casting swooping shadows like bats' wings, Krazy Kat staircases that turned themselves inside out halfway up like optical illusions on the puzzle page of the Sunday magazine, forcing me to hang on to the railings to avoid pitching into an abyss. The soundtracks had torn loose from the filmstrips, putting the lines in the mouths of all the wrong actors: John Garfield spoke in Gloria Grahame's falsetto and Barbara Stanwyck snarled with Humphrey Bogart's trademark lisp. Train whistles brayed from typewriter keyboards. Steam calliopes tootled through tender love scenes. Telephones sounded like ricocheting bullets.

The images were even more disorienting. Automobile grilles spiked with chrome bulged into fish-eye close-ups. Driving rain turned windshields into opaque jewels. Wet asphalt reflected skyscrapers like mirrors, so that it was impossible to tell which were the skyscrapers and which the reflections. Demonic grinning faces appeared upside down in the bowls of spoons. Whoever was in charge of the dispatching department had sent me Orson Welles's D.T.'s by mistake. I wondered where mine had wound up, and if Welles, straining a canvas chair in Directors' Valhalla, was having Dwight D. Eisenhower's.

I gripped the sides of the mattress in a desperate spread eagle through a delirious flying carpet ride, singeing myself in the torch held by Columbia's overdressed Lady Liberty, dodging Monogram's charging locomotive, slaloming between the broadcast rings rippling out from RKO's radio tower, recoiling from the matzoh breath of the MGM lion.

Lay off the movies, Walker. One of these times your face is going to freeze that way.

The telephone rang at least twenty times before I pried loose of the bed and hurtled out into the living room. I half expected to hear Peter Lorre in the earpiece.

"Mr. Walker, this is Gay Catalin."

Her crisp voice sounded like something from the other side of civilization: starched table linens and sparkling crystal as seen through a smeared window by the Dumpster. Dust motes kicked and tumbled in the sunlight pouring into the room. I had slept straight through another storm. My watch had migrated to the wrong side of my wrist. 10:05.

"I was going to come see you later today," I said. "There have been developments."

"I know. The police just left. I'm sending you a check for twenty-five hundred dollars. Please tell me if that isn't enough to cover your fee and expenses."

I peeled off my coat, changing hands on the receiver. My shirt stuck to my skin like a wet Kleenex. "I take it I'm fired."

"No, that would mean I'm unsatisfied with your services. Now that the police regard Neil as a wanted fugitive, I no longer consider employing a private detective to find him a positive use of my husband's money. I'm calling our lawyer instead."

"Your husband's no murderer."

"That's for the lawyer to prove. Thank you for all your hard work, Mr. Walker. Please feel free to use me as a reference." The connection broke.

I cradled the receiver and rummaged in my sodden shirt pocket for the pack that wasn't there. I broke a fresh one out of the drawer of the telephone table, found a book of matches, and killed a couple of hundred brain cells, but that wasn't enough to make me stop thinking. Then I spotted the TV set.

I don't own a remote, so I surfed barefoot, with my hand on the old-fashioned knob. Three or four talk shows, all featuring men in miniskirts. A couple of reruns of sitcoms I hadn't bothered to laugh at when they were fresh. An infomercial hosted by the former star of one of the sitcoms. *I Love Lucy*, which killed five minutes until the feminine hygiene spot. A soap opera. A war. A political round table discussion that incorporated the best of those two art forms. Pepe LePew and the cat.

The VCR was long overdue at the store, but it didn't know that. I punched it on, turned the channel to 3, and hit PLAY. The tape in the deck happened to be *Pitfall*. I sat down and watched it from the beginning until the scene where Dick Powell took over the controls of Lizabeth Scott's boat. Then I got up, turned off both machines, and dialed the number of Vesta Mannering's apartment. The hello I got on the sixth ring came from the same sub-basement I had crawled out of when Gay Catalin called.

"When did the cops cut you loose?" I asked without salutation.

"Who's this?"

"Amos Walker, alias the money fairy. Did they at least give you a ride home?"

"They offered. I called a cab. I prefer the brand of disinfectant the Yellow people use. Hold on a second."

I held on a little longer. Paper and cellophane and foil crackled. Steel scratched flint. A pair of lungs filled and emptied. In the suburbs another couple of hundred brain cells died without a whimper. Then:

"What did you say about money?"

"Later," I said. "I wanted your undivided attention. Are you a suspect?"

"Not unless I hired it done, and I guess all those original Rembrandts in my three-hundred-buck-a-month walkup don't put me in the right tax bracket for that. I was slinging menus in front of a hundred witnesses all the time Leo was getting himself shot in my bedroom. Did you do it?"

"No, and neither did Neil, but that's how Detroit's handling it. How much of what you told me did you tell them?"

"If you mean did I tell them about Orvis Robinette slapping me around, the answer's no. They didn't ask." She paused. "Oh, hell. Would they tap my phone?"

"Not for a couple of little victims like Elwood and Webb. Anyway, Detroit hasn't had the case long enough to get the court order, and in Iroquois Heights it's last season's catch. We're safe to talk. Are you working today?"

"I doubt I'm still employed. Two big Detroit cops in uniform plucked me out from behind the registration desk in the middle of the evening rush hour. That doesn't add up to four stars in a restaurant review."

"If you're rested up enough to see me in half an hour, you may not need to look for another job for a while."

She paused again. "I've gotten exactly two hours' sleep in the last twenty-four. Even when I'm rested I'm not good at riddles. Spell it out."

"What would you do if you had nine thousand dollars in your hands right now?"

"Oh, please."

"Indulge me. You're up already."

"I'd get a new wardrobe and have some pictures taken by a good photographer and hire a booking agent and get my acting career out of the toilet. While I was at it I'd pick a religion I liked and find the church most in need of a new roof and drop nine hundred in the collection plate. Miracles don't come cheap."

"Are the cops still hanging out at your place?"

"They took down the seal, but I've still got Leo's picture in masking tape on my bedroom carpet. I slept on the couch."

"Not there, then. The Detroit cops knock usually, but that Iroquois Heights gang thinks every little murder gives them a ninety-nine-year lease on private property, especially when there's a chance of catching a beautiful woman naked. Where can you meet me?"

"If you're serious about the money, you pick. I need the laugh."

I thought. Then I had it. "Got a pencil?"

She went to look for one. When I gave her the address she asked me to make it an hour and a half. "I've got bags under my eyes you could pack shirts in."

"Wear dark glasses."

She made a noise with her lips. "Give me a hint about this nine thousand."

"Ninety-two hundred," I said, "to put the fine point on it. That's the ten percent finder's fee the insurance companies will pay you when you return the money your ex-husband stole from the video stores downriver." I hung up.

Twenty-four

I LEFT WHAT I COULD of the Monday From Hell in the shower drain and the sink basin, dressed fresh from the skin out, ate breakfast for the first time all year, and rolled out. The air smelled scrubbed and rinsed. This had been the rain we'd been waiting for since July, the one that broke the cycle of pressure and heat and swept the sky as clear of clouds as a china bowl. The temperature was in the low seventies. Tops were down, bare midriffs were in, businessmen walking back from lunch swung their briefcases and whistled. I might have joined them if I could think of any tune but "The Song of the Volga Boatmen." It had been a long hard row, the boat had landed in the wrong spot, and I was the only one who seemed to care.

I dropped off the VCR and the Debbie Reynolds movies I hadn't gotten around to watching and wrote a check to ransom my good name. The clerk, a different kid this time with the same skin condition as his predecessor, didn't send up any flares. There were four identical machines on a shelf behind the counter and, incredibly, no one had been in over the weekend asking for *Tammy and the Bachelor*.

For the film aficionado and the student of architecture, the Michigan Theater in downtown Detroit is the place to go to be depressed. Built in 1926 along the soaring Art Deco lines of the Albert Kahn buildings sheltering the police department, the two daily newspapers, and the Fisher Theater, the Michigan had packed its auditorium for Rudolph Valentino, Charlie Chaplin, Greta Garbo, and Clark Gable, eked in enough viewers to cover the rental fees for James Dean and Marilyn Monroe, shut down through the entire film careers of Ryan O'Neal and Karen Black, and then in the time of disco and Jimmy Carter was gutted of its velvet seats and rosewood stage and turned into a parking garage. Now Luminas and mini-conversions and Nissans blackened the crumbling ornamental plaster at the tops of the ceiling columns with monoxide and dripped oil and transmission fluid on the mosaic floor tiles. What the ghosts of the Sheik and Cleopatra and the crew of the battleship *Potemkin* made of it all was anybody's guess.

I parked under the remains of a green-gilt false balcony, its bottom burst from water draining off the roof and trailing clumps of horsehair plaster, got out and wandered around for a while. I was ten minutes early, an old detective habit. By all rights my veteran's pension should kick in ten minutes before my sixty-fifth birthday and my casket should be lowered into the ground ten minutes ahead of the time advertised in the obituary, not that anyone would be there to notice. When I got to the gates I would smoke a cigarette while waiting for St. Peter to come back from lunch.

It was a big old echoing shell of poured concrete and red iron girders, with enough space overhead to house the phantom population the city bribed the census takers to report to Washington. Pigeons fluttered among the flies like bats in a cathedral. My footsteps slapped back at me from vaults and groins where the treble of a pipe organ long since gone to scrap might still be reverberating, as unaware of the change as a Japanese soldier on a remote island in the Pacific. I thought I smelled hot buttered popcorn under the guano and gasoline, but that was probably race memory. It was just a place to park cars.

I leaned against the Cutlass' rear fender, smoking and watching the entrance. I wondered if Neil Catalin had been watching the same way when his wife came here to meet him four days ago, when this was just a missing-person case and there were two more people in the world. I wondered if he had arranged to meet her at all. If I was right, and Webb had called Gay, successfully imitating his partner's voice, to keep us busy while he killed Brian Elwood and pinned it on Neil, then sent us to the DIA while he went to Vesta's place to kill her, I couldn't work up much indignation over Orvis Robinette. All he wanted was the money he thought he had coming to him, and all he had done was kill a killer.

I was thinking these thoughts, like God on His cloudy mount, when a red Triumph convertible turned in from the street, paused while the driver took a ticket, and rolled up the aisle between the rows of parked vehicles. I lifted a hand. Vesta saw it and cranked into a handicapped slot two cars over. She swung a mile of smoothly shaved tan leg out of the seat and came my way, hugging herself as if she were chilled, her high-heeled sandals clicking in the great empty space. She wore a white sleeveless blouse knotted above two inches of brown midriff and black shorts. Her hair was gathered inside a white silk scarf tied under her chin and she had on black-rimmed glasses with gray lenses through which I could just make out her eyes.

"I see you took my advice about the glasses," I said.

"Occupational necessity. I can't afford to squint in bright sunlight. Every fresh wrinkle knocks fifty bucks off my base salary." She glanced around. "This is the first time

I've been in this building. It doesn't look like your usual parking structure."

"It's not. We're standing in the orchestra pit. The screen was there, with a stage in front of it where Astaire and Rogers danced during personal appearances. It's kind of hard to envision now."

"A movie house." She smiled without enjoyment. "I might have guessed. You're the right person to go looking for Neil. You share an obsession."

"Don't think I'm on the trip I seem to be on. That comes in handy when I run up against someone who expects me to react like a Hollywood sleuth of the old order. It confuses them when I break from the script, and that levels the playing field. Anyway, I'm not looking for Neil anymore. His wife fired me this morning."

"I can't say I'm surprised. You're kind of a blunderer."

"What I am is a redundancy, with the police of two cities already looking for Catalin for murder. And just what kind of blunderer I am is something you really don't know much about."

She took off her glasses. She had made up her eyes, but there were tiny threads of blood showing in the whites. "You'll have to excuse me if I've bruised your feelings. I've had just enough sleep to make the amount I haven't had that much worse. There's fingerprint powder all over my apartment. I don't have a career. I probably don't even have a job. If I kept a biorhythm chart, which I don't because I'm the only actress east of Catalina who doesn't believe in that sort of thing, it would read like a Russian tragedy. I'm here for only one reason." She put her glasses back on and folded her arms, waiting.

"Why didn't you tell the cops about Robinette? Don't tell me again it's because they didn't ask. That one's as old as greasepaint."

"They let me know in a hundred little ways that they had it all figured out and that my input was just for the boys in the computer room. Introducing Robinette into it would just snarl things up. It seemed simpler to let them go on thinking what they thought. Otherwise I might still be there. Did you tell them?"

I shook my head. "Same reason, different motives. If they thought this connected to the shotgun robberies, they'd think you knew where the money was and tank you as an accessory."

"That was taking a chance. What if I had told them? They'd tank you for withholding evidence."

"I've been tanked before. It's worse than you expect, but not as bad as you fear. I figured you had enough angst for all of the Barrymores to draw from without a stretch in the county hotel."

"Zorro in a ninety-dollar suit. What makes me your damsel? I'm trying to sleep my way to the top."

"You're not having much luck at it. Anyway it's a narrow market."

"Thanks for the compliment."

"You're no femme fatale," I said. "You just look the part. From where I sit you're the only fly in this web who thought it was just an innocent doorway. An expert I talked to about Catalin's fix said if anything jolted him out of it, reality would. The world is a lot more complicated than noir fiction. Bad guys turn out to be just determined survivors, like Phil Musuraca. Some of them even get to be heroes; Robinette may have saved your life. Bad girls are just good girls in trouble. It's something to think about."

"Sometimes things are just the way they seem. I'm nobody's idea of a good girl."

I grinned. "That's quite a pep talk you give yourself. Stanislavsky or Stengel?"

"You said something about ninety-two thousand dollars."

Happy hour was over. I snapped my expired butt in the general direction of the VIP seats. It bounced off a van that had rusted through all its fenders and rolled toward the iron grating over the drain. "Trust me, you don't want the whole shot. The law will never leave you alone, and even if it does, Robinette won't. That kind of hero he isn't. Ten percent's customary from the insurance companies. A crafty lawyer might be able to jack them up for another five plus his fee. If you want someone to run interference and you're allergic to lawyers, I'm between assignments at the moment."

"And what might your fee be?"

"I get five hundred a day and expenses. There won't be any expenses. Hour's work over the telephone. Fifty ought to cover it."

Her brows shot up above the dark glasses. "That's all?"

"You were right about one thing," I said. "Sometimes the good guy is just as honest as he looks."

"Of course, this is all theory so far. Where's the money? How'd you find it?"

"Neil helped."

"So you did talk to him."

"Communed would be the word. I watched the same pictures he did. *Pitfall* in particular. Did you see it?"

She shook her head. "I don't own a VCR, and we couldn't exactly visit Neil's basement. He *talked* about old movies a lot. I wasn't always listening."

"I'll sketch it out: Married man, single dish, boyfriend in the slammer, fat sleazy private dick. Sound familiar?"

She said nothing.

"Coincidence maybe," I went on. "For sure when he found out the rest of it, his interest level went up: Here was his chance to lead the life he'd only been able to experience secondhand. It fascinated me too, but only because the resemblances sharpened the deeper I got into your relationship. There were differences. Raymond Burr went after Lizabeth Scott for purposes of lust, while Musuraca was only interested in the missing money. Your ex-husband gave you a car. Scott's boyfriend bought her a boat. But those were only questions of props and continuity."

"Car." She was starting to get it. She was a lot more intelligent than her past behavior indicated.

I said, "The same guy who told me about the difference between a movie and the real world pointed out the significance of the boat in *Pitfall*. I didn't need that, because you'd already told me about the one condition Ted Silvera had made in your divorce. I even took pity on Fat Phil, who'd been trailing you for days and didn't realize he was never more than a block away from what he was after. I recommended he read Poe. A half-smart guy, Phil. He got the drift, but he missed the point. He thought I was talking about your apartment.

"The night before he was busted for the shotgun robberies, Silvera met with Ernie Fishman, the fence from Flatrock. That much you know. What you didn't know, but that Robinette knew, was that Ernie dealt in stolen jewelry as well as everything else that can be carried away in one trip and turned into quick cash. Ninety-two thousand dollars in the small well-circulated bills found in video store cash registers is bulky and hard to conceal. Silvera traded it to Fishman for something a lot more portable. He must have known the law was close, so he hid the merchandise somewhere they wouldn't be likely to look when they came around with a warrant. They were looking for cash, remember. They'd ignore the places that are too tight or wet. You said the only thing Silvera asked for in the decree was the option to buy back the car he gave you."

She turned around, looking toward the Triumph. "I've cleaned that car a hundred times, inside and out. I had it in twice for detailing. If he—"

"He wouldn't put them anyplace where they'd be found during normal cleaning and maintenance." I walked past her and around to the front of the little convertible. It was a miniature version of a 1930s roadster, complete with running boards, a doughnut cover over the spare tire on the trunk, and a hinged straddle type hood.

I'd thought about the gas tank, but stickup men are a lazy lot, and anything like a string that would make a package easy to retrieve would be obvious every time the tank was filled. Magnetic boxes under the fenders and chassis fall off too easily and call attention to themselves up on the hoist. Just for fun I unscrewed the radiator cap and peered down inside, but that had all the same drawbacks as the gas tank, so the disappointment didn't disappoint me.

The windshield solvent reservoir was a blue plastic box mounted under the wipers with a cap the size of a jar cover. I removed it and stuck my hand down inside, groping along the smooth sides and saturating my shirt cuff with the blue-tinted liquid. When my fingers found a lump the size of a baby's fist I felt for the edges of the tape. It tore loose with a noise like Velcro and I withdrew the package and shook off the excess moisture.

It was a common pint-size Ziploc refrigerator bag, doubled over twice and secured with wide waterproof transparent tape. I peeled away the tape, unfolded the bag, zipped it open, and told Vesta to hold out her hands. When she complied I tipped ten lumps of what looked like quartz crystal into her cupped palms. The diamonds ranged in size from raisins to lemon drops, cut in pear shape and sparkling in the light they hadn't seen in three years.

I was wrong about one thing, and I learned that the next morning when I opened the *Free Press*. The police in Iroquois Heights found a body identified as that of Philip Francis Musuraca, curled into a fetal position in the roomy trunk of his 1960 Buick Invicta, parked behind a Chinese restaurant. He'd been beaten to death.

REEL THREE
Dissolve

Twenty-five

"A. WALKER INVESTIGATIONS."

"Mr. Walker, please."

I changed ears on the receiver. "This is Amos Walker."

The short silence on the other end told me I hadn't fooled anyone. If I'd really been trying I'd have answered the telephone with Judy Collins' soprano. "Mr. Walker, this is Ashraf Naheen. We met last week at Balfour House. On Mackinac Island?"

I recognized the British accent now, too precise to have been acquired in the country of origin. I put down my Smith & Wesson and the midget screwdriver. I'd located a screw to replace the one I'd lost when I threw the office at Orvis Robinette. It was Wednesday morning. Eighteen hours had passed since I'd left Vesta Mannering admiring her sparklers in the ruins of the old Michigan Theater. "I remember you, Dr. Naheen."

"I have a little matter I'd be pleased to discuss with you this afternoon, if you plan to be in your office. It isn't related to what we spoke about last week. I wish to consult your services."

"I'll be in. Do you know the address?"

"I still have your card. I'm catching the ten-thirty flight to Detroit City Airport. Look for me about two o'clock."

When we were through talking I sat back and thought about the Pakistani psychiatrist, brown and pleasant-looking, sitting in his green office and not discussing the nervous breakdown that had placed Neil Catalin in his care eighteen months ago. I thought about Tom Balfour, the island brat and all-around dogsbody, and his suspicions that Naheen videotaped his sessions with his patients for purposes of shaking them down. That didn't get me anywhere, so I stopped thinking. I finished putting together the revolver, loaded the cylinder from the box of cartridges I kept in the safe with my change of shirts, and returned to the morning edition of the *Free Press* and the article about Phil Musuraca.

It wasn't much, just two and a half inches in the Local section without a picture. Brian Elwood and Leo Webb had received more play, and no connection was made between them and Fat Phil. I supposed I was indirectly responsible for his beating death. If I'd fingered Orvis Robinette for the Webb killing, he wouldn't have been available to pay off Musuraca's blackmail try with his fists. On the other hand, if the Iroquois Heights detective hadn't tried to cash in on Webb's homicide, I wouldn't have had any reason to feel guilty. So that was one more thing to stuff into my little internal box of angst and sit on the lid until it locked.

The second murder had moved the Elwood story from the police column to a spot below the fold on Page One. The Freep had dug up photos of the three principals: a flattering three-quarter portrait of Webb in suit and tie that I had seen in a frame hanging in the hallway leading to his office, a high school yearbook shot of Gay's baby brother Brian, retouched to mask facial blemishes, and Catalin's driver's license picture, face front and sweating guilt through every pore. The article bore as much resemblance to the facts as the Hollywood version of an eighteenth-century novel did to its source. Journalists. Even when they got it right it didn't sound like anything you'd had something to do with. I turned to *Tank MacNamara* for my minimum daily requirement of truth and committed the works to the circular file.

My own reporter's instinct awakened, I cranked my Paleozoic Underwood down from its perch atop a file cabinet and typed up a report on the Catalin missing-person case for Gay Catalin to throw away without reading. It read like a screen treatment for Jack L. Warner to drop his cigar ashes on and then hand over to Ben Hecht and W. R. Burnett for rewrite. I stuck it in a manila envelope, stamped and addressed it, and sailed it at the floor in front of the mail slot. Then I wrote out checks for the rent, utilities, and membership dues in the Blunt Instrument of the Month Club against a checking account balance that didn't exist yet and dispatched them after the report. That carved twenty minutes out of my hectic workday.

Break time. I started a pot of coffee on the little four-cupper in the water closet, washed my hands and face and smoothed back my hair, tracking the progress of the gray in the peel-and-stick mirror tile above the sink, filled a Chrysler Corporation commemorative mug from the pot, and carried it to the desk. The coffee tasted weak. I hoisted the working bottle out of the file drawer of the desk and put a nail in it. My watch told me another eleven minutes had swept past. If this kept up I was going to have to hire an assistant.

Ashraf Naheen was sitting in my reception room when I got back from lunch. Small, round, and brown in his rimless glasses and a cocoa three-piece gabardine, he looked up pleasantly from a two-year-old copy of *Police Times* and stood, offering his hand. He saw me glance at my watch before I took it.

"We're ahead of schedule," he said apologetically. "We arrived at the airport in time to take an earlier flight. This is Gordon, my head orderly. I never travel without him."

I had already noticed Gordon, for professional reasons. He took up all the space in the oversize club chair I'd promoted from a curb on St. Antoine, and when he laid aside the *Entertainment Weekly* with Emmanuel Lewis on the cover and stood, he filled the gap between the crown of his head and the ceiling. He had the spotty tan of the infrequent island goer-outer, black hair sheared close to the skull, probably by himself, and slabs of muscle on his shoulders that threw off the lines of his Big and Tall sportcoat. His face was a plank with features penciled on. We didn't shake hands.

"Does Gordon ride with the passengers, or do you check him through?"

Naheen was pleasant. "Some of my less successful cases harbor resentments. Even a doctor of psychiatry must sometimes resort to prehistoric methods for his protection. And Gordon is an agreeable companion. He seldom speaks, but when he does, what he has to say is invariably significant. May we go into your office?"

I unlocked the door and the doctor and I went through. Significant Gordon stayed behind to sort through the selection of *New York Times* crossword puzzle books on the coffee table, starting with the back pages where the answers were. I scooped up the mail—two or three circulars and a thick mailer—and carried it to the desk. The mailer was as heavy as a brick.

Naheen wandered the office like a visitor to a gallery, stopping in front of the Anheuser-Busch print of Custer's Last Stand.

"Interesting choice," he said, "and possibly a revealing one. Are you a defender of lost causes, Mr. Walker?"

"Only when it pays."

He smiled his pleasant, noncommittal analyst's smile. "I ask your pardon. When I see an office so aggressively generic, containing only one item of personal expression, I'm tempted to read much into the item. It's a professional gaucherie that has cost me a number of valued friendships."

"We're not friends, Doctor. I'm just the help. I inherited the office and the furniture in it. All I changed was the magazines and the wall art. A target silhouette used to hang there. The print was just the right size to cover the spot where the wall didn't fade."

"Any number of less provocative prints would have done the job just as well. I suspect you're obfuscating. But I am tilling another's soil. Cigar?" He produced a leather case shaped like three torpedoes and opened it. When I shook my head he selected one, returned the case to his breast pocket, and went through the ritual. When he had it burning he dropped the match and the band in the ashtray I slid across the desk and sat down in the customer's chair.

I took my seat and didn't smoke. The fumes from the doctor's cigar were thick enough to have texture.

"The news from Detroit makes its way into our little island paper on a regular basis," he said. "It always saddens me to learn the fate of a guest I was unable to help. Is Mr. Catalin still at large?"

"He was as of yesterday, when the case stopped being mine. As I remember, you thought it was unlikely that his personality would split this wide."

"I make no apology. The brain is not a mechanical device. You can't just identify the defective component and replace it. Which in a roundabout sort of way brings me to the reason I'm here."

"One of your guests skip out on his bill?"

"They are all accounted for," he said pleasantly. "My problem is with a former employee. His name is Miles Leander."

He spelled it. I wrote it on my telephone pad. "Canned or quit?"

"I had to let him go. He was an orderly on my staff. He developed a hostile attitude and it was communicating itself to the guests. That was two weeks ago. Now he is attempting to extort money from me."

"Extort how?"

He leaned forward, propping his cigar on the edge of the ashtray. The afternoon sun canting in through the window behind the desk made opaque circles of his spectacles. "I must assure myself of your confidence. Some of the people I help at Balfour House are public figures. I will not remain in practice for long if they misjudge my motives."

"I wouldn't be in business a minute longer if I went around repeating what's said in this office."

He was still for a moment. Then he nodded. "I record some of my sessions with guests on videotape. It's purely for my own use, for reviewing later. Gestures, expressions, body language often reveal much about a person's emotions and thought processes that words do not. I find it useful to examine them for these things in private, without distractions."

"Do the patients—excuse me, the guests—know you're filming them?"

"Absolutely not. People behave differently when they're aware their words and actions are being recorded. By the time I subtracted suspicion and self-consciousness, I wouldn't have much left to work with."

I doodled on the pad.

"No one views the tapes but me," he went on. "When I am not watching them I keep them locked in a fireproof vault I had built into the closet in my office. I possess the only key. I put them away, I take them out. No one handles them but me."

"How many are missing?"

He hesitated. Then he nodded again. "I suppose I had no business coming to you if I did not expect you to behave like a detective. Forty-eight tapes are gone, Mr. Walker. They represent ninety-six one-hour sessions spent with a total of thirty guests. Some were prominent, many were not. The one thing they have in common is they are no longer guests at Balfour. The tapes were removed from the rear of the file, where the old case records are stored prior to destruction, and replaced with blanks."

"That's a lot of tapes to smuggle out all at once. What kind of security do you have?"

"The doors and windows are wired to alarms, for which the orderlies have codes. Gordon oversees a staff of four to discourage promiscuous comings and goings. These precautions are merely to keep the guests from coming to harm outside; I do not treat dangerous cases, only nervous disorders. It's my opinion that Leander spread out his theft over a long period to avoid attracting notice. He stole from the defunct file because I would not be likely to review those tapes. What I cannot figure out is how he got into the vault. That key is never out of my possession."

"Anyone can take an impression of a lock and have a key made to fit. When did you find out the tapes were gone?"

"I suspected nothing until ten days ago, when he sent me a copy of one, along with this note." He removed a fold of ruled paper from his inside pocket.

I took it. It was ordinary drugstore stock, with holes punched along the left margin for a ring binder. There were five lines block-printed in soft pencil:

DOC NAHEEN'S GREATEST HITS
$50,000 IN SMALL BILLS TO MR. BELL
15001 VERNOR, DETROIT
SALE ENDS AUGUST 31
OR WAIT AND TAPE THEM OFF TV FOR FREE

"Mr. Bell?"

He made a face and picked up his cigar. "My office is equipped with an old-fashioned sash-pull. It was there when I moved in and I decided to keep it as a charming alternative to the impersonal electronic buzzers one finds in institutions. Whenever an orderly is needed I tug on it and a bell rings at the other end of the house. Leander obviously chose the alias to mock me."

"What about the envelope?"

"It was a common mailer, addressed to me at Balfour in that same hand. It bore a Detroit postmark."

"That bell thing is shaky. What makes you so sure it's Leander?"

"He was bitter when I dismissed him. He called me a fraud and a charlatan and said it was about time the rest of the world knew what he knew. I have questioned the other orderlies and I'm satisfied none of them had anything to do with the theft. I have no doubt."

"I suppose you checked out the Vernor address."

"It belongs to a private messenger service, Spee-D-A Couriers. The person I spoke to on the telephone knows nothing about a Mr. Bell, but said I could check back Thursday when the manager returns from vacation. That's tomorrow."

"Being a trained detective I probably would have figured that out. Any idea where Leander is now?"

"He rented a room in one of the older homes on the island, but the owner informed me he moved out the day after he left my employ, without leaving a forwarding address. The employee application he filled out two years ago listed his sister as next of kin at eleven hundred Sherman in Detroit. When I tried to call there a recording told me the number had been disconnected."

I entered the address among the doodles. "What exactly do you want me to do, Doctor?"

"Get back the tapes, of course. I have no intention of paying fifty thousand dollars for my own property, even if I had that sum."

"That's a tall order. Even if I find him, he won't have the tapes with him. Even if he does, I can't separate them from him without committing theft."

"But they're my property!"

"The cops may not see it that way at first. He might call them just for spite. By the time it's sorted out, the tapes will be public record. Since your guests didn't sign releases allowing you to film them, you're in violation of federal law. Losing your license to practice psychiatric medicine will be the least of your headaches."

He scowled through a dense cloud of smoke. "What do you suggest?"

"Pay the fifty thousand."

"I don't have fifty thousand. Most of what I bring in goes into the upkeep of Balfour House and my malpractice insurance. I could not possibly raise more than twenty thousand, and I will not pay that to a thief. There is no use pressing me."

"How much will you pay?"

"Ten thousand. No more. But I must have every tape and every copy he may have made."

"Nobody can guarantee the last part," I said, "unless I deal with him directly."

"And if you do?"

"Then our options broaden."

Twenty-six

SITTING BACK in his chair, with one hand resting on one of his heavy thighs and his cigar pointed at the ceiling, Naheen was in listening mode. It would be the attitude he adopted when one of his guests was stretched out on the green leather couch in his office.

I swiveled away from him, got up, and slid the window up as far as it would go, sucking in the greasy air from the diner down the street, which was fresher than the smoky air inside the office. I propped open the sash with the discarded barrels from a sawed-off shotgun someone had once tried to kill me with—an item of personal expression the doctor had missed—and sat back down, swiveling to face him.

"I could put the fear of God in him," I said. "Make him see how lucky he is to have ten thousand dollars to spend on something other than traction and physical therapy. If he comes back on you later with copies to sell, he can count on all of that with interest."

"Do you think that would work?"

"Ask your head orderly. You don't get to be Gordon's size in his line of work without having had that kind of conversation a couple of times."

"Why do I need you, if I have Gordon?"

"You came to me. You didn't need six years of medical school and a year of residency to come up with the same scenario I just sketched out, so I assume you thought you needed someone with a couple of skills Gordon doesn't have, like chewing with his mouth closed and tracking down Miles Leander in a city of a little less than a million. How soon can you get the ten grand together?"

He inhaled through his nose. The cloud actually shrank. "I can have it next Monday."

"Friday would be better. The less time Leander has to think about it, the better for us."

"You both seem to think my finances are more liquid than they are."

"Maybe he's heard the same rumors I have."

I could see his eyes now, large and brown and floating in the magnification of his thick lenses, like olives pickled in their own juice. "What rumors are those?"

"Your camcorder's a pretty big secret for such a small island. I was there less than two hours before I heard that you videotape your sessions and then use what's on the tapes to shake down your guests after they return to the outside."

"I've heard those rumors. Mackinac is a resort community. The people who run it advertise it as a place to escape from the complexities of the twentieth—and soon the twenty-first—century. The presence of a loony bin in their precious Shangri-La is a distinct irritant. They will do and say anything to discredit me. I am proud to report that Balfour House is the only structure on the island that conforms to all the local building and safety codes. If it did not, I would not still be in business. Unannounced inspections are frequent and remarkably thorough." Using his finger, he carefully broke off a two-inch column of ash in the tray. "It would not surprise me to learn that Miles Leander is behind most of the rumors. Our relationship has not been cordial since I was forced to upbraid him sharply for his lack of courtesy toward certain of our more troubled guests."

"And yet you kept him on for two years."

"I am a patient man. Perhaps too patient at times for my own good. It comes with the territory."

"Then you deny you're a blackmailer."

"I know nothing about that enterprise beyond what I've seen in cheap melodramas. Common sense suggests a blackmailer would be a most difficult person to blackmail. One expects him to take the precautions his victims overlook."

"Funny thing about scavengers. They spend so much time angling to put the bite on other people they never think someone might be angling to take a bite out of them."

He leaned forward again and pressed out the cigar in the bottom of the ashtray. His expression was pleasant. "I could spend the rest of the afternoon protesting my innocence. Possibly in the end you would be convinced. Meanwhile the reputations of thirty unsuspecting people would have moved that much closer to destruction. I am sworn to regard their suffering as my responsibility. Are you prepared to share it?"

"Just because no one ever asked me to raise my right hand doesn't make it any less true for me, Doctor. I don't suppose you'd care to tell me their names."

"That would be a serious breach of ethics. Will you accept the job?"

I glanced at the Auto Show calendar. "Next Thursday's the thirty-first. With any luck I'll have this wrapped up by Monday. Give me a thousand for a retainer. It's something to wave under Leander's nose if I turn him before you can raise the other nine."

He adjusted his glasses, uncapped a fat fountain pen, and wrote out a check in a folder with a marbled leather cover: green, to match the decor of his office. He blew on the ink to dry it, then passed the check across the desk. He had a fine, calligraphic hand.

He rose. "I'll be at the Westin until this is resolved. I'll call you when I have the cash in hand."

"Who's minding the store?"

"The vacation season is always quiet. The orderlies can manage the few guests on hand, who are there mainly for the rest. The horses, you know: clip-clop, clip-clop. One wonders where the Victorians went for respite."

"The Khyber Pass comes to mind."

I escorted him to the outer office, where Gordon stood up quickly from the upholstered bench. The springs were slower to react.

"Thank you, Mr. Walker." Naheen held out his hand. "You impressed me upon the occasion of our first meeting as a man of wisdom and discretion. I've seen nothing today to make me change my mind."

"Whatever." I took the hand and gave it back.

I waited long enough for them to reach the second landing, then used the smoking stand to prop open the door to the hall and disconnected the pneumatic closer on the inner door. When the place smelled a little less like a bus station in Havana, I closed the doors and went back to the desk.

The mailer I'd picked up from under the slot was still waiting to be opened. I pulled the tab and tilted it over the blotter. My unlicensed and unregistered Luger slid out.

I peered inside the envelope. A rectangle of white paper clung to the lining. I reached in and pulled out a half-sheet of Detroit Police Department stationery containing John Alderdyce's thick scribble:

You Owe Me.

Twenty-seven

THE HOUSE WAS IDENTICAL to all the others on that block of Sherman; not that it had been planned that way, as in a suburban tract, with architects, developers, and builders working in harmony to present a soothing uniformity to a postwar world, but in the way that old people from different families and varied nationalities grow to look like one another from years of being forced to coexist under a communal roof. The sidings, once painted a variety of colors, had puckered and gone a monotonous shade of gray, all the panes in all the windows peered out through a milky opacity created by decades of discoloration, like cataracted eyes, and the squares of lawn, although recently cut, shared the malnourished sepia brown of winter-killed wheat. The cancer came from within. Give the houses a fresh coat of latex, replace the windows, fertilize and manicure the grass, and within a season everything would have reverted to what it was before the improvements. It would be like painting the leaves of a dead tree.

I parked against the curb and walked up the front walk, which had begun to crumble like cake. The day was hot but not sultry; the sun felt good on my back after the air-conditioned chill in the car. The front door was open. Through the screen I saw the oblong glow of a black-and-white TV and heard the soporific voices of a pair of announcers discussing the recent play in a Tigers game as if it were a shard of pottery discovered in a dig in Ethiopia. I rapped on the screen door's wooden frame.

Someone cursed, got up with a grunt from a deep chair, and scuffed up to the door carrying a sawed-off length of baseball bat. He was white, a rarity in that neighborhood, with dirty gray hair, hammocks of skin under his eyes, and white stubble on his chin. He was wrapped up in an old green bathrobe too heavy for the season. A sour smell of medicine and mildew crept out through the holes in the screen.

"Miles Leander?" I asked.

He coughed into his fist, a deep, hollow lung-rattler, dripping with congestion, and cleared his throat. "Who wants to know?"

I pressed one of my cards against the screen. "The name's Walker. I'm not with the police or the city. I'm not working for a collection agency. All I want is talk."

"What about?"

"That depends on whether your name is Miles Leander."

A sly look swam up to the watery surface of his eyes. "I'm Leander."

"I doubt it. You're kind of old to be prying epileptics off the floor of Ha-Ha High."

"You're kind of new to this neighborhood to be calling anybody a liar."

A woman's voice came from the back of the house. "Who is it, Roy?"

Neither of us reacted at first. Then a baggy leer spread across the stubbled face.

"Aw, hell," he said. "I guess the cow's clear out of the corn."

A new face appeared over his left shoulder. The woman's dusty-copper hair was ratted straight out from her scalp, giving her a surprised appearance. The set of her tired features said it was artifice, that there wasn't much left that could surprise her. I decided neither of them was as old as I'd thought at first, that we were almost contemporaries. I felt nothing about that at all.

She squinted at my card, then opened her eyes to read my face. "Can we help you?" She sounded doubtful.

"You can if you're Miles Leander's sister," I said.

"I'm Susan Thibido. This is my husband, Roy. Miles is my brother, but we haven't seen him in days. He stayed with us a couple of days last week, but I don't know where he is now. Is he in trouble?"

"Tell him not to come to us if he is," Roy said. "We got trouble enough to last."

"We wouldn't if you'd go back to work."

"I'm sick." He coughed, providing evidence. "I been sick three weeks. How's a man supposed to look for work when he's sick? I don't see you bringing home no steaks."

"I've got a job."

He made a noise in his nose. "Delivering papers. Scab work. All the regulars are on strike, or didn't you notice?"

"You're a steamfitter. The steamfitters aren't on strike."

"They ain't sick, neither." He coughed again.

I scraped the screen with the edge of the card, just to make noise. "Miles isn't in trouble yet. He might be if I don't talk to him soon. He's playing a dangerous game."

"Drugs?" Her voice dropped an octave.

"Not to my knowledge. He's got a chance to climb out from under and make a couple of bucks besides, but the clock's ticking. I won't be able to help him once the cops come in."

"I told him not to take that job. You can't work around crazy people without it rubbing off. Is it about the job?"

"Kind of. I'm doing some work for his old boss. There's a sum of money involved. For you, too, but only if I get to speak to him. Are you sure you don't know where he is?"

"How much money?" Thibido asked.

"He's always been independent. We only see him when he needs a place to sleep. He might be staying with one of his old girlfriends, but I don't remember any of their names. Some of them came and went so fast I never knew what they were called. Is this money honest?"

"Who the hell cares, Sue? When did you start growing a halo?"

"Money doesn't have moral standards," I said. "The sum I'm talking about is enough to change Leander's life, but not enough to affect my client's. No one will suffer from the transaction. There are no drugs or white slavery involved, no guns or government cover-ups or child pornography or treason. No foreign democracies will fall. Call it severance pay from a generous former employer."

"It can't be that easy," she said. "Nothing that's right is that easy."

"Christ." Roy scuffed back to his game, the cut-down bat swinging at his side.

I wedged the card between the screen door and the frame. "Next time Miles gets in touch with you, please give him my number. He's an adult. You should let him decide."

"I always have. I wish I could say his decisions have always been sound." She nodded then. "I'll give him your number and tell him what you said." But she made no move to claim the card. She was waiting for me to leave before she unhooked the door. I thanked her and went away.

On Michigan I stopped and used a pay telephone to call Spee-D-A Couriers and confirm that the manager, whose name was Mr. Blint, wouldn't be in the office until the following day. Fresh out of leads, I cashed Dr. Naheen's check, caught supper down the street from my bank, and went home.

I was dozing in front of an oil fire in Madagascar when my telephone rang. I got up and turned down the sound on the set.

"Walker?"

A low voice for a woman and even some men, with fine grit in it, like a cat's lick.

"Vesta?" I sat down and groped for a cigarette. I was awake now.

"I went to see a lawyer like you said. He thinks I ought to be able to get at least fifteen percent out of the insurance companies, plus his fee. That's almost fourteen thousand for me."

"Congratulations."

"I need to make sure you're not mad because I didn't use you as a go-between."

"You don't owe me any explanations."

"I don't owe anyone anything. I don't intend to ever again. I made that decision before I knew anything about the money. I especially don't want to owe you. That's no way to start a relationship." After a short silence she said, "Hello?"

"I was just lighting a cigarette. Are we starting a relationship?"

"That's what I called to ask. You don't have to be polite. I mean, I don't even know if you're married or involved or dead set against women. I'm pretty sure you're not gay."

"I'm not any of those things. Are you asking me out?"

"Hell. I'm no good at this. I guess I'm not a woman of the post-feminist era after all. Please forget I called."

"Don't hang up. I'm not any good at it either. Half the women I meet are clients. The other half I'm following for the first half. I spend most of my Saturday nights in my car watching a window with the shade pulled down. Incredible as it may seem, the few women I run across who don't fit either category aren't interested in watching it with me."

"So is that a yes?"

"Where would you like to go?"

"Someplace where we won't trip over anyone either of us knows. I know a neat little place in Brighton, if that's not too much of a hike. Tomorrow night?"

"As it happens, my calendar is clear. Who picks who up?"

"You drive. I've done my bit for the sisterhood. Six-thirty's comfortable if we want to make an eight o'clock reservation."

"Aren't we civilized."

"Only where it counts." She said good-bye.

I put out the cigarette and went to bed. The telephone rang again as soon as I got in.

"Change your mind?" I asked.

"About what? Who do you think this is?" It was John Alderdyce's voice.

"My wake-up service, apparently." I sat down. The chair was still warm. "Thanks for the package, John. I was starting to think I'd spend Labor Day in the Iroquois Heights lockup."

"I don't know what package you're talking about, and neither do you. You're still dreaming."

"I get it. So who's dead now?"

"A fourteen-year-old girl in a crack house on Woodrow Wilson and an old man who took a midnight walk into the River Rouge, for two; but you're not hooked in with either of those. At least I don't think you are. I thought you'd like to know you can stop looking for Neil Catalin."

"You found him? Where and in what condition?"

"He's still missing, but his car isn't. We found it parked in the long-term lot at Metro Airport. That puts it in the FBI's wheelhouse. He's now wanted for unlawful flight to avoid prosecution. So there's nothing you can do or think that the boys and girls in suits didn't think of first and follow up on yesterday."

"Did the county boys pop the trunk?"

"That's always the first order of business. No body. No blood on the upholstery either. He took a flyer on a big silver bird and now he's Fed bait."

"It doesn't matter. I got my walking papers yesterday. Did Ballistics kick back anything on those slugs where Webb was killed?"

"I thought it didn't matter."

"I'm writing my memoirs."

"Webb and Elwood were killed with the same gun, a nine-millimeter. The slug from the staircase wall was too messed up to be anything but a probable, but the one in Webb's chest matched. Catalin registered a nine-millimeter S-and-W year before last. We searched his house and office yesterday, but we didn't turn it. That's because he's either still got it on him or he chucked it in the sewer after he shot his partner. He's getting better. He only fired once at Webb."

"What about powder burns?"

"Webb had 'em on his shirt. That just means there was a struggle. *You* think the shooter wrestled the gun away from him and it went off. *We* think Webb wrestled the shooter for the gun. We'll let the lawyers sort it out once Catalin's extradited back here."

"If he's arrested."

"Like I said, that's a federal headache now. I've got enough on my hands with the teenage girl and the old man."

"Thanks, John."

"That's another one you owe me. I mean, if you owed me one before." The line clicked and hummed.

I was deep asleep the next time it rang. I clawed my way up from the bottom of a shaft filled with black crankcase oil, untangled myself from the bedding, and stumped on raw nerve-ends into the living room, shaking circulation back into the arm I'd been lying on.

"This damn well better be good."

"Is your name Walker?"

A voice unknown to me, male with an edge. I had a premonition. It was still there when I switched on the floor lamp. "I'm Walker."

"This is Miles Leander. My sister says you went to her place looking for me. Why?"

"I've been retained by Dr. Ashraf Naheen to talk to you about the tapes."

"What tapes?"

I let that one wither on the branch.

"I'm not interested in talking to anyone who'd take a dime from Naheen," he said finally. "Tell me something. What do you call someone a snake pays to do his slithering for him?"

"A private detective. When and where can we meet?"

"Never and nowhere. I only called you because Susan asked me to."

"She worries about you."

"She should worry about herself. I'm not married to a lump like Roy."

"My client has authorized me to offer you a lot of money. Not as much as you're asking for, but without fear of prosecution. Running from the law is expensive."

"Who the hell needs money? I'd rather have a good opinion of myself and three squares a day in jail. Look, I don't know what Doc Schlock has told you, but you can tell him for me he's through. I don't have the tapes. I sent them to all the people who should have them."

"Who would that be?"

"You're the detective. Work it out."

I was growing weary of that one. "You didn't send a copy of one of the tapes to Naheen along with a fifty thousand-dollar price tag for the originals?"

His end was quiet for a beat. Then he made a nasty laugh and hung up.

I stood there in my robe for a long moment, jigging the receiver in my hand. Finally I cradled it and reached over to switch off the lamp. Just then the glass pane in the window across the room separated into three pieces and fell with a clank. The report came right behind, as loud as the first shot at Fort Sumter.

Twenty-eight

I GAVE THE LAMP a shove, hit the floor hard on my right shoulder, and rolled behind the chair. The room was dark now. I listened to my heartbeat and waited for my pupils to adjust. Gradually I began to make out features in the room in the dusty starlight, the slightly lighter oblong of the broken window in the black expanse of wall.

It was quiet outside, or as quiet anyway as a suburban neighborhood entirely surrounded by a great city ever gets in summer. Crickets stitched in the yard, traffic whirred past on the Chrysler and Ford freeways nearby, one of my neighbors was watching Letterman by an open window with the sound cranked up, the eternal dog went on barking long after it had given up hope.

My .38 revolver, shiny new screw and all, was in the bedroom, where I would have to cross in front of the window to get it. I decided to wait.

I was good at that. In Cambodia I had remained in a crouch for nearly three hours, waiting for a sniper I wasn't sure existed to make a move of some kind. Then a branch had stirred, halfway up in a hardwood tree without a breath of air moving between me and Saigon. I shot him out of it, an irregular not more than thirteen years old, wearing a dirty loincloth and sandals made from U.S. Army Jeep tire recaps and armed with a Russian AKM, rate of fire six hundred rounds per minute. I had used one in a hundred and eighty.

But in Cambodia I had been twenty years old, and I knew who the enemy was.

Ten minutes crept past, one by one on their bellies.

The dog barked and barked.

The telephone rang and kept it up twelve times before it quit. I hadn't been this popular since the end of the sexual revolution.

A dull ache awakened in my right hip and began the slow blind crawl toward the knee, burning as it went. When the time came to move, the whole leg would be as dead as I was supposed to be.

A door slammed, loudly enough to make me flinch. A motor started. Rubber scraped asphalt. A pair of high beams swept the room like the light on the conning tower of a U-boat. The engine growl climbed to a thin whine and became someone else's disturbance down the block. I had heard that sound once before.

I waited two minutes, just in case he'd left a friend behind. Then I stood up, went to the bedroom for the Smith & Wesson, and went out the back door.

The blue mercury light on top of my neighbor's garage made snipers out of every shadow. It took me five minutes to work my way around to the front of the house, and five more to satisfy myself that I was the only living thing awake on the street, not counting the dog. Even if the shot woke someone up, he had had time to convince himself he was dreaming and turn over and go back to sleep. He wouldn't have any reason to look out his window and see one of his fellow taxpayers standing in his bathrobe in his own front yard, a gun hanging at his side like Wyatt Earp's after the civil infraction at the O.K. Corral. I went back inside.

I righted the floor lamp, found the bulb had a broken filament, and replaced it. I searched the living room walls for a half hour and had begun to wonder if I'd been dreaming myself when I found at last where the slug had gone. On my hands and knees in the same spot for the fifth time, I happened to look up and saw a fresh white scar in the walnut finish on the underside of a curio shelf left over from my marriage. The curios had departed along with the other half of the union, leaving me with a convenient place to stand a beer bottle when I went back in the kitchen to make a sandwich. The thing had been invisible for years.

I got up, placed my palm under the shelf, and lifted. The nails securing the board to the wooden brackets were loose in their holes and the board moved easily, exposing a neat round hole in the painted plaster behind it. The slug had burrowed along the bottom of the shelf with just enough pressure to nudge it upward half an inch, then buried itself in the wall. The shelf had then settled back into its original position, concealing the hole. Malicious destruction of property had never been more discreet.

I retrieved my Swiss Army knife from the litter on the bureau in the bedroom and performed surgery. After shattering the window, crossing the room, and hoicking up the shelf, the lump of lead had nearly spent itself by the time it came to rest against a stud. I pried it out and examined it. It might have come from a nine-millimeter weapon. It might have been a .38 Special or a freak European caliber. I'd left my slide rule and calipers back at the lab. I tossed it up and caught it a couple of times and when the novelty went out of that I dropped it into the pocket of my robe.

It was strictly a souvenir. If I went to the cops with it and it turned out to have come from the same gun that had killed

Brian Elwood and Leo Webb, the investigation would come back to Detroit and sit on me like a fat drunk on a bar stool. They would want to know why Neil Catalin had it in for me, and when I didn't give them the answer they were looking for they'd tank me as a material witness, or stake me out like a goat on a lion hunt. Either way my days as an effective investigator were over until they had their man.

And they would never have their man as long as they thought he was Catalin.

While I was working all this out, a moth the size of a kite sailed in through the broken window, splatted against the lamp shade, and plopped to the carpet, dead as the USSR. I had some home maintenance to do.

I found some scraps of plywood in the garage, but nothing that would fit the empty window frame. I picked up a hammer and a sack of nails, punched the bottom out of the silverware drawer in the kitchen, and nailed the piece over the hole. After picking up and throwing out the broken glass I took the hammer and nails into the bedroom and pounded a nail into the bed's wooden frame halfway between the head and foot, leaving an inch and a half of shaft sticking out.

The telephone rang. I carried the revolver with me into the living room.

"Walker's All-Night Construction."

"Are you okay?"

It was Vesta.

"It depends on what scale you're using. Did you try to call earlier?"

"You didn't answer. I was worried."

"Why?"

"I had a visitor right after I got off the phone with you. After he left I went to bed, but I couldn't sleep. I got to thinking he might be on his way over to your place. I was right, wasn't I?"

"I'll guess. It was Orvis Robinette."

"I kept the door on the chain all the time we were talking. He could have broken it, but he was on his good behavior. I told him I didn't have the ninety-two thousand, that my lawyer had it and he'd put it in a safe deposit box and that we were giving it back."

"Was he still on his good behavior?"

"For him, I suppose. He didn't call me anything I hadn't heard before, but he didn't try to break in. That means he believed me. He wanted to know whose idea it was to give the money back. I wouldn't tell him, but I think he figured it out for himself. He left then. When you didn't answer your phone I thought—"

"He was here. I didn't see him, but I know the sound of that souped-up Camaro he drives. I heard it at your place the night he killed Leo Webb. He wasn't as lucky with me. He missed."

"Did you call the police?"

"What for? I've already been violated."

"But you're okay."

"Okay enough to do a little midnight carpentry. He won't be back tonight. I'm pretty sure he won't be back at all."

"What makes you sure?"

"He's hotheaded, but he's no psycho. He went into crime for the money, not the buzz. The cash is gone. There's no percentage in carrying on a vendetta. That doesn't mean he won't try again if I happen to cross his path, but he won't go out of his way to cross mine after the risk he just took. By now he's planning his next heist."

"I hope you're right. All my relationships lately seem to wind up in jail or wanted by the cops or dead. I'm starting to wonder if I'm the opposite of a rabbit's foot."

"Let's just say your biorhythms are due for an upswing. Go back to bed; that's what I'm planning to do. I'll see you tonight."

"Just don't walk under any ladders between now and then, deal?"

I grinned and told her good night.

When the receiver was in the cradle my grin faded. With the gun in my hand I checked the locks on every door and window in the house. In the bedroom I draped my robe over the footboard, hung the revolver by its trigger guard on the nail I'd hammered into the bedframe, and stretched out on the mattress, checking a couple of times with my hand to make sure the weapon was within reach. A gun under a pillow is too hard to get to. A gun on the nightstand is too easy for the wrong people to get to. And as confident as I'd sounded when I spoke to Vesta, too many of my assumptions had gone wrong lately to trust any of them as much as I trusted that nail.

Twenty-nine

IN THE MORNING I showered, cleaned my gun, shaved, loaded the cylinder, dressed, checked the load, drank coffee and juice, snapped the holster to my belt, and went to work. Nobody shot at me when I fished the *Free Press* out of the junipers, so I counted it the start of a good day.

A high-speed early-morning chase involving a stolen car, three Detroit police cruisers, and an innocent thirty-three-year-old mother of two killed crossing with the light at an intersection had bumped the Elwood-Webb murders to an inside page. The story led off with the discovery of Catalin's car at Detroit Metropolitan Airport, went from there to an all-purpose quote from the FBI special agent who had inherited the case, then went on to rehash the familiar details. The same trio of pictures of Elwood, Webb, and Catalin ran as filler.

The respite of the last few days had ended. The ventilating breezes from Canada had shifted to the North, bringing up the stale air from Ohio and Kentucky and below that sopping Dixie: It smelled of kelp. A bank of sullen, dirty-faced clouds was working its way upriver from Lake Erie, preparing to screw down the lid once again. Humidity, storms, and blackouts were predicted. The officers of the Tactical

Mobile Unit busied themselves polishing their face shields
and checking the expiration dates on their cans of Mace.
Every summer and every winter, the Pleasant Peninsula
pays a price for avoiding the earthquakes out West and the
flooding in the East.

I stopped at the office long enough to check my service
for messages and call Spee-D-A Couriers. Mr. Blint, the
manager, was at his desk and expected to be there throughout the day. After just ten minutes parked in the sun, I could
have broiled a steak on the hood of the Cutlass. When I
turned on the radio, Nat King Cole sang "Those Lazy, Hazy,
Crazy Days of Summer." I punched a button to change stations and got Sarah Vaughan on WEMU: "Ain't No Use."

I wondered if it was going to be such a good day after all.

The messenger service was set up in a glass-brick building on Vernor that had housed an Italian restaurant, a throw-
away newspaper discarded after eighteen months, a
Mexican restaurant, a police mini-station, a Thai restaurant,
an accounting service, a Japanese restaurant, a Republican
campaign headquarters, and some kind of restaurant. It was
a palimpsest of a structure that bore some evidence of every
business that had passed through its portals. The windows
were made of bulletproof Plexiglas from the mini-station
period, an electronic megaphone belonging to the political
incarnation still poked out above the door, and the button to
push for service reposed between the jaws of a brass-plated
Japanese dragon.

The building was less than twenty years old. It had replaced a hotel that had been in operation constantly since the
Cleveland Administration.

A sign mounted perpendicular to the front of the building
read SPEE-D-A COURIERS, the S fashioned after a lightning
bolt. A row of bicycles was chained to a rack next to the entrance. I stood back out of the way as a lanky teenage girl

in Spandex shorts, a halter top, a cork helmet, and shin guards punched open the door, dumped an armload of packages into the basket of the first bike in line, unlocked the chain, and took off, swinging a leg over the seat after the vehicle was already in motion.

The shallow customer area was painted blue and orange to match the colors of the sign out front and ended abruptly before a counter with a swing gate. The room beyond was a chaos of stacked packages in Fiberglas crates, cases of pigeonholes, canyons of boxes, and a granite-topped table like a printer's stone where a dozen or so young people dressed like the girl who had just left stood wrapping and stamping bundles with that combination of wasted movement and superior efficiency that belongs exclusively to the under-twenty set. Just watching them made my corns ache.

A copper bell with a handle stood on the counter. I picked it up and gave it a jingle. In a little while one of the workers, a boy with cropped blonde hair and a gold stud in his right nostril, came over.

"Mr. Blint?" I asked.

He shook his head and jerked it toward the back. "Is it a complaint? Sorry, mister. Some of these kids are a little slow. They don't stay here long enough for us to sort out the lazy ones from the Spee-D-A material."

"How long have you worked here?"

"Almost four weeks."

"I guess that makes you the assistant manager." I gave him a card. "Please take this in to Mr. Blint. It's important I talk to him."

He went back without glancing at the card or asking questions. He was Spee-D-A material. Thirty seconds later he came back and opened the gate.

"Mr. Blint's at his desk."

After the bicycles and printer's stone I suppose I expected

an old crotch in a green eyeshade surrounded by carrier pigeons in cages. I got a graying longhair in granny glasses and a fringed leather vest, seated at a keyboard in front of an electronic screen. He shared the back third of the building with fourteen monitors, six fax machines, eight printers, and a board containing a row of digital clocks representing the world's time zones, including the daylight savings holdouts. A bulletin board shingled with notes and memos featured a color reproduction clipped from a magazine of the melting clocks of Dali's *The Persistence of Memory.* The screen saver marching across the blue glowing faces of all the spare monitors put it more directly: TEMPUS FUGIT.

"I think I'm getting it," I said by way of greeting. "Gepetto Plugged."

"Actually, my home page handle is Huygens. He was the Dutchman who designed the first clock pendulum." Blint's attention remained on the screen in front of him. "What you're looking at is a three-dimensional oxymoron. Fax, Internet, E-Mail, World-Wide Web, and the good old under-appreciated Don Ameche." He patted the console telephone at his elbow. "Who the hell needs a messenger service? I wonder if the frontier ferrymen who contracted with the Union Pacific to carry their rails and men and equipment across the rivers of this great land ever paused to consider that they were putting themselves out of business."

"I think they did. You don't turn down paying work. Speaking as one oxymoron to another," I added.

"That crossed my mind when I saw your card. Why employ a shamus when you can get all the information you need at the touch of a key?"

"Not all. You can't swap confidences in cyberspace. You can't buy a drunk a drink or wave a fin under the nose of an underpaid clerk or fix up a city councilman with the barmaid or muss someone's shirt. At forty cents a minute you can't practice diuturnity."

"Diuturnity." He sat back then and looked up at me. His eyes were oyster-colored above the wire rims of his Ben Franklins. "Such an impressive vocabulary in such an unremarkable suit."

"I gave myself a word-a-day calendar last Christmas. And I never discuss tailoring with anyone who dresses like Jimi Hendrix."

"Hendrix. There was someone who made full use of the time he had. Yes, child?" He looked at the girl in Spandex who had materialized from the other side of the pigeonholes.

"Devon just quit. He said Burger King pays more and the hours are better."

"He's probably right. Give Rebecca his route."

She left.

"Big turnover?" I asked.

"Tip of the iceberg. The wages I can afford to pay restrict me to the MTV generation. They have the attention span of a housefly."

The girl returned. "Rebecca says there are too many hills on Devon's route."

"Tell her she's fired. Corinne," he called, after a moment.

She'd started to turn. She turned back. "I'm Janet. Corinne quit last week."

"Noted. How are you on hills?"

"They're easy. I'm a gymnast."

"Congratulations, Janet. You just inherited Devon's route and a raise."

"Who gets my old route?"

"Rebecca. I decided she's not fired."

When we were alone again, Blint sighed. "Have you always been a detective?"

"Probably not. If I were born wearing a shoulder holster I'd have heard about it."

"I was a mail carrier in Royal Oak for twenty years. Then a clerk I barely knew well enough to talk to came in and sprayed the place with lead just as I was tying out. Now I'm self-employed." He pushed himself away from the computer console and I saw the wheels on his chair. "But you're not here to waste *Tempus.*"

"My client had some property stolen. Someone's offered to sell it back to him, payment to be delivered to this address. Is it usual for a messenger service to accept deliveries as well as make them?"

"Not if I suspect hot merchandise is involved, or drugs. The authorities are here on a regular basis because of the minors I employ. I always test clean."

"But you do accept deliveries sometimes. I'm investigating a customer, not you."

"On occasion, yes. We charge more for the convenience than the postal service does, but you need identification to rent a post office box. Anyone can walk into any post office and find out who belongs to a particular box number. That never fails to upset the people who advertise for partners in alternative-sex publications; they almost always find out from their employers or spouses. We don't ask for ID unless the customer pays by check. That almost never happens. It doesn't do to have your monthly dividend from the Marital-Aid-of-the-Month Club arrive at your front door in full view of the neighbors."

"The customer I'm interested in goes by Mr. Bell."

He was silent for a moment. Then he slid his cheaters back up his nose. "How do I know you're not just working some divorce case? I figure I've got two more years before the whole world's on line; just enough time to make a difference between a comfortable retirement and Little Friskies every Friday. That goes west when my customers find out I can't keep a secret in a cage."

"This isn't evidence. It would just be a hell of a lot of trouble to go to when there are easier ways to get what I'm after."

I took out the sheet of notepaper Naheen had given me containing the fifty-thousand-dollar ransom demand, folded back the top to conceal the doctor's name, and held it in front of his face.

Blint read it, then took off the glasses and rubbed his eyes. He had a cast in one and a white scar along that temple that a bullet might have made. It reminded me of the mark on the underside of the curio shelf in my living room.

"Works for me." He put his glasses back on. "I remember Bell. None of these kids would; most of them weren't working here then. It was a couple of weeks ago. I could look it up."

"Not necessary."

"He paid cash. I told him I couldn't hold anything longer than thirty days. He said if it hadn't come by September first, it never would."

"What did he look like?"

"It was a busy day. I was shorthanded, as usual, and working the counter always gives me a stiff neck. He had on a baseball cap, bill to the front, and I think a Windbreaker. I don't remember the colors, so don't ask. Pair of shades, the neon kind the kids like. He was young. A kid. When he came in I thought he was looking for a job."

"Race, height, weight, facial hair?"

"White. A smudge of beard, maybe. I'm not sure. I don't notice people's height as a rule. They all look like basketball players from down here. Medium to tall, I guess. Skinny. This sucks, doesn't it? I was a much better witness the time I was shot."

"You had more reason to notice details then. I wouldn't sweat it. Witnesses who remember too much are worse than witnesses who don't remember at all." I frowned at my notebook. "He sounds young for the guy I'm thinking of. Could he have been disguising his age? A cap and snazzy glasses can go a long way in that direction if there's some doubt."

"I'm around kids all the time. This one wasn't much past twenty, if he was that."

"He didn't give you any information beyond calling himself Bell?"

"No, and I didn't ask. He didn't behave like a druggie, and he didn't dress the way kids that age deck themselves out when they're making more money than they should; not enough flash. So I figured he was ordering back issues of *Anal Delight* and didn't want his parents to know. If I'd thought he was using my business for a blackmail drop, I'd have thrown him out on his ear."

"How was he going to claim delivery without some kind of ID?"

He twisted in the chair, tore the top sheet off a square pad on the corner of the desk, and held it out.

I took it. It was a receipt blank bearing Spee-D-A's logo in blue and orange.

"I wrote 'Mr. Bell' on it, initialed it, and gave it to him," Blint said. "All he had to do was show it at the counter. It didn't even have to be him. The receipt is all that's needed."

I couldn't think of any more questions. I didn't like the answers I'd gotten to the ones I'd asked. I gave him back the blank and put away my notebook. "If you hear from him again, I'd appreciate a call."

"What I'd like to do is call the cops and jail his young ass."

"They won't thank you for it. My client will, and he's in a better position to help out with your retirement."

Turning, I almost bumped into Janet.

"Rebecca quit," she told Blint.

"Why?"

"She's mad because I got a raise and she didn't."

Driving back to the office, I felt like a white rat in a maze designed by a sadistic scientist. None of the directions I took led to a pellet. Mr. Bell wasn't Miles Leander. Miles Leander didn't want money. I had a blackmail case without a blackmailer. I wonder what Blint's computers would have made of it, or if they would just shut down their circuits in protest.

On Vernor west of Grand, I picked up a Detroit police cruiser in my rearview mirror. I glanced down at the speedometer, but I wasn't violating the limit by much; certainly not enough to attract official attention in a town where they let you drive. The car lagged twenty feet behind me for two blocks. Then it closed the distance and kicked on its flashers.

Thirty

"WHAT'S THE TROUBLE, Officer?"

"Step out of the car, please."

That old cop *please,* lined with steel and backed up by DPD blue filling both side windows and their thumbs on the checked butts of their revolvers.

I stepped out of the car.

"Hands on the roof, please. Lean forward."

I put my hands on the roof. The metal scorched my palms.

"Spread your feet."

I spread my feet, knowing they would be kicked farther apart. Now I couldn't abandon the position without falling.

"I'm carrying a revolver. The permit's in my wallet."

Hands thumped me from armpits to waist and jerked the .38 from its holster. After that there was no more please. My feet were kicked out from under me. I fell forward, splitting my lip against the doorpost. A hand snatched my collar, another hand twisted my right arm back and up, and I was hustled forward and flung across the blistering hood. In another second my wrists were cuffed behind me. Only then did one of the officers yank my wallet from my hip pocket and rummage through the contents until he came to the concealed weapons permit.

"Looks legit."

"Put him in the car."

They were both black, and efficient with the nerveless efficiency of the veteran who knows his job well enough to have lost his passion for it. One of them forced my head down to clear the roof of the cruiser and pivoted me into the back seat while his partner leaned against the door and radioed the precinct house. I sat and sweated and bled onto my shirt and ignored the curious gaping of passing motorists. The unit was new, but the showroom smell had already begun to retreat before the onslaught of tobacco smoke, take-out barbecue sauce, and the bodily effluvients of the chronically busted.

After a long time the pair climbed into the front seat and we began rolling.

"What's the beef?" I asked after a block.

The driver, who was the older and bulkier of the two, with white temples and a thick roll of hard fat at the base of his skull, glanced up at the rearview mirror, then returned his attention to the windshield. He said nothing.

I tried again. "When did the Supreme Court strike down Miranda?"

The younger officer—who wasn't young—rode with his window down and his elbow resting on the sill. "Just kind of shut up, okay?"

I kind of shut up. We were heading down Woodward now at a cop clip, eeling through spaces in the traffic and pinking all the lights. The broad main stem's infinity of rathole bars, overgrown lots, and empty storefronts gaping toothlessly whipped past like a Third World documentary on fast forward. Pedestrians stumped along carrying laundry in duffels and decaying baskets, indistinguishable from the homeless who punched in at twilight. We passed the public library and across from it the Detroit Institute of Arts, where I had watched *Pitfall* and spoken with Gay Catalin, three days and a hundred years ago. A banner stretched across the front advertised the motion picture festival leading up to the premier of Austin Alt's new movie tomorrow night at the Fox.

A voice crackled over the two-way radio, too low for me to make out the words from behind the grid separating the front and back seats. The officer who had spoken to me unhooked the microphone and said something into it. The voice crackled in response. He returned the microphone to the dash and spoke to his partner, who nodded and swung the car into a tight right turn from the inside lane. The car behind us in the right lane stopped with a chirp.

The officer on the passenger's side propped his elbow on the back of the seat and looked back at me. "Your lucky day, perp. No lockup for you just yet. We got a little detour to make first."

"Where to?"

"Detroit General."

"The hospital?"

"If there's another one I sure don't know about it, and I was born on Adelaide right where the Grand Trunk crosses."

"How'd you wind up on that side of the badge?"

"I guess I ain't as lucky as you."

"Cut the gab," his partner told him.

Adelaide took his elbow off the seat and faced front.

We parked outside the emergency room in a slot reserved for ambulances. Adelaide helped me out and took me by the arm. Inside his partner spoke to a black nurse who hadn't seen anything new that day. She said something back and we caught the elevator to the second floor.

The recessed-lit, linoleum-paved hallway was congested outside the door to Intensive Care: uniformed Detroit officers, hospital personnel in white, and Inspector John

Alderdyce, a black hole in an unstructured silk jacket and foulard tie. I felt a tingle.

"Officers Thompson and Olready, Inspector," said the younger half of my escort.

"Which one are you?" Alderdyce asked.

"Thompson."

The inspector barely glanced at me. There was no recognition in the glance. "Did he resist?"

"No, sir. We had a BOL on a blue nineteen-seventy Cutlass with a pick-up on the driver. Headquarters didn't say what about. Precinct policy in a case like that is to go in heavy and save the baby oil for later."

"What precinct?"

"Ninth."

"That's Zabrinski's yard, isn't it?"

"Yes, sir."

"Your skipper's a horse's ass, Thompson. The reprimands in his jacket go all the way back to before they broke up STRESS."

"I wouldn't know about that, sir."

"Take the cuffs off."

"We found this on him, sir." Thompson pulled my revolver from his belt.

Alderdyce took it from him. "Was he carrying paper?"

The officer produced my wallet from his hip pocket. He took that too. "The cuffs."

Olready unlocked the manacles. The blood charged back into my hands, prickling like a fistful of straight pins.

Alderdyce handed me a handkerchief. "Want to file a complaint?"

"It's hot. Everybody's boiling over. Anyway, a complaint's not much good these days without video accompaniment." I daubed at my torn lip. "An apology would be nice."

The inspector looked at the officers.

"Sorry about the hard handling." Thompson wasn't looking at me.

Olready said, "Sorry."

"Now we're friends." Alderdyce gave me the wallet and gun and watched me put them away. I offered back the handkerchief. "Keep it. Care to tell me where you were this morning between midnight and two A.M.?"

On my knees in my living room, looking for a bullet. "I was at home in bed."

"Anybody with you?"

"I got a couple of telephone calls. What's the squeal?"

He took out a spiral pad. "You had contact last night with a party named Leander?"

I felt a tingle that had nothing to do with my hands. "He called me. We spoke. Is this about Leander?"

"His sister, Susan Thibido, told officers you came to her place yesterday looking for her brother. She said you made threats."

"She's mistaken."

"She's inside." He tipped his head toward the door to Intensive Care.

"I said I could keep him out of trouble if he agreed to meet me. It's a stretch to call that a threat."

"It's a bigger stretch to call you a fortune-teller," he said. "But you came close."

"What happened?"

"The sister's phone rang a little after two this morning. She couldn't make out what he was saying, but she knew it was him and he didn't sound good. She'd spoken to him earlier. He was staying at an old girlfriend's apartment on Watson while the girlfriend was out of town. Mrs. Thibido called the police. They found him on the floor of the living room with most of his bones broken and not much of what you would call a pulse."

"How is he?"

"How would you be?"

"He's conscious," I said. "If he weren't you wouldn't have had me brought here for him to identify."

"Will he?"

"Not unless his brains have been shaken loose. We only talked on the telephone."

"About what?"

"The heat and the storms. What else is there to talk about this summer?"

"Try attempted murder. It could still be murder if those machines he's wired into start flashing *tilt.* "

"Let's go in and talk to him before they do."

He put away his pad and squashed the button next to a speaker mounted flush to the wall.

"Yes?" A woman's voice, as flat as the speaker.

"This is Inspector Alderdyce. I need to bring someone in for Leander to see."

There was a short silence. Then the speaker crackled.

"One minute. Just the two of you."

A muted buzzer sounded. He twisted the broom handle on the door and we went in.

We passed a pair of nurses, one female, one male, seated in front of a bank of monitors. On the way down the short quiet corridor we encountered Roy and Susan Thibido. Her red hair was still ratted, but she had put on a clean cotton dress and strap sandals and orange lipstick. Roy wore a green twill worksuit and blew his nose into a blue bandanna handkerchief as he passed us. If he felt his wife's fingers digging into his upper arm when she recognized me, he didn't react.

The room was just big enough to contain the bed, an IV

stand, a cartload of monitoring equipment, and two visitors of moderate proportions, which Alderdyce was not. He left me standing in the doorway while he approached the bed.

Miles Leander looked like a character in a potentially hilarious scene from a slapstick comedy, although nobody was laughing. His head wore a helmet of bandages and he was in a total body cast with all four limbs hoisted upward on pulleys. Various wires and tubes trailed from holes in the plaster. He might have been a balloon drifted away from the Thanksgiving Day parade.

Alderdyce leaned over him and spoke his name gently. One eye opened in a ring of blue-black bruises. The other was swollen shut. It took him a moment to focus on the face inches from his. Again the inspector spoke. There was a pause, then the eye slid toward the doorway where I stood. After a while he grunted and shook his head. The grunt ended in a groan; even that tiny movement was excruciating.

"That narrows it down," said Alderdyce when we were back out in the main corridor. "He won't be able to give us any kind of description until they unwire his jaw."

"It's not the way I work, John."

"People lose their tempers in the heat. You said it yourself." He put a hand on the back of his neck and stretched. "I wouldn't want to take on whoever it was without the whole TMU for backup. Doc says the fractured skull and internal damage would have killed most people. Leander's a big guy, and his sister says he worked as an attendant in a mental institution. It takes muscle to subdue a psycho."

"I know someone who could take him," I said.

Alderdyce gave me a cop look.

I shook my head. "Not evidence. You can't tank anyone for withholding a hunch. If it turns out to be anything more I'll run to you."

"That I'd like to see. I'd pay to see that." He stretched

again. "It's not my squeal anyway. I only took it because I was close by on my way to lunch. If Leander croaks and it's tied to something else he was involved in, it goes to Felony Murder. You can sing your old sad song to Mary Ann Thaler."

"Now I know how a pinball feels," I said.

"I'll have Thompson and Olready take you back to your car."

"I'll call a cab."

Passing a small waiting room down the hall, I spotted Susan Thibido seated in a chair upholstered in tan vinyl. She tensed up when I went in.

"Relax," I said. "Your brother cleared me. Where's Roy?"

"Getting a cup of coffee. They don't know if Miles will ever walk again, if he does survive."

"I'm sorry."

She made a short dry laugh. "Yeah."

"I mean it. When I spoke to you I thought Miles was dirty. Something he said last night started me wondering."

"My brother is an honest man, Mr. Walker. He's impulsive, and that gets him into trouble sometimes, but he'd never do anything he knew was wrong. I may not have been the world's best big sister, but I taught him that much."

"How'd you know where to send the cops?"

"He called me earlier and told me where he was. That's when I gave him your number."

"Who else knew besides his girlfriend?"

"I don't know. He might have told anyone, although he doesn't have many friends. Most people think he's too serious. No fun to be around."

"Did you tell anyone?"

"No. Well, Roy."

I touched my lip, where a scab had begun to form. "Where'd Roy go for coffee?"

Thirty-one

I FOUND Roy Thibido treating his condition in a little ante-room off the hospital cafeteria, pouring the contents of a pint of Southern Comfort into a waxed cup of coffee from the vending machine. He put on his baggy leer when he saw me.

"Found out where they empty the bedpans." He lifted the cup in a toast and drank.

"What did you expect for eighty-five cents?" I asked. "Juan Valdez?"

His face flushed when the liquor hit his stomach. It had been red to begin with. "They sure hung a hurt on Sue's baby brother. I like to of puked when I saw him."

"Maybe it's the brand you drink."

"Huh?"

"Nothing. Your wife thinks I'm the one who hung the hurt on him. Or she did."

"You? Nah." He poured himself another hit.

"Why not? I'm big enough."

"You're a cub scout. I guess I know a pro job when I see it. I was on the line a time or two."

"I thought maybe it was because you saw the guy who did it."

He took a swig and squeezed his eyes shut. "Now how would I do that?"

"I thought maybe you got a good look at him when you told him where he could find Sue's baby brother."

He opened his eyes, swirled the liquid around in the cup, looked down at it; thought better of that and said, "I guess maybe you spend too much time thinking. A thing like that can put all the wrong thoughts in your head."

"I'm pretty sure you saw him. You're too cagey to give away valuable information like that over the telephone. You'd insist on having the cash in hand. How much was it? I don't really have to know. I'm just curious what price a heel like you would put on the life of his own wife's flesh and blood."

He had priorities. He reached up and set the cup and bottle on top of the coffee machine. Then he pivoted on the ball of his left foot, bringing his big knob-knuckled right fist around in a broad arc at the side of my head.

I sidestepped it. Stumbling on, he made a wind like a passing cattle truck, lost his balance, and fell hard, emptying his lungs with a woof. He was drunker than he looked, or maybe he was just clumsy. I reached down and gave him a hand up. When he had his feet under him he tried again, with his left fist this time. I ducked it, caught his wrist, dug my shoulder into his armpit, and boosted him on over. He did a complete flip and piled up against the base of the vending machine. A cup dropped into the slot and filled with gurgling coffee.

"Next time bring the baseball bat, Roy."

Again I bent to help him up, and this time he didn't resist. Just then an intern came along—he wasn't dressed loudly enough for a doctor—and hesitated at the sight of one man supporting the full weight of another with his arm across his back.

"Inner ear," I said.

He nodded, all understanding. "Should I call an orderly?"

I shook my head. "Happens all the time. He's got surgery in an hour. He'll be fine once he's got a scalpel in his hand."

"He's a *surgeon?*"

"Best chest-cutter in Vienna."

When the intern had gone into the cafeteria, adjusting his glasses, I dragged Thibido into a corner next to a potted fern and sat him on the floor with his back against the wall. He was dazed but conscious. The exertion had accelerated the effects of the liquor.

I took the bottle down from the top of the machine, wiped the mouth with the heel of my hand, and helped myself. The bitter-honey taste catapulted me back to college, before I learned to distinguish good booze from bad. I went over to Thibido and bent down and gave him a swig. He sucked on it as if it had a nipple.

I pulled it away. He whimpered and reached for it, but I straightened up out of his range. "I'll get you started, Roy. A real kick-sand-in-your-face type: broad shoulders, bent arms, bad haircut, neck like a leg. Answers to Gordon. Did you go to him or did he come to you?"

"Why should I tell you?" His speech was starting to slur. In another minute he'd be weeping all over himself.

"Nobody has to tell me anything. I'm just a private citizen with a plastic badge. All the metal ones are upstairs. You don't have to tell them anything, either, but then you don't get to go home."

"Shit."

"An overused word today." I wiped off the bottle and drank. "But in your situation it's appropriate."

"Nothing I do don't turn to nothing but shit."

There was one too many double negatives in that for me,

so I let it alone. "Gordon," I prompted. "Who kicked, who received?"

"He must of been watching the place." It was barely audible. He was staring at the floor between his legs with his chin on his chest.

"What place? Your place?"

"He come up on the porch when I went out to get the paper. You say his name's Gordon. He didn't introduce himself. Looked like you said. I'm thinking, shit, this is it. I left my bat inside."

"When?"

"Last night. Sue was upstairs. He said he just wanted to talk to baby brother. Just like you, only he wasn't so shy about saying how much. Thousand bucks, he said. 'How much up front?' I said. 'All of it,' he said. I said, 'What if I give you a bum steer?' 'You won't,' he said. Then he grabbed my wrist—Jesus, he near crushed it—and turned up my hand and counted the bills right into it: fifty, a hundred, two-fifty—like that, right up to a thousand. Only he didn't let it go when he had it all counted out."

"Not until you told him."

The little room got quiet. Fine antiseptic dust settled into the wrinkles in his shirt and pants and the spaces between the linoleum tiles on the floor. The summer grew old and stale.

"Yeah," he said.

I was tired then. I felt myself getting old with the summer. I'd already felt stale. I didn't even feel like kicking Thibido's chin through his scalp. I leaned down and set the bottle on the floor between his legs and walked out of the hospital, where the hot untreated air lay on my back like plagues on Egypt.

The Renaissance Center.

Symbol of Detroit's regeneration from the ashes of rage,

poverty, and the Stanley Cup playoffs. A cluster of glass and copper towers rearing above the brick-slobbering warehouses on the river separating the United States from Canada (and didn't the Canucks thank God every day for that). Dreamed up by Henry Ford II, who when he sobered up was as surprised as anyone to find that the rest of the city had bought into it. Constructed along purely anti-Renaissance lines, with one way in and out (and that on the second floor), it needed only a bar dropped across the entrance and snipers deployed at the windows to withstand a siege from among the workforce that had built it. What it couldn't do was prevent the shops and businesses that paid rent from trickling out when all the customers moved to the suburbs. Pull-down doors in the mall masked exposed wires and unwanted fixtures from the spectral shoppers who haunted the hallways, looking like dead cells in an extinct organism. A Manilow dirge was playing over the loudspeakers when I entered and made my way to the Westin.

I shared the lobby of the 740-foot hotel with the desk clerk and the proprietor of the gift shop, seated in a folding chair smoking a cigarette outside the entrance to his place of business. Neither of them paid me an ounce of attention as I picked up one of the house telephones and asked the operator to connect me to Dr. Naheen's room.

"Yes?"

I heard classical music in the background.

"This is Walker, Doctor. I'm in the lobby. I have some information about Miles Leander."

"Please come up." He told me the room number. "I'm in twenty-three-oh-six."

The elevator took me almost to the roof. I heard violins behind Naheen's door. They stopped when I knocked.

When he opened up I stepped inside and pushed the door

shut behind me. Most of Windsor spread out below the broad window on the opposite side of the room. Gunmetal clouds were rolling in from across the river. The city was lit up in their shadow, as in a kind of false night.

The psychiatrist wore a brown mohair smoking jacket with a pale silk scarf around his throat, tan trousers, and cordovan slippers. He had one of his cigars in one hand and a balloon glass in the other. He looked like a chocolate Easter Bunny pretending to be Noel Coward.

"Where's Gordon?" I asked.

"He has a room down the hall. We're both heterosexual, in case you were wondering."

"I wasn't."

"Can I interest you in some cognac? I'm afraid I haven't a proper glass to spare, but the kind the hotel provides are serviceable." He lifted a squat bottle from a tray on the low chest of drawers.

"It's a little early for me." I pushed open the door to the bathroom and stuck my head in. It was unoccupied. That left under the king-size bed; but Gordon wouldn't fit there.

"We're alone, Mr. Walker. No camera equipment." Naheen chuckled.

I went over and looked down at the river. The water was as black as oil.

"Didn't they have anything closer to the ground? Another couple of feet and you'd need an oxygen tank."

"I like heights. I selected Balfour House because of its position on a hill. I enjoy looking down."

"Kind of like God." I turned around.

He touched his glasses with the hand holding the cigar. "No, Mr. Walker. There's no deity complex here. I'm as entitled as anyone to take innocent pleasure from a view."

"How long have you been taking pleasure from this one?"

"I don't think I understand."

"Have you been in this room ever since you checked in yesterday?"

"I went down to dinner last night, in the hotel dining room. I haven't been out today. I hope I don't offend you when I say I dislike this city. I only come here when I must, and I avoid being on the streets as much as possible. My years on the island have made me acutely sensitive to the honking of automobile horns and the casual profanity of pedestrians."

"I know: Clip-clop, clip-clop."

"The doctor is no less human than those he treats. I am sorry to disillusion you on that point."

"So you hang around here in your underwear and watch the soaps."

"Hardly." He indicated a litter of professional-looking journals on the rumpled bed. "I catch up on my reading and listen to good music. You have an excellent classical station in this area. Would you like to hear?" He stepped toward the cabinet containing the combination TV and radio.

"I'm a Spike Jones fan myself. Did Gordon join you for dinner last night?"

"I gave him the evening off. Is there a reason for all these questions? I understood you came here to give me information." He sat down in a deep chair and adjusted the crease on his trousers.

"I spoke to Leander. He doesn't have your tapes."

"I see. He told you this?"

"He said he sent them to all the people who should have them."

"And who would that be?"

"He told me to work it out for myself. I did."

He tilted his head back and blew a smoke ring at the ceiling. Waiting.

"He sent them to the people who are on them," I said.

"The patients whose psychiatric sessions you videotaped without their permission or knowledge."

"Why would he do that?"

"Because he's no blackmailer. He didn't send you that ransom demand. Someone else did."

"And you believed him?"

"I didn't have to. I went to Spee-D-A and talked to the manager. The man who called himself Mr. Bell, who arranged for the messenger service to accept and hold the package containing the fifty thousand he was demanding for the return of the tapes, wasn't Miles Leander. His description wasn't even close."

"Perhaps he has an accomplice."

"I don't think so."

Naheen held up his cigar and admired it in profile. "Apparently you found Leander convincing. I wonder if he offered you a partnership in his little enterprise."

"Right now he's not in a position to offer anyone anything," I said.

"No?"

"No. Last night the cops scraped him off the floor of his girlfriend's apartment. He's in Intensive Care at Detroit General Hospital."

That bought me nothing satisfactory. His profession had prepared him to intercept disturbing information without cracking his game face. He propped his cigar in the glass ashtray on the lampstand beside the chair and took a sip of cognac. "What is his condition?"

"Critical, serious, take your pick; it's all doctors' jargon. He's not in a condition to communicate."

"That's unfortunate."

"Is it?"

Again he didn't react. "What happened is one more reason to believe he had a partner, and that the two fell out.

Sociopaths are not herd animals. Sooner or later their misanthropy will surface, causing them to turn upon one another. Physical beating is particularly indicative. The *animus,* as Jung termed it—"

"Who said he was beaten?" I asked.

Thirty-two

SOMETHING THIS TIME: the slightest tremor in the dark amber liquid in the bottom of the glass he was holding. The light reflected off his spectacles in flat circles, concealing his eyes. "You," he said. "You said he was beaten."

I shook my head. "I said he was in the hospital. I didn't say what put him there. He could have been shot or stabbed. How did you know he wasn't?"

"It was an obvious assumption, given the psychosis I described." He took a healthy swallow. I thought of Roy Thibido, gulping his cheap sweetened whiskey from a vending machine cup. They were brothers in spite of the difference in vintages. "The conclusion was logical."

"Bad save, Doctor. You need a new line of work. You rattle too easily for this one. You know for a fact Leander was beaten, because your pet ape told you all about it. Gordon found out from Leander's brother-in-law where he was staying and went out there and bounced him around to get him to tell what he did with the videotapes. Maybe he told him and Gordon didn't believe him. Or maybe he did believe him and kept on bouncing anyway. Having gone that far, he had to finish the job so Leander couldn't finger him. It was more than just an assault rap now. It might as well be murder.

"Well, he didn't finish the job," I went on. "When a man's lying in his own blood and excrement it's kind of hard to tell, especially when your own heart's pounding from the exertion and you can't tell if you're getting a pulse."

He managed to drain the glass and set it down without shaking. It took all his training to do it.

I said, "That's too bad for you. If he recovers, he'll talk. Even if he doesn't, the cops will be here soon, because I told Leander's sister I was working for her brother's former employer. I'm only one telephone call ahead of them. That's all they'll need to find out from your people at Balfour House where you're staying. You don't have what it takes to stonewall your way through a professional grilling. I've tripped you up twice, on a pair of tricks so old they ought to be chiseled on stone tablets, and I don't do this every day. The cops do. Say I'm all wet and you tough it out. Gordon won't. Why should he? He'll turn you for the chance to bargain his case down from murder one to assault with intent to cause great bodily harm less than murder. The judge will buy that. Battery's not an exact science, and one more loose cannon rolling around a crowded deck won't change the crime statistics. He'll want the guy who loaded it and pointed it and pulled the string."

As I spoke, I watched him crumble. It was all inside, and if I hadn't seen him trying to battle back from unsure ground before, I might not have detected it. He looked older. The pleasant expression was gone. Clearly it was just something he put on for the occasion, like the elegant jacket, which at the moment made the man in it look that much more pathetic. He was someone to feel sorry for, if you went in for that kind of thing.

"I didn't pull any strings." He was watching the smoke toil upward from the end of his parked cigar. "I didn't want anyone hurt. I certainly didn't want anyone killed. Gordon said he could persuade Leander to give up the tapes. I thought he just meant to intimidate him."

"That's what you wanted to think. You just didn't ask Gordon the questions you didn't want to know the answers to. That strategy's been tested and failed. It brought down a president and an Olympic skater."

"I wanted to protect my patients."

"You wanted to protect your racket. That bus has left the station. The well-heeled patients you've been blackmailing with the information on those tapes have kept silent so far, but once you're busted and the press gets hold of it they'll come streaming out of the woodwork. Thanks to Leander, the tapes are in their possession. They don't have to worry about them leaking out, and the law won't need them for evidence as long as your victims are willing to testify."

"God. Dear God. What do I do?"

"The same thing you should have done when you realized the tapes were missing. Call a lawyer. And stay away from Gordon. You're on different sides now."

He said nothing. He hadn't heard.

The first drops struck the window, noiselessly on the other side of the cushion of air between the double panes. I changed my mind about the cognac and went over and poured some into a hotel glass.

"The question is, who tried to shake you down if it wasn't Leander? Who is Mr. Bell, and how did he lay hands on the videotape he copied and sent you to put teeth in his demands? Where is the tape? Did you bring it with you?"

"Why should I help you?"

"No reason, except you don't have a choice. If you left it up on the island, that's that. Your lawyer might be able to get a court order restraining the cops from raiding your video library on the grounds of patient confidentiality. If they find it here in your possession when they come for you, it's a bird from a different flock. It could air on tonight's Six O'Clock News. One more nail in your coffin."

"It's in my suitcase."

A pebbled brown American Tourister lay in state on the folding stand in the closet with its latches undone. I opened it and rummaged among the odd items of clothing he hadn't unpacked until I felt something solid in one of the side pockets. I took it out. It was an ordinary TDK VHS videotape in the manufacturer's sleeve, without a label or any other kind of identification. The tab had been broken off so it couldn't be taped over by accident.

A VHS videocassette player rested on a shelf below the TV in the cabinet. I switched on the set, turned to Channel 3, and poked the tape into the slot in the player. It began turning immediately.

At first there was a lot of video noise. Then the screen flipped and the interior of another room in another building slid down from the top, blurred, and focused. I recognized the green leather sofa in Ashraf Naheen's consulting room on Mackinac Island. A man was seated on the end of the sofa with his knees together and his hands gripping them. It was plain he was unwilling to stretch himself out across the cushions like a character in a *New Yorker* cartoon. The man was a representative specimen of middle-aging American manhood: sad-eyed, hesitant in the jaw, hairline in retreat. I recognized him instantly, although we had never met. At one time the clothes he wore had been chosen for their style and the statement they made, but today they were just something to place between him and his nakedness. He'd neglected to fasten two buttons on his shirt.

Dr. Naheen's pleasant voice came from offscreen. "At what point did you feel you wanted to get up out of your seat and walk into the light?"

The response was awkward and shambling, a man opening his private trunk in front of a stranger. "I—well, that is, it was never a question of wanting, exactly. I just sort of did. I mean, here I was here, and then there I was there. I don't recall ever having given it anything like what you would call a conscious thought."

I was standing in front of the set, not paying attention to anything but what was taking place onscreen. Naheen didn't stir from the deep chair where he sat slumped in the wreckage of his self-esteem, not looking at anything. He had nothing in common with the confident, controlling voice prompting the man on the tape from just outside camera range.

"I remind you that the conscious and the unconscious are my province. Don't try to analyze yourself, or to say what you think I want to hear based on psychiatric examinations you may have seen dramatized on television. I realize finding words for your feelings is difficult. We have plenty of time."

He must have had a key, and he must have suspected the doctor wasn't alone, because I never heard so much as the scrape of the latch or the doorknob rotating in its socket.

"I'm trying, Doctor," said the man on the tape. "I want to get well."

There was a sudden weight on the carpet behind me, bending the floorboards beneath my feet, and before I could react, a thick bare arm with a spotty tan dropped down across my throat from behind and pressed back against my larynx. I wasn't breathing. I reached up with both hands to pry it loose, but it was like hauling on a tow bar. Then the other arm crossed the back of my neck in a scissors.

"No one is ill here," explained Dr. Naheen pleasantly. "We just need to identify the source of your trouble and remove it."

I wasn't breathing. I knew the hold from my training in

the military police; only then it involved the use of an oak baton. This one didn't need artificial aid. With or without the stick, when applied correctly it was described in the manual as unbreakable.

I had never liked the manual. I brought my knee up almost to my chin and stamped my heel down hard on his instep.

Nothing happened.

I wasn't breathing. My vision checkered as if someone were twisting a steel net taut against my bulging eyeballs. I reached back for my gun and closed my fingers on the handle, but the body that went with the girderlike arms and iron instep was pressed up against it and I couldn't work it loose. I sobbed, but no one heard it. The sound had no place to go and died in my throat. I wasn't breathing.

The TV screen went black, only it wasn't the TV.

My hearing was the last thing to go. The voice of the man on the tape said, "I guess I always just knew I belonged up there."

"In the light."

"In the light. . . ."

Thirty-three

RAIN FLOGGED MY FACE.

Not individual drops, but in great stinging knouts with ice crystals mixed in, like the barbed ends of a cat-o'-nine. It burned my eyes and numbed my skin, saturating my clothes, whose weight tugged me toward earth. The rain was blowing sideways; every fresh surge struck the side of the building with a whump that seemed to rock it. The hailstones were as big as marbles, as big as shooters, bouncing knee-high off horizontal surfaces and falling hard enough to raise welts on naked flesh. They rattled like buckshot. There was a brimstone stench of water striking heated asphalt, and drifting steam. Hell was in office. A broken bolt of lightning shattered the molecules in the air, followed closely by the concussion of the blast. The entire building trembled like the cognac in Dr. Naheen's balloon glass.

I was not connected to the building, but floating above it. In the first confused seconds of consciousness I thought I was back home in bed, dreaming of flight, but the cold water and screaming wind were too real, too frightening for fantasy. I was being carried.

I knew at once by whom. Gordon, Naheen's head orderly, the man who had beaten Miles Leander nearly to death and strangled me senseless in Naheen's hotel room, had me slung over both shoulders in a fireman's carry. He was stronger even than he looked; strong enough to have lugged close to two hundred pounds of dead weight out of the room, down the hall, up the fire stairs, and across the roof of the 740-foot-tall building. I saw the edge coming up, and beyond it, below it, the tops of the cylindrical towers of the shopping and office complex that ringed the hotel. Below them, spreading out from their foundations, lay Detroit and Windsor and the fragile thread of river that kept the world's two largest democratic nations from each other's throat. Through the downpour, scores of lighted windows twinkled like sequins on a blanket. A traffic signal on Jefferson changed from green to yellow to red. In another moment I would be part of the sprawl.

I did the hardest thing I've ever done in my life.

I did nothing.

Played dead while the priceless few moments that remained between me and the abyss melted away in the rain.

Gordon stopped at the base of the low retaining wall. He shifted his burden, spreading his feet and bending his knees as he prepared to pitch me over. He went down and up, down and up again and ducked his head. I felt his muscles bunching beneath me like rocks shifting.

I grabbed a fistful of his face and squeezed.

It caught him unaware. He'd thought I was out or already dead, and it was the surprise as much as the pain that made him stagger backward, almost dropping me. I twisted loose, landing on my feet hard enough to feel the sting to my knees and jarring my fingers loose from his eye sockets.

For a big man he had quicksilver reflexes. He must still have been blinded, but he lashed out in the pain and darkness with an open right hand that caught me on the side of the head with the force of a shovel. A bulb burst in my head.

I went down, half deliberately, and rolled out of his reach. Lightning flashed again. It outlined his bulk against a bleached sky and pinned me to the roof like a bug to a board. He was seeing now. I braced myself, but he didn't charge. Instead, he snaked my way, one foot in front of the other like a tango dancer, half crouched with his arms bent up at the elbows and the edges of his hands foremost. That was just plain unfair; karate was invented to tilt the odds toward the smaller man. Out of instinct I reached back for my gun, even though I knew the holster would be empty. I hated being right.

The rain and my own grogginess threw off my timing. Before I thought he was inside range, he pivoted on the ball of his left foot and kicked me with his right. I backpedaled in time to lessen the impact, but not nearly fast enough to duck the blow. His heel caught me an inch above the solar plexus. My wind went out, I slipped on the wet asphalt and fell and rolled again as he moved in for the kill. He spun in mid-spring, staying with me. He maneuvered like a cheetah.

I gasped for air. I wondered if one of my lungs had collapsed. Blackness filled my head. I shook it out. He kicked again, with his left foot this time, and this time the lightning saved me. The sudden white light blinded him; he missed. His foot whizzed past my right ear and I reached up and caught his ankle in both hands and pushed. He hopped back two yards on one foot, arms windmilling for balance. I charged in, a tenth of a second late. The fingers of a stiffened right hand caught me in the arch of the rib cage. I doubled over, and the callused edge of a hand as hard as a splitting-maul struck the back of my neck, a fraction of an inch from permanent damage. Another bulb burst. I went down on my face.

His next move was as predictable as inflation: a heel would come down on the top of my spinal column, severing it. After my body was flung off the roof, the medical examiner would roll the injury into the general inventory and declare it consistent with a fall from a great height. I wondered if it would be Albert Chung.

Out of the corner of my eye I spotted a grail. It didn't have to be *the* Grail. I was lying next to the narrow outhouse-shaped shelter that had been built over the stairs. After carrying me up the last flight, Gordon had propped open the fire door with an object that had been left there for that purpose. It was a wrecking bar, thirty-two inches of iron gone sandy with rust. I swept out my arm, closed my fingers around the cold rough shaft, and followed through. When the iron struck the knob of bone on the outside of Gordon's knee I felt the shock clear to my shoulder.

Forget the groin. As any cop knows who has carried a baton into a fight, the most vulnerable points on the human body are the joints. The big man took in his breath and crumpled. He was still rocking from side to side on his back, clutching his knee with both hands and groaning, when I got my feet under me and took a swipe at his head with the bar. I was out to kill. There was no stopping him any other way.

His reflexes were still good. Blinded with pain and sick to his stomach, he ducked the blow and scrabbled out of range on his hands and one knee, dragging the injured leg behind him. My own empty swing carried me off balance. I stumbled, and by the time I found my footing, Gordon was upright, the calves of his legs pressed against the retaining wall on the edge of the roof for support.

He closed his stance and waited. His eyes reflected what light there was in a feral glow.

This was where my self-defense plea went south. The enemy was at bay, the stairs and escape were within easy reach. All I had to do was walk away.

I wasn't interested in walking away. In the space of a few

hours I had been handcuffed and badgered and strangled and batted around. A little before that I had been shot at and grilled by the police of two cities. The hero business was getting old. It was my turn to be the villain.

I lunged, aiming the forked end of the bar like a javelin at the thickest part of Gordon's body. I had all my weight behind it, but the big man's hands were faster. He caught it in both fists, stopping my charge as abruptly as a concrete abutment. I nearly gored myself with the blunt end.

He braced himself to wrench the weapon from my grasp, but this one time I anticipated him.

I let go.

The iron bar went flying over the surrounding rooftops, end over end, twirling and flashing like a drum major's baton. He bent backward, arms flailing. I saw the white flags of panic in his eyes.

That wouldn't do. The cops preferred their murder suspects alive and talking. I couldn't be the bad guy after all. I hadn't the wardrobe for the part. I reached out and caught hold of his belt.

The belt broke.

The fire door hadn't locked when it swung shut. I set the button so that it would when I closed it behind me. That was a point in my favor if I went with self-defense. For all I'd known I couldn't have escaped if I'd wanted to. I might care later. I didn't now.

I leaned on the railing going down. My clothes were soaked clean through. The cuffs of my trousers dragged against the stair grids. My coat and shirt weighed sixty pounds. Every muscle in my body was sore. My throat was scratchy from strangling and I had a deep pain in my abdomen from two blows beneath the sternum. My head

throbbed. The scab on my lip had broken and I was bleeding again. I didn't feel like looking in any mirrors.

The door to Ashraf Naheen's room was ajar. He was still
sitting in the chair where I'd seen him last, but now he had
my revolver in his lap. The videotape was still playing on
the TV set. The man on the green sofa was saying something
about staying up past his bedtime to watch the Late Show
after his father had passed out in his easy chair.

"I don't know where my mother was," he said. "She
was out a lot, and then she stopped coming home when I
was thirteen."

Naheen looked up when I came in, but he didn't seem
surprised to see me coming back from the roof alone. He
was beyond such emotions. He looked as bad as I felt. He'd
removed his spectacles, and his eyes had the pinkish swollen
naked look of eyes that are accustomed to wearing glasses.
The cognac smell was strong in the room. The balloon glass
on the lampstand was empty. I was pretty sure it was a new
empty. He'd been getting ready to do something.

Seeing me told him he was ready. The gun lay on the palm
of his hand as if someone had placed it there. I wondered if
it had been Gordon, and what he had expected his employer
to do with it. Suddenly the psychiatrist closed his hand
around the butt and thrust the muzzle into the soft flesh
under his chin. He moved fast; much faster than seemed
possible coming out of a state of near catatonia, and if I
hadn't still been pumping adrenaline he might have caught
me flat-footed. I lunged and batted the gun out of his hand.
It struck the long mirror over the chest of drawers, cracking
a corner, and bounced off onto the carpet.

I went over and scooped it up, but Naheen had spent his
roll. He leaned forward in the chair and planted his elbows
on his knees and put his face in his hands and began blub-
bering into them. He seemed to be saying something, but I

wasn't paying attention. I lifted the receiver off the telephone and pushed the button for Security.

While I was waiting I stopped the tape and started it rewinding. I peeled off my sopping coat, slung it over a floor lamp, and switched on the bulb. In the bathroom I stripped and wrung out my shirt and pants and socks over the sink. I scrubbed my hair with a towel and used my comb. My face didn't look as bad as I'd thought; it probably wouldn't stampede a classroom full of third-graders, although the teacher might faint. A dirty-yellow bruise was blooming in the area of my solar plexus. I got dressed and left the bathroom.

Naheen was standing in front of the chest of drawers, rummaging with both hands in a brown morocco-leather toilet case with his initials on it in gold. I wrestled it away from him, backhanding him across the face when he tried to snatch it back. He fell sprawling to the bed and lay there whimpering.

The case was a cornucopia for suicides: razor, iodine, barber shears, prescription sleeping tablets, plenty of dental floss in case he felt like braiding himself a noose. I zipped it up and tossed it onto the top shelf of the closet out of his reach.

Someone knocked on the door. "Security."

"Just a second." I went over and popped the rewound videotape out of the machine and tucked it under the waistband of my pants in the small of my back. I put on my coat, which was a long way from dry but felt warm from the electric bulb, and left it unbuttoned.

The hotel dick was one of the modern breed, politely impersonal in a tailored maroon blazer and black wool slacks with a stripe up the seam. He had smooth walnut features and short black hair with a spray of gray at the widow's peak. He carried a walkie-talkie and said his name was Brockburton.

"Amos Walker." I shook his hand. "This is Dr. Naheen.

He's registered here. He should be in a hospital. He's had a shock."

Brockburton barely glanced at the man on the bed. "This wouldn't have anything to do with a report we got ten minutes ago about someone falling off the roof."

"It would. The victim's name is Gordon. He's registered too, but I don't know his last name. He worked for Naheen."

"Who do you work for?"

"The same, or I did until a little while ago, when Gordon tried to throw me off the roof. I'm a detective. Private, like you."

"Not like me. I'm employed to discourage the guests from throwing each other off the roof. The language isn't specific, but that's sort of covered in the job description." His eyes took in the room. "You know it's the second time for this building. A woman jumped off it while the place was still under construction."

"I remember reading about it."

"Sure put a damper on the Renaissance. I'm not going to have any trouble with you, am I? It's been a tough day. The lights went out twice during the storm."

I shook my head. "I suppose someone called the police."

He tipped the walkie-talkie toward the window. "Those aren't air raid sirens."

I heard them now, growing louder as they took the turn from Woodward onto Jefferson. "You wouldn't have a cigarette? Mine got wet."

"No-smoking room. Sorry."

That was the end of conversation between us. I offered him the bottle of cognac, but he shook his head. I drained it into the hotel glass I'd used earlier and took a seat by the window to sip and watch the rain letting up. I shifted around to keep the edges of the videocassette from digging into my back.

Thirty-four

BY THE TIME I got away from the cops it was late afternoon. I had barely an hour to go home and get ready to go out. The sun was back, as hot as it had been before the storm broke. Steam rose from the water standing in the gutters. I wondered if I would ever again look at the rain without thinking of the roof of the Westin.

Several traffic signals were out. One that wasn't had been blown down by the wind into the middle of West Grand River. There it stood at a tilt in the pothole it had made when it struck, as tall as most of the cars that maneuvered around it, still going through its cycle of green, yellow, and red. It didn't seem to matter that everyone else had stopped paying attention. I stopped and waited for the green, ignoring the horns bleating behind me. Professional courtesy.

The glass elves hadn't paid the house a visit while I was away. On the other hand, no burglars had, either; the square of plywood was still in place where the window pane had shattered. I had a hard time convincing myself that had happened just last night. The shabby easy chair and the inexpensive rug and the hunting prints on the wall looked like things that had been picked out by someone who wasn't me.

I might have been standing in a stranger's house. A stranger who couldn't afford a decorator.

I went into the bathroom. My clothes were almost dry, but I hadn't seen so many wrinkles since I did bodyguard duty for the Detroit Democratic Irish League. I looked at the videocassette I'd smuggled out of Ashraf Naheen's hotel room. So much dynamite in such an ordinary-looking plastic case. Four people dead and counting. I put it in the hamper under the dirty laundry. I shoved my suit and shirt into a bag for the cleaner's, stood under the shower for fifteen minutes, shaved around the cuts and bruises, checked my watch, and padded back out into the living room in clean shorts and a new shirt to call Vesta and tell her I was running late.

"Are you all right?" she asked. "You sound wiped out."

"Just a long day. The details would just put you to sleep."

"We can postpone."

"No, I need this. I'll be there at seven."

I worked the plunger and dialed my answering service. I hadn't been in the office since Pluto was a pup.

"Just one call, Mr. Walker." I couldn't tell if I'd heard this particular female voice before. Speech impediments, regional accents, and anything else that might smack of dangerous individuality seemed to be against company policy. "Inspector Alderdyce called at eleven-fifteen. No message."

Alderdyce hadn't been among the cops who had come to investigate the swan dive from the top of the hotel. I'd been on my way there when he'd called. I tried his extension and got his voice mail. He sounded even more surly on tape than he did in person. I didn't leave a message either.

I put on a Frank Lloyd Wright tie and the black pinstripe double-breasted I'd bought for security work in Grosse Pointe and deducted from my taxes, shined my black Oxfords, picked up the snap-on holster containing my .38

from the bureau, then put it back. It had been a long time since I'd needed a gun to enter a restaurant.

On Telegraph I pulled the Cutlass into a car wash and ordered the works. During the rinse cycle, the water gushing against the windshield and windows reminded me of the Westin roof. Watching the attendants buffing the hot wax to a glassy finish in the mirrored bay at the end, I started to feel reborn. I overtipped them and joined the thickening home-bound traffic, avoiding puddles as if they contained toxic waste.

She must have been watching at the window when I turned into the little parking area. She emerged from the side door just as I was getting out of the car, wearing the same deep-indigo dress she'd had on when we met, only this time she was walking out of the shadows into the sunlight. Her black hair was swept up and she wore a thin silver band around her throat and matching bobs in her earlobes and no other jewelry. Her face was fresh under the makeup and she was smiling.

The smile faltered when she saw the marks on my face, but she covered up quickly. "You clean up nice," she said, looking me over from head to foot. "Where do you keep the bazooka?"

"Left it in my other suit. You don't look so hideous yourself. Did you cut your hair?"

"I considered it, but at the last minute I lost my nerve. I pinned it up. Do you approve?"

"I hate it. Now I have to go out and rent a Cadillac." I walked around to the passenger's side and opened the door.

We took Telegraph down to the Reuther. When we were entering the expressway she said, "Do you want to tell me what happened, or do I assume you moonlight as a sparring partner for a steam thresher?"

She was looking straight ahead through the windshield. I

didn't speak until a space opened in the rat race and I wedged inside.

"It's not the best start for a relaxing evening out," I said. "Once it begins you have to listen all the way through to the finish, like 'The Star-Spangled Banner.' "

"I'm as patriotic as the next girl."

I told her the whole story, starting with Dr. Naheen's visit to my office, including my conversations with Miles Leander and Mr. Blint at Spee-D-A Couriers, and ending with Naheen's attempts at suicide after Gordon's fall. I left out only the identity of the patient whose session was on the videotape. I was saving that for later. By the time I wound up we had shifted to I-96 West, where the cars began to thin out. The first coppery streak of sunset appeared in the froth of clouds on the horizon. It reminded me of Susan Thibido's hair.

After a short silence Vesta said, "So does this kind of thing happen to you often?"

"I'm pretty sure not. I'd remember if I ever had another fight on top of a skyscraper."

"You know what I mean."

"It's a little easier for a private investigator in this state to get a permit to carry a concealed weapon than it is for an orthodontist."

"But you must like that part of it. Orthodontists charge ten times more for their services."

"It evens out. I don't have to wear a paper coat."

She was looking at me now. "I didn't notice it before. You and Neil are a lot alike. The only difference is you're actually leading the life he can only dream about. You get a buzz out of all this derring-do."

"I don't suppose you've heard from Neil," I said.

"Don't change the subject."

I slid into the outside lane to pass a truck. "I was an M.P.

stateside after my tour in Cambodia. When I was discharged I joined the police department here, but that didn't take. This did."

"So it doesn't scare you."

"Only when I might get killed."

"How often is that?"

"Not as often as in the movies. A little more often than people think who are always saying it's not like the movies. What about acting?"

"Does it scare me? Only when I might forget my lines."

"How often is that?"

She looked out her window. "Now you're making fun of me. Flopping on your face on a soundstage isn't the same as being thrown off a building."

"I didn't say it was. No two jobs have less in common than actor and detective."

We were quiet for a couple of miles. Then she said, "I do, though."

"Do what?"

"Get a buzz out of it. Being afraid I might forget my lines."

I slowed down for a traffic snarl. A state trooper had pulled over a van and the flashers had brought out the innocence in all the other drivers. "We're pretty much screwed up," I said.

"Pretty much."

The ice was broken. We could relax for the rest of the trip.

For a small town, Brighton was lively of a Thursday night. All the spaces were taken along the main drag, so we pulled around behind the restaurant and parked in a municipal lot badly in need of resurfacing. Inside the entrance we found a packed bar area and a grinning blonde hostess in white puff sleeves and a green vest, incipient panic showing in the

whites of her eyes. We followed her between tables filled
with chattering customers to a booth in another room and sat
down. Paintings and photographs of movie stars and un-
knowns, all wearing hats, covered the walls. The music
playing over the speakers was fifties jazz, Bird and Coltrane
and Gillespie and Brubeck.

"I didn't expect it to be this crowded." Vesta had to lean
across the table to avoid shouting.

"Anything that doesn't resemble a roof in a rainstorm is
swell with me."

"Did you notice the hostess? She's that close to a nervous
breakdown."

"You wouldn't be."

"I've been pinched by too many male customers in too
many places to lose it over a little thing like traffic control.
She's probably the owner's daughter."

Our waitress came. Vesta ordered orange roughy. I asked
for the Australian steak and we had drinks while we were
waiting. By the time the food arrived, some of the early
diners had left and the decibel level in the room went
down. The music came through clearly: Art Tatum playing
"Ain't No Use" on the piano, but it was an upbeat rendi-
tion.

"Food service is rotten work," Vesta said between fork-
fuls. "Acting's worse. The rejections are devastating and
you have to work around a lot of pumped-up egos. The producer always seems to have a son-in-law who thinks he's
Brando. It's draining emotionally, but it's also hard physical
labor, as bad as digging a ditch. I lose five pounds in a day's
shooting. The hours are long, but the pay stinks."

"Hardly seems worth the buzz." I washed the steak down
with plenty of water. Apparently they liked it spicy there in
the Outback.

She shrugged. "It has its rewards. I was asked once for my autograph."

"Did you give it?"

"No. The piece of paper came with the key to his hotel room." She put down her fork. The candle on the table heightened the color on her cheekbones and painted shadows in the undercurves. "I'm sorry for that crack I made the other day about you being a blunderer. I guess if you were you wouldn't have lasted this long."

"I blunder my way out of as many tight places as I blunder my way into. Sometimes stupidity is an asset. Outsmarting yourself can get you killed. Look at Phil Musuraca."

"I read about that. Is that what happened?"

"He thought he'd caught the brass ring, but it was attached to the wrong bull's nose. The bull being Orvis Robinette."

"Oh."

"Robinette killed Leo Webb. Fat Phil saw him bail out the window of your apartment house after Robinette and I traded shots. He thought that entitled him to a silent partnership in Robinette's criminal career. He as much as told me so himself, not long before his body turned up beaten to a pulp in the trunk of his own car."

"I wish I could say I feel sorry for him. I'm not that good a Christian."

"I'm not either, but I do. I felt the same way for the scabs who tried to go pro during the baseball strike."

"The police still think Neil killed Leo."

"Impossible."

"Why?" she asked. "I mean, *I* know he didn't do it, because I know Neil, and he'd never hurt anybody, no matter what a psychiatrist might say about delusionary behavior. I'm an actress and I understand consistency of character. But you've never met Neil. What makes you so sure he didn't kill Leo or Brian Elwood, when the police are so sure he did?"

"Because Neil's dead. He's been dead since before I started looking for him, and probably since the day he vanished."

you'd a never can tell. What makes you so sure he didn't kill me first then Flowee... when the police are on their way?"

"Because she's dead. She's been dead since Sunday should love me for that, and probably since the day we met."

REEL FOUR
Smash Cut

Thirty-five

THE WAITRESS CAME OVER to ask if everything was all right. Vesta asked for another drink. I stood pat. The help left. Art Tatum's chord progressions seemed to have taken a sinister turn.

"Neil's dead?"

I said, "It's the only answer that plays. Why would Webb frame him for the Elwood murder if he were alive and in condition to talk when he was arrested? Why would he drive Catalin's car to your place except to make whoever was watching think he was still alive, while giving him a good reason to walk away from his respectable life; one that this particular watcher would buy? And how did he get the car, if Catalin were alive to refuse it to him?"

"But how could Leo know Robinette was watching me? He couldn't have known he existed."

"He didn't. That was a fluke. Phil Musuraca was the one who was supposed to be watching. He was the one who was supposed to testify he saw Catalin's car drive up to your place and someone who might have been Catalin going in the night he disappeared. Webb made sure to wear a floppy hat to make him harder to place in the dark. He expected Musuraca to be there, because he faxed him two words he knew would put him back on your case: VESTA KNOWS.

"He and Neil went back all the way to college," I said. "He'd have heard all about his partner's former peccadillo from the source. Just to be sure that whoever investigated Catalin's disappearance couldn't miss Fat Phil's story, Webb dialed Musuraca's number on the telephone in Catalin's office so it would show up on the redial. All he had to do was hang up when someone answered: The fact that the number was called would be in the electronic memory."

"But Musuraca wasn't there. At least I don't think he was. I didn't notice him following me until the next day."

"That's because he didn't get the fax until the next day. He was away working a divorce case the day it came. But Webb didn't know that. As it happened, things worked out his way, but then he had to kill you to keep you from swearing under oath that it was Webb and not his vanished partner who went to see you. That was already in the plan."

I pushed my plate away. "Webb called Gay Catalin, imitating Neil's voice, and arranged to meet her at the old Michigan Theater Friday night. By now he was looking for Catalin, and he expected me to accompany her and be out of the way while he killed Elwood. I didn't, because I didn't know about the call, but Webb caught another break because I was busy elsewhere. He went to the Michigan just long enough to leave a ticket on Gay's windshield admitting her to the Monday night opening of the film festival at the DIA. Then he left to take care of Elwood on Ferry Park. Monday night the DIA appointment tied both of us up while he went to see you.

"That was where his string of luck ended. You weren't in. Orvis Robinette was."

"Would you folks like dessert?"

Vesta jumped as our waitress set her drink in front of her. She shook her head. I said, "Just the check, please."

"I'm still not understanding why Leo killed Brian," Vesta said when we were alone again. "It was Neil he tried to blackmail."

"It all seemed pretty elaborate just to snuff someone for stealing equipment from Gilda Productions," I said. "I didn't put it all together until I saw who was on the tape that was sent to Dr. Naheen. That was when I put a name to the description Blint gave me at Spee-D-A Couriers. The man who arranged to accept the package containing the fifty thousand was too young to be Miles Leander, the man who removed the tapes from Balfour House. Put dark glasses on Brian, cover his New Wave haircut with a baseball cap, and you get something that sounds a lot like Mr. Bell. B. Elwood. Get it?"

"I'm beginning to," she said. "It was Neil on the videotape, wasn't it? From when he was there last year."

"Leander was telling the truth when he said he sent the tapes to the people who should have them. He meant the patients whose sessions the good doctor had recorded so he could shake them down for what was on them. Most of them kept silent when they received the tapes; if they went to the law they risked exposing their deepest secrets to a legal system with more leaks in it than a wicker bucket. Only one tape got a response. That was the one Leander sent to Neil Catalin.

"Only Catalin didn't get it. Either Leander sent it to him at Gilda and Webb intercepted it, or Elwood did when it came to the house he shared with his sister and brother-in-law. I think Webb saw it first. It didn't contain the kind of dynamite he could use against his partner even if his partner were well enough off to bother blackmailing, but the very fact that the tape existed gave him leverage against Naheen, a member of a respectable profession and owner of his own psychiatric clinic on Mackinac Island, where there is no such thing as a low-rent district.

"Webb needed a go-between to arrange the ransom drop and to pick it up," I went on. "He used Brian, who he knew to be a sleaze and not too bright. He probably didn't even cut him in, just gave him the key to the Southfield studio and told him to help himself to as much equipment as he could fence. Somehow, probably during that last meeting with his partner, Catalin found out what was going on and threatened to blow the whistle. Webb followed him away from the office, killed him, disposed of the corpse, and stashed Catalin's car so he could use it later to make people think he was still alive and involved once again with you. Neil's extramarital affair and the nervous breakdown he suffered afterward were the only glitches in his long record of social respectability; it would make sense that you were somehow connected to his disappearance.

"Maybe Brian suspected his brother-in-law had been murdered. Maybe he was even part of it and decided he was entitled to more than he was getting. Remember, he tried to blackmail you and Neil once. Having already committed his first murder, and penciled in yours to follow, Webb wouldn't waste much sleep wondering what to do about young Elwood. Probably he arranged to pay him off at the house on Ferry Park where Brian was planning to exchange the studio equipment for cash. What better place to kill him and make it look like he fell out with his buyer?

"Only Webb got cute, and instead of leaving it at that he planted Catalin's video rental card at the scene to pin Elwood's murder on his brother-in-law. Those cards are always getting left around; he could have found it in Catalin's desk. With Neil implicated in one homicide, the cops would be more likely to accept him as the killer. Of course Webb would have been sure to get the Spee-D-A claim ticket from Brian so he could pick up the fifty thousand."

The waitress brought the check. I left the amount together with a fifteen-percent tip and we left. It was a warm night. The stars dangled low in a cloudless sky.

"Fifty thousand dollars is a lot of money," Vesta said. "It doesn't seem enough to kill three people for."

"The blackmail scheme just started things moving. There was more involved. I don't have enough bricks yet to build a case, but this has all the earmarks of something that was in motion long before anyone ever heard of Miles Leander. A lot of material things change hands when the senior partner in a going business drops out."

"I just don't see Leo hatching a murder. Embezzlement, yes. That doesn't take as much nerve."

"I suspected him the day I met him. He admitted he liked nice things, and he was a little too eager to explain away Neil's absence as some kind of lark.

"So far his investment was low, with a high yield," I went on. "The stolen equipment would be returned, or if not, the company's theft insurance policy would reimburse him for the full amount. That's why he arranged for Elwood to spirit the stuff away instead of just paying him off. Webb couldn't lose."

"But he did. He lost everything, including his life."

"Only by accident. He didn't know you were working late that night, and he couldn't know Robinette would pick that night to toss your place looking for the ninety-two thousand Ted Silvera stole during the shotgun robberies." I unlocked the door on the passenger's side of the Cutlass and opened it.

She hesitated. Her pupils were huge and glossy in the dim light of the parking lot. "But he did know. Or he should have. I was expecting him that night, but I found out when I got to work that I had to stay for the late shift. I left a message on the answering machine at his house."

"Maybe he didn't get it. If not, it would still be on the machine. The cops would consider it evidence Catalin killed Webb out of jealousy. Or maybe he got it and decided to let himself in and wait for you."

She sat down. "You know what's wrong with your theory? Too many 'maybes' and 'probablys.' It wouldn't hold up in a court of law."

"It doesn't have to. The defendant has already been tried and sentenced and executed. You can't cop a plea with a gun in your face." I shut the door and walked around to the driver's side, feeling my brow furrowing. Something stank, and it wasn't coming from the Dumpster behind the restaurant.

We stopped at a nightspot in Birmingham, an L-shaped place with a converted Wurlitzer standing in for the band that appeared there weekends, had drinks, and used the dance floor. She clung to me firmly, smelling of pale blossoms under a full moon.

"You're a good dancer," she said.

"My boxing coach made us take lessons. I notice you don't trip over your feet."

"My mother mortgaged the house to get me the best voice and ballet teachers she could find. I danced the Dying Swan at a recital while other girls my age were still learning to use the potty."

"Did you manage to work in a childhood?"

"Uh-uh. When you're brought up to think of Let's Pretend as a business, you don't play with dolls and little teacups on your own time. I thought the Kansas parts of *The Wizard of Oz* were romantic."

We drove to her apartment house. With her hand on the

door handle on her side she said, "I'd invite you up for coffee, but I'm out. Can I offer you anything else?"

"Yes."

Up in her living room she dealt us each a glass of Scotch
from a bottle equipped with a pourer. She saw me looking at
the broken windshield hanging over the false fireplace. "My
baloney period. I took out a loan and hired a decorator to impress all the Hollywood producers I was going to bring back
here when they came through town shooting chase scenes.
God, he was a bitch." She drank.

"Did the producers like it?"

"I never met one. Only the second unit ever comes to
Detroit: pimple-faced assistant directors and stuntmen in
trusses. Meanwhile I'm still paying off the loan."

"The producers don't know what they missed."

"How would you know? You've never seen me act."

"I think I have."

She watched me for a moment. Then she set her glass on
the fireplace mantel and moved in close. "Am I acting
now?" She melted into me, closing her eyes.

I kissed her. Her lips were soft and tasted of strawberries
and her teeth were sharp. When we came apart I said, "I
don't think so. But you might be better than I think."

"When will you know?"

"These things take time."

She smiled. We kissed again.

The first time was hot and frenzied, without finesse; we were
both greedy and took more than our share. Her nails were
claws, her body lithe and sinuous, blue-white in the moonlight coming through the bedroom window. The second time
was slower, more controlled. We gave more, made discov-
eries, and commented on them in whispers punctuated with
kisses. Afterward I lay on my back with her head on my

chest, listening to her even breathing and thinking what a difference a wrecking bar made.

Right about then a car turned the corner at the end of the block, slowed to an idle as it passed the building, then accelerated to take the hill, and I stopped thinking. I knew the sound of those twin pipes.

Thirty-six

"AGAIN?" Vesta raised her head from my chest and smiled without opening her eyes. "You *are* a good guy."

"Later. Do you own a gun?"

They were open now. "Why?"

"I'm probably wrong. There have to be a thousand juiced-up wagons in this area that sound just like Robinette's Camaro. Just in case I'm right, tell me where you keep the gun so I can find it without turning on any lights."

"I don't have one. Where's yours?"

"I've got too high an opinion of my animal magnetism to bring one along on a date. What have you got that works like a weapon?"

"A can of Mace. It's in the handbag I carry to work. I'll get it. You'll never find it. That good a detective you're not. No man is." She slid out of bed into a silk robe and opened her closet.

I got dressed and went over to the window, sinking down on one knee to peer around the half-drawn shade. The moon threw a trapezoidal patch of light onto the floor of the bedroom where I'd found Leo Webb's body and spilled shadows of liquid velvet into the parking lot where my Cutlass nestled beside Vesta's little Triumph. Both cars looked black. Nothing was moving there.

"Here it is." She started toward me.

"Stay there."

She stopped while I drew the shade down the rest of the way. When the room was nearly pitch black I stood and went over to her. The can, short and squat like a container of shaving cream, felt cold when I closed my hand around it.

"Make sure you know which way it's pointing before you use it," she said. "This stuff can blind you permanently."

I found the hole with my finger, pointed it at the floor, and tested the sprayer. It worked.

"Stay here and keep an eye on the parking lot," I said. "If you see anything moving, let me know. Leave the lights off."

"Where will you be?"

"Bottom of the stairs."

She put a hand on my chest. "Don't get killed, okay? One more murder and I lose my lease."

I grinned, shook the can, and left her.

There was almost no light at all in the stairwell. I waited on the landing for my eyes to adjust to what there was, then went down, feeling each step with the ball of my right foot before trusting my weight to it. The air was stale and smelled of Victory Cabbage and Meatless Tuesdays and nouvelle cuisine and pensioner cat food, all the cooking fads of seven decades rolled into one depressing meal. Every tweak and groan of a geriatric building settling into the earth sounded as loud as a gunshot. I had spent entirely too much of my life on this staircase thinking of death.

At the bottom I groped for the doorknob, cool to the touch, and determined with the ball of my thumb that it was locked. I unlocked it. Then I locked it again. I didn't want whoever came to the door to suspect that anything waited for him inside but a sleeping building; also I needed some kind of warning. My reflexes weren't what they were twenty years ago in another hemisphere, or for that matter twenty minutes ago in another room. I positioned myself to the left of the door on the opposite side from the knob and wanted a cigarette but didn't light one. More important than not giving myself away with smoke, I needed the heightened nervous system that came with the craving for nicotine. I wondered what the nonsmoking detectives did to sharpen the edge.

I forced my mind blank, which in my case was like clearing space in a dusty storeroom. Mostly I tried not to think that of the three men I knew of who had been with Vesta, two were dead and one was in jail.

"Amos!"

Vesta's whisper from the top of the stairs went up my back like a jet of ice water. I hadn't heard her open the door of her apartment. It took me a minute to convince myself she hadn't been reading my thoughts.

"How many?" I spoke in a murmur. Whispers carry too far.

"Just one. I think he's got a gun. A short rifle or something."

"Get back inside."

This time I heard the door draw shut.

And silence settled inside the little foyer like a fall of fresh snow.

A foot fell outside, or maybe not. I tensed up, then willed my body to relax. The can of Mace felt slippery. I parked it under my left arm, rubbed my palm down and up my thigh, wiped the can on the front of my shirt, and returned it to my right hand. I didn't make any more noise in the still night air than a runaway dump truck.

The doorknob turned, grating ever so slightly in its socket, and stopped.

I took in my breath and held it. Then I changed my mind about the Mace. I transferred the can to my left hand and flexed the fingers of my right.

Something hard struck the door in the area of the knob. The molding around the inside of the frame cracked. A pause, and then the something struck again: the heel of a man's shoe. Wood splintered, the door came free and flew at my face, and I threw up my left forearm to block it. Something long that gleamed in the moonlight spilling in from outside poked through the opening. I grasped it in my right hand and wrenched it toward the floor, at the same time leaning into the door with all my weight. A molecule-shattering roar filled the little space, a gush of blue-and-orange flame destroyed my night vision. The man on the other side of the door had reflexes as quick as mine and shoved back. I took a step backward to avoid the collision, but kept my grip on the fat barrel of the shotgun and pulled, jerking him across the threshold and off his feet. He cursed and tried to catch himself, but I pivoted on the ball of my right foot and thrust the Mace into his face and sprayed. He made a gaspy whimper and let go of the shotgun to claw at his face with both hands.

Now I had the weapon. I dropped the can, took the shotgun in both hands, and rammed the stock into the side of his head. He made another little noise and fell at my feet.

Silence again, although my ears were still ringing from the blast.

I stooped, felt for his collar, and dragged him the rest of the way inside. I pushed the door shut and propped his feet against it, which seemed appropriate since he'd used one of them to kick apart the latch. I groped for the switch on the wall of the stairwell, but before I found it the foyer flooded with light. Vesta stood on the landing with her hand on the upstairs switch. A number of other tenants huddled behind her in robes and pajamas, awakened by the racket.

The shotgun was a twelve-gauge Winchester pump, less than twenty-eight inches long. The wood was still white where the stock had been sawed down to the pistol grip and fresh steel shavings clung to the end of the barrel.

"Is it Robinette?" Vesta asked.

I grasped the back of his head by the hair and lifted it to expose his face. It was a pale face, too pale by a race to belong to Orvis Robinette. I didn't know him from the Four Freshmen, but I made a pretty good guess based on his preference in weapons.

Vesta confirmed it. "It's Ted," she said. "My ex-husband, Ted Silvera. I didn't know he was out."

The Shotgun Bandit was wearing a tan jacket that was at least a size too large for him. It might have been the one he had worn on his way to Jackson; prison food is a good diet to lose weight on. In the time it took me to lower his head to the floor I had a plan. I was taller by a couple of inches, and his hair was a shade lighter than mine, but it was nighttime and if I moved fast enough I might survive the plan.

I laid the shotgun on the stairs. Silvera groaned and stirred, but the stinging in his eyes would keep him busy long after he regained all his senses. I wrestled the jacket off his shoulders and down his arms and put it on. It was almost a perfect fit, just a little short in the sleeves. I found the can of Mace against a baseboard and summoned Vesta down from the landing. When she was a couple of steps from the bottom I handed her the can.

"He shouldn't give you any trouble," I said. "This stuff is designed to stop a tiger in mid-pounce. But if he does, give him another dose."

"What are you going to do?"

"Play Trojan Horse." I picked up the shotgun and racked a fresh shell into the chamber.

I kicked Silvera's feet out of the way and let myself out the door. On the concrete step I turned up the collar of the jacket, then started toward the street at a brisk trot. There was a bare chance the pair had arranged to meet on the other side of the block, in which case I was out of luck; but I doubted it. If everything went according to plan, Silvera would need the shortest, fastest route of escape, and that would be right out front.

He must have circled the block and parked at the base of the hill, where he could see the driveway to the apartment house. As soon as I got to the end, carrying the shotgun with my shoulders hunched and my chin tucked inside the collar of the tan jacket, the Camaro's motor sprang to life with a rippling growl and the green car rolled into the pool of light shed by the streetlamp near where I stood in the shadows.

I leaped forward, pulled open the door on the passenger's side, slid in, and thrust the muzzle of the shotgun under the chin of the man at the wheel.

"Hands on the dash," I told Robinette, reaching out with my free hand to turn off the ignition. "Let's talk."

Thirty-seven

"THROUGHOUT OUR HISTORY, the only authentic American art has emerged in times of repression," the bald man was saying. "We've been conditioned to regard the sixties as a period of freedom from pernicious Puritanism, and what came of it? Designer jeans. Warhol's immortal soup can. Sam the Sham and the Pharaohs. Ryan O'Neal. *Ryan O'Neal,*" he repeated, to a chorus of mock-horrified snickers. "Conversely, that very Puritanism we've been conditioned to despise gave us Hawthorne, Melville, Thoreau, Emerson, Poe, and Dickinson. When Hitler came to power in Germany, the great *Mitteleuropean* directors—Lang, Preminger, the Siodmaks, and my beloved Billy Wilder—fled to Hollywood, where they brought their expressionist techniques to bear in complying with Hays Office restrictions. Couldn't show graphic violence onscreen? Say it with shadows. Couldn't film biographies of actual criminals? Use allegory. No sex? Steam up the innuendo. Remember, it was the survivors of Vichy France who spotted these strains when Europe was inundated with *verboten* American movies after Liberation and codified them under the heading film noir. We had to be told by a people who had experienced the worst kind of repression that we'd invented something special."

"But isn't that just the male view?" asked one of the bald man's listeners, a thin woman in a man's tuxedo with her hair mowed to within a quarter-inch of her scalp. "All the women in those films were objectified and exploited. How can we justify that as art?"

Austin Alt measured her out a benign smile. He was a tall, pudgy sixtyish with a milk-chocolate California tan in aviator-style bifocals with gray-tinted lenses. His white fringe of hair waved back into an elaborate ducktail over his starched formal collar. He emptied his champagne glass and handed it to someone. "I never engage in gender politics. However. In nineteen forty-four, Lauren Bacall curled up on Humphrey Bogart's lap in *To Have and Have Not,* stroked his cheek, slapped it, told him he needed a shave, and walked out of his room. Compare that single image against the number of times you've seen Kim Basinger raped and beaten and explain to me how far we've come from the objectification and exploitation of the forties."

The woman silenced for the time being, I drifted away from the edge of the large group that had gathered around the director and wandered through the grand lobby of the Fox Theater, sipping flat champagne and sunning myself in the light reflecting off the carved Chinese lions, golden grapes, plaster eagles, jeweled monkeys, fluted sconces, and brass-buttoned ushers that populated the restored building. The organ, a three-manual Moller, was merely a backup for the lordly four-manual Wurlitzer in the auditorium; faux pipes of molded plaster above the inlaid double doors leading into the theater proper represented the genuine articles, two stories high and built into the structure out of hollow pine without knots, because the bass chords were powerful enough to punch them out.

The Fox was more than a motion-picture palace. Along with the newly refurbished State Theater in the next block of

Woodward, it symbolized Detroit's latest attempt to drag it-self out of the ashes, one fueled by big money belonging to the city's new rich. The hookers displaying their legware along the main thoroughfare and the dealers in their big hats seated in Lincolns parked at the curb were already having a tough time making themselves seen against the flashing lights on the towering marquees and had started the slow migration uptown. Where they stopped, if they stopped, de-pended on how long the new reform administration man-aged to remain relatively honest. The wheel had made this same turn before.

There were at least a hundred people in the lobby, decked out in black tuxes and gold and red and blue and white sequined gowns with the occasional red ribbon to commemorate the plague currently in fashion; but it would take three times that number to make that echoing grotto seem crowded. They formed clusters under the cherubs and Greek masks, shifting position only to admit new ar-rivals and to select canapes and drinks from trays carried by the catering staff, got up in Highlander costumes com-plete with kilts in honor of Alt's new film, a historical set in Scotland. I recognized the deputy mayor, the police chief, several city council members and their spouses, a couple of Pistons in Forty Extra Longs and size fifteen patent leathers, and a local news anchor, three sheets to the wind with a two hundred-dollar call girl on his arm. The conversations were conducted in rapid, high-pitched voices that died short of the great vaulted ceiling, which seemed appropriate.

I spotted Asa Portman, waist-deep in conversation with a Ford Foundation matron in diamonds and chins, and drifted that way. The University of Michigan professor of psychol-ogy and I were the only males present not in evening dress; I had on my black double-breasted with a fresh shirt and tie and he wore gray tweed and a bow tie on a plaid shirt. He'd trimmed his beard for the occasion and done something to keep his unruly hair in check. When he saw me he excused himself and came over to shake my hand.

"Have you met the Great Man?" he asked.

"Not quite. I didn't want to interrupt his lecture."

"Art and repression, right? He's been giving it for years. All his interviews sound the same. Are you planning on watching the show?"

"I haven't thought about it."

"The reaction from the sneak previews isn't encouraging. Malcolm the Third couldn't ditch his Dodge City twang and I understand there's a honey of a jet trail in the sky over the Battle for Northumbria."

I sipped from my glass, watching the Detroit Symphony conductor describing the size of his baton for a model from the auto show. "Did you get it?"

"They were backed up at the film lab. I bribed a technician to move it up on the list. You owe me twenty dollars."

"When?" I got out my wallet and handed him a bill.

"He said seven. It's almost that now. I left a student behind with instructions to bring it here as soon as it's ready. I gave him your description. He'll come to the street door."

"He'd better not get caught in traffic. I've only got the auditorium from ten to eleven."

"I hope you thought this out," he said. "I had to call in every marker I've got in the Detroit area film community to set this up. I'm counting on your having something interesting to say when you come to address my class."

"After tonight I should. Thanks, Professor."

"Portman will do. I'm not a castaway on Gilligan's Island."

He left to join the group gathered around Austin Alt and I went off in search of a telephone. I waited for a Hollywood type with long hair and ruffles on his shirtfront to finish blowing long-distance kisses to his Yorkie, then dropped a coin and punched out a number I knew by heart.

"Hello?"

"This is Walker. We need to talk."

"I can't imagine what about, but go ahead."

"Not over the telephone. I need to meet with you. Tonight."

"Can't it wait till tomorrow? I'm planning to turn in early."

"This won't keep. I know what happened to Catalin. I've got a witness."

Silence crackled. A platinum-haired aircraft tower in a black velvet dress whom I recognized as a hostess of one of the local TV talk shows clattered up, stopped when she saw me on the line, glanced down at a thin gold watch strapped to the underside of her wrist, and sighed.

The voice came back on the other end. "Can you come here? I really am too tired to go out."

"I believe you. You've been busy. Come to the Fox Theater at ten. There's security at the door but it's been greased. Just tell them you're here to see me."

I worked the lifter and offered the receiver to the lady in black, cradling it formally across the crook of my arm. She snatched it out of my hand, nearly strangling me with the cord, and shoved me aside with a padded shoulder.

The conditioned air in the lobby had gone stale. I stepped outside to breathe some fresh smoke. There was still plenty of light, and would be until past ten o'clock, most of Michigan being on the extreme western edge of the Eastern time zone. It looked as if the storm front had broken at last. The sky was a painful shade of blue and the meteorologists couldn't find a cloud between here and Toronto. No more blackouts.

I was still standing there twenty minutes later when a gray Ford Bronco rolled up to the curb and the driver leaned over and cranked down the window on the passenger's side. In the right circumstances the vehicle could have been mistaken for Brian Elwood's Black Jeep Cherokee; for a fleeting moment I thought I was having a flashback to the sodden evening in front of my house where this whole thing had started. But the head was too bushy for Elwood, the body that went with it too chunky in a University of Michigan Wolverines T-shirt.

"Are you Mr. Walker?"

I nodded. "Got something for me?"

He scooped something off the passenger's seat and held it out. I took it. It was a flat metal can about eighteen inches in diameter, the kind reels of film come in. I tipped him ten dollars. He grinned his thanks and drove away.

Before I went back in I glanced toward the green Camaro parked in the loading zone across Woodward Avenue. It had been there all the time, but I had avoided looking in that direction. Now I made eye contact with the man sitting behind the wheel, whose expression didn't change. I nodded then and took the film inside.

Thirty-eight

THERE IS ABOUT the Fox auditorium a heart-sickening enormity, dwarfing its best features and reducing the lone visitor to the status of a beetle plodding across a golden bowl. The trumpeting elephant's head mounted above the proscenium measures twenty feet from eartip to flaring eartip, but in the cavernous proportions of the room it looks as if a man of ordinary size could span it with arms outstretched. The electrified stained-glass globe hanging from the Arab tent of the ceiling, fashioned after a Fabergé egg, appears no larger than a beachball, yet my entire living room could fit inside it, with space for a big-screen TV as well. It weighs two tons. The false arched balcony-boxes that march around the room's upper level might have sheltered the fierce-looking oversize saints of a medieval cathedral, and a gathering of one thousand people in the orchestra and balcony would leave four fifths of the seats empty.

It is a palace in every sense of that overused term, conceived and constructed on the massive, impossibly opulent scale accessible only to mad Russian monarchs and the demented monopolists who flourished during Hollywood's Golden Age. William Fox was noted for his refusal to wear a watch under any circumstances and for keeping the blinds drawn over his office windows day and night to make time stand still. It didn't work; the stock market crashed anyway and his creditors hounded him out of the industry before he had a chance to collect a nickel from his showpiece theaters in Detroit, Brooklyn, St. Louis, Atlanta, and San Francisco. He'd missed his best opportunity for greatness by two hundred years and a continent. Catherine the Great would have applauded his lunatic vision and offered him a place in her harem.

Onstage, the movie screen hides behind curtains bearing a screen-printed Japanese landscape, with swags of wine-colored drapery above and enough space between the painted acacias and the footlights to park a symphony orchestra—a frequent event whenever the Stokowski of the season comes through town. From my vantage point, I could see the cleaning crew bagging up litter from the aisles and between the rows of seats; the Alt premiere had finished ten minutes ago. I'd caught the tail end of the historical epic, standing just far enough back to avoid getting any blood spattered on my tie. My ears were still throbbing from the French horns and bagpipes. Movie sound has come a long way since Jolson, but I doubted it could demolish even a small city.

In a little while the last of the cleaning crew left, carrying his broom and long-handled dustpan. Someone switched off the overhead lights. Only the sapphire bulbs glimmering in the sconces on the walls remained to define the room's boundaries. The hum of voices coming from the direction of the grand lobby subsided to a buzz, then broke off into tinkling notes, like a faucet dripping itself dry. Silence fell with the sudden reverberating boom of a great door slamming. The ghost of Valentino walked once again.

I fought the urge to fidget. The huge room was acoustically perfect, designed years before the advent of electronic amplification by an architect who understood the configuration of the human ear as well as any audiologist; the smallest clearing of a throat could be heard two hundred feet away.

I waited years.

I waited as much as ten minutes.

At the end of that time, one of the inlaid double doors at the end of the center aisle tipped open and a lone figure stepped in from the lobby. A few yards in, the newcomer stopped, waiting for a pair of wary eyes to accustom themselves to the dimness of the room.

"Hello?"

The greeting sounded as close as if it were spoken into my ear.

A light slammed on in the projection booth above the balcony. A white beam shot through the darkness and exploded onstage.

Instinctively the new arrival turned to look up at the booth. But human nature is as strong as it is predictable. The head came back down and swiveled around to stare at the screen.

And the screen was visible now, white as righteous wrath and spreading like daylight as the printed curtains glided noiselessly apart.

White, that is, except for the figure standing at the bottom wearing a black double-breasted suit, with his hands in his pockets.

"Mr. Walker?"

But Mr. Walker said nothing. Numerals and letters appeared behind him, unsteady, three frames to the shot and then whiskaway for the next, the smallest five times the size of the man standing in front of them:

10
NINE
8
7

SIX
5
4
3
2

And then white no more, but black and white, a man's handsome troubled middle-aging face filling the screen, big as a barn door. Dick Powell, alone in the half-light of his suburban living room, waiting for the jealous boyfriend of his former mistress to break in; waiting for him with his old service automatic in hand while his wife and young son lie asleep upstairs, oblivious to the drama about to take place one floor below.

The last reel of *Pitfall.*

Two things were different from the last time I'd watched the feature. Then there had been tense background music, composed to work the audience up to an emotional high pitch just before the suddenness, the awful unredemption of the shot. This version, however, was silent; the soundtrack was missing. The other difference, obvious in the tight shot of Powell's face, was the blemish on the point of his chin. It might have been a fly, attracted by the bright silvery light to the surface of the screen. Instead it was a man, disappointingly life-size, and now nothing more than an annoying irregular surface for the projected image to wrap itself around like wallpaper on top of an overlooked nail. Just a man. Not Humphrey Bogart, eighteen feet high and thirty-six feet wide. Not John Garfield or Robert Mitchum or Richard Widmark or even Elisha Cook, Jr. The guy who had to find his keys when the lights came up and go home.

"I've already seen this picture," Gay Catalin said. "Is this what you dragged me down here for?"

She looked as she had the night I first laid eyes on her in

the house she'd shared with her husband in West Bloomfield: trim, blonde, beginning to show her age, but all the more attractive for refusing to fight it through heroic measures. Tonight, however, she had abandoned her customary yellow for a simple knee-length dress of deep purple that appeared black in the light reflecting from the screen, with shoes and a purse to match.

"It seemed appropriate. It's where I came in."

"You said you know what happened to Neil. I didn't know you were still looking for him. Isn't it enough that the police are looking? I've lost him whether he stays missing or he turns up to stand trial for murder."

"Catalin didn't murder anyone. He couldn't."

"That's what I said, but the police didn't believe me. What makes you think they'll believe you?"

"When his body turns up they won't have any choice. Especially when the coroner tells them he's been dead since before your brother was killed."

She remained unmoving. "Neil's dead?"

"He died the day he walked out on a meeting with Leo Webb at Gilda Productions. We'll never know the reason he walked out, since Webb was the only other person present and what he said before he was killed can't be relied on, because he was an accomplice after the fact. My guess is Webb told him that Webb and you and your brother were trying to blackmail Dr. Ashraf Naheen."

She flinched. Onscreen, Dick Powell had just shot the intruder, and she may have been startled by the muzzle flash. "Can you turn that off? I'm having a hard time understanding what it is you're trying to say."

"You're not that easily distracted," I said. "You certainly weren't the day a disgruntled former employee of Naheen's sent a videotape of one of Neil's psychiatric sessions to your home. I thought at first it was delivered to Gilda, where

Webb intercepted it, watched it, realized what it meant, and sent a copy to Naheen anonymously, indicating that he had others and that he'd go public with them if the good doctor didn't pony up fifty thousand dollars. He was greedy, but he wasn't that devious. Only someone who had watched almost as many complex crime films as Catalin had could come up with a plan like that."

"Those plots aren't plausible. Nothing ever works out like that in real life."

"You should know. You must have had some inkling of it when Catalin came home and confronted you with what Webb had let slip during their meeting. That was when you killed him."

"I explained why I terminated your services. If you're trying to torment me—"

"My guess is you used Neil's own gun, the nine-millimeter Smith and Wesson he registered and that the cops didn't find when they searched your house. The same one Leo Webb used to kill Brian. Or was that you?"

She shook her head slowly. "I didn't kill my husband. I certainly wouldn't kill my brother. My own brother. I raised him myself."

"You did a rotten job. He was a sneak and a would-be blackmailer. Maybe his attempt to shake Neil down when he was running around with Vesta is what gave you the idea to put the bee on Naheen. Anyway, I don't suppose Brian gave you any argument when you and Webb chose him to set up the ransom drop at Spee-D-A Couriers. The pay was okay: twenty thousand bucks' worth of electronic equipment, just asking for anyone who had a key to carry it out the back door of the Gilda studio. That's where Webb came in. He had a key."

The light quality changed onscreen. Jane Wyatt, playing Dick Powell's wife, had come downstairs and switched on a lamp. She was listening to her husband telling her to call the police; that he'd just killed someone. Mouthing it silently, because there was still no soundtrack.

I said, "Did Baby Brother change his mind about his end? Did he refuse to give up the Spee-D-A claim ticket unless you promised him a fatter slice, or did you just suspect he'd get a bright idea and fly with the cash as soon as he had his mitts on it? Doesn't matter. The point is you couldn't afford him, because sooner or later he was bound to screw up with the law and sell out both of you for a reduced plea. A thing like that plays hell with family. I still like you for that sloppy shoot-up on Ferry Park, a real duffer's job; but Leo was even less of a hand at killing than you. You gave up your amateur status the day you snuffed Neil.

"You trumped up a telephone call from Catalin offering to meet you at the old Michigan Theater to give you an alibi for Brian. Then you set me up with a ticket to the first night of the DIA film festival to keep me busy while Leo took care of Vesta. He was already in deep as an unsuspecting accomplice to Neil's murder. Faking a tryst between Neil and Vesta using Neil's car to explain his disappearance was minor. After that he was committed too far to balk at killing Brian and then doing Vesta to keep her from swearing under oath that it was Webb who came calling the night Catalin vanished. You probably made it clear to him he'd share the fall for the first murder. No one saw Neil come home that day, and Webb left the office shortly after his partner stalked out, plainly upset about something."

I stopped talking. There was an emergency exit on either side of the stage, marked with a neon sign. One of the arched doors was ajar.

"It's a theory," Gay Catalin said. "But that's all it is. As far as the police are concerned, Neil killed Leo at the Mannering slut's apartment to eliminate the competition."

"Old news. Orvis Robinette shot Leo with the gun Leo planned to use on Vesta. He had the bad luck to interrupt Robinette while he was tearing the place apart looking for the ninety-two grand he and Ted Silvera, Vesta's ex-husband, stole from several video stores downriver. They fought, of course. Robinette won; also of course."

"More theory."

"Would you like her to say something else?" I asked.

"No, I heard enough."

The new voice drew Gay's attention away from the stage for the first time, to the emergency exit. The door opened the rest of the way and Robinette came in. His big right hand was wrapped around the butt of an automatic pistol.

Thirty-nine

THE BIG ROOM was as silent as only a room can be where the slightest sound is as loud as an explosion. The bandit's great height and bright orange hair looked right at home in the dimensions and glitter of the aging movie house. The pistol was pointed at Gay Catalin.

"I heard enough," he said again. "That's the voice from the phone."

"Who are you?" There was a thin edge of hysteria behind the question. She knew the answer.

"You've spoken," I said, "although not in person. Robinette came back to see Vesta last night. He brought his old partner with him. Silvera got out of Jackson yesterday, four years early for behaving himself. When Robinette told him his ex turned in the money he went to prison for—turned it in on my advice—he got upset and decided to take us both out. He bought a shotgun, violating his parole, and cut it down just like the one he used in the robberies, but he was out of practice. He's in jail in Iroquois Heights.

"The cops don't know about Robinette just yet. I told them Silvera's ride took off when things didn't go as planned. I let him go when he agreed to come here tonight and identify you."

"I've never had any contact with this man in my life."

"Sure you did," Robinette said. "You and me contacted Monday night. You called me at my dump and told me the money was in a locker at the YMCA and the key was hid at Vesta's."

She was looking at me. "How would I know where to call him? I didn't even know he existed."

I said, "You knew. He was following you around because he saw your husband's car parked at Vesta's. You got the license number off his Camaro, as I did, and ran it through channels. You recognized the name, because you saw the tape of Neil's session with Naheen. He mentioned the whole affair with Vesta, including her ex-husband's crimes and the man he committed them with. Getting a telephone number is easy once you have the name.

"That was smart, but it was also a mistake. You tipped Robinette anonymously about the money and then you sent Webb to Vesta's place the same night. You knew I was beginning to suspect Webb. When I told you he'd ducked me at his office that day you knew he'd crack under questioning. Chances are you already suspected that and planned to set him up from the start. You knew he was no match for someone like Robinette, with or without a gun. So the only other person who could finger you for Catalin dropped out of the picture, and because he was shot with the same gun that killed Brian Elwood, the cops pinned it on Catalin. Smart. It was so neat it deserved a gold star. Mistake.

"Because it was too neat. Things never tie up that sweet except in the movies Neil loved. What was Webb doing at Vesta's place when she was working late? How did Robinette happen to pick that night to ransack the place? Robinette answered the second question last night when I braced him with his partner's shotgun. As for the first, Vesta told me she left a message on Webb's answering machine telling him she'd be hung up at the restaurant. How is it you got that message and Webb didn't?"

"Talk, lady!" Robinette gave the automatic a twitch. He'd been eager for this meeting ever since he learned he'd been set up as thoroughly as Leo Webb, and by the same person. "If your mouth ain't big enough for the words to get out I can always make another hole."

She was as cool as the sapphire lights. "Clearly, this is duress. I was at Leo's house that day, talking him out of a bad case of nerves. The phone rang while he was in the bathroom splashing water on his face. I let the machine get it. Afterwards I erased the tape. Of course I'm making all this up at gunpoint."

"There was more than fifty grand involved," I said. "Gilda Productions is incorporated for tax purposes, and corporation documents are public record. Webb and Catalin were each insured for half a million dollars, the amount to go to the surviving partner in the event of death or inability to fulfill one's obligations to the firm. That covers being wanted by the law, so you and Webb stood to split a chunk. Then when Webb got killed without leaving a legal heir, the whole amount went to you as Catalin's next of kin. He must have really got your goat that time he strayed."

"You don't know what it was like. How could you? You're as bad as he was. Look at what you chose to get my attention." She tilted her head toward the screen, where Dick Powell was walking the midnight streets, working up the courage to turn himself in to the police. The same shadows and light that were playing over his face slid a cargo net over hers.

I said nothing.

"I've been a widow for years, eating alone and watching television or reading a book, evening after evening, while he lived in the basement with those morbid films. Even when he wasn't watching them he was talking about them: mise-en-scéne, bitch goddess, automobile as weapon, telephone as instrument of intimidation; nattering away his life on trivia while the business he built to support us rotted from neglect. I invested my inheritance in Gilda to keep it from defaulting. I pawned my grandmother's engagement ring. And all the time I was making these sacrifices, all those evenings I thought Neil was working late at the office to attract new customers, he was cheating on me with an actress. An *actress*. It was as if all the clichés and contrivances he put up with in his old movies had taken over his life.

"That's when I got the idea. He was already half crazy on the subject. What was to stop him from going the rest of the way?"

Neither Robinette nor I moved. The last reel was playing itself out, and nobody was paying any attention to what was happening on the screen.

"Neil thought it was his decision to check himself into Balfour House," she said, "but I'm the one who brought it up when I read an article about it in a Sunday magazine. He was just stressed out enough over what was happening downtown to give it serious consideration. Believe me, there are a thousand little things one spouse can do at home to make the other spouse decide to slip away to a picturesque island for a long rest cure. I was laying the groundwork for an incompetency hearing and a conservatorship, but just taking away his business and his bank account wasn't enough. I stewed over it for a year and a half after he got back. Then that videotape came in the mail. I watched it—on Neil's personal altar, the big screen in the basement—and I saw the whole plan, just as clearly as if it were playing out in front of me instead of Neil's mewlings about his grotesque childhood."

"That's cold." Robinette was grinning broadly; one pro appreciating the performance of a peer. "You are one cold bitch. Run."

She blinked at him. "What?"

"I said run. I was going to dice you right where you stand. Slavery's done ended, or didn't you get the memo? We don't gots to sit still for getting used by no rich white women, not no more. But I like the way you think, so I'm giving you a one–two–three lead. If you can get through that door behind you before I finish counting, I won't shoot you in the back."

She looked at me. "Is he serious?"

I said, "That's not the plan, Orvis."

"You the man with the plan. I'm the man with the gun. Go, lady. One!"

"Drop it!" I shouted.

Robinette turned and shot me.

At the same instant, Lizabeth Scott shot Raymond Burr onscreen. The muzzle flashes were simultaneous. Burr fell. I didn't. A round hole opened in the middle of my double-breasted jacket, through which light showed. My hands stayed in my pockets and my lips continued moving, even though nothing was coming out: mouthing the Preamble to the Constitution over and over, a dozen miles away in a studio in Southfield that had been closed for five hours.

Gay Catalin turned and ran.

Robinette forgot about counting to three and fired. But he was rattled by what had happened and the bullet went high, nicking the railing of the balcony six feet above her head. She hit the door running and pushed on through to the lobby.

I stepped out of the shadows inside the emergency exit opposite the one Robinette had entered by and shot him in the side. He staggered and turned to shoot back, but he was still confused. The barrel of his automatic wavered between the image on the screen and the exit. I fired again. He doubled over and sank to the floor.

The echoes of the reports racketed around the auditorium for a long time. For all I know they're still going. I looked up at the projection booth. "All right, Professor?"

A hatch opened next to the beam from the projector and Asa Portman leaned out. "Ready when you are, C.B. And don't call me Professor."

I crossed to the other exit with my gun out and looked down at Orvis Robinette. He was lying on his side with his knees drawn into his chest, clutching his abdomen with both hands. He squinted up at me, outlined against the flickering screen. For a moment he wasn't sure which image of me to focus on. "How?" It came out in a gasp.

"Judy Yin. Leo Webb's secretary at Gilda Productions. She liked him. When I told her my plan to snare the man who killed her boss, she offered me full use of the studio facilities. A fellow named Portman got me a print of *Pitfall*. You wouldn't know him; he never did time. I spent all afternoon talking in front of a camera with the last reel of the film playing behind me. No microphone, just my mouth moving so you and Gay Catalin would think my voice was coming from the stage. That's one of the miracles of the Fox, the way sound carries. From a little distance you couldn't tell that I wasn't just standing in front of the screen." I shrugged. "It bought me two seconds."

His eyes closed. I didn't know if he'd heard anything I'd said. He was going into deep shock.

All the doors at the back of the auditorium opened simultaneously and twenty uniformed Detroit police officers streamed up the aisles, some of them carrying riot guns. I laid my revolver on a theater seat and clasped my hands on top of my head.

John Alderdyce strolled in while I was being frisked. He

said I was okay and the officer let me push myself away from the wall. The officer bending over Robinette straightened.

"This one's pretty bad, Inspector. I'll radio EMS."

"If you like." The inspector watched Lizabeth Scott, the movie's only authentic victim, being escorted to her cell by a city matron. Dick Powell, the source of most of her grief, rode away with loyal Jane Wyatt at the wheel, free to live whatever remained of the respectable life he had been leading when the story began. The reel ran out. The screen went white.

"Good picture?" he asked me.

"I thought so the first couple of times I saw it. I've seen it so many times now I don't even see it anymore. Did you get Mrs. Catalin?"

He nodded. "Mary Ann Thaler's checking her for weapons."

"The kind she carries won't turn up in a frisk." I looked around, spotted the checked butt of the automatic poking out from under a seat, and used my handkerchief to pick it up by the barrel. "The serial number on this ought to check out with the gun Neil Catalin registered. The prints are Robinette's. Meet Robinette." I waved the butt at the man on the floor.

"Thanks. We've met a time or two."

"You may not have to meet him again, even if he survives. If the slugs that killed Brian Elwood and Leo Webb didn't come from this piece, I'll retire and write my memoirs."

"I almost hope they don't." He took the gun by the handkerchief end.

"Robinette didn't kill Elwood; Webb did. But then Robinette beat to death a P.I. in Iroquois Heights named Musuraca, and you may not be able to make that one stick."

"Any murder will do. I hear you found out they sprang Ted Silvera from Jackson. I tried to call."

"You should have left a message."

"That'd make one more you owed me. This brings us almost even for the Luger. If you'd told me Saturday what you called and told me today, you'd be a little ahead."

"I needed you to catch him in possession of the gun. He didn't have it with him last night or I'd have called you then. I was pretty sure he'd have it today. Nobody resents being taken more than a taker."

"I'm not sure we can hold the woman. Anything she told you in here is inadmissable."

"Try this," I said. "Gay Catalin was too smart to risk taking her husband's body very far from their house. The gun's enough to shake loose a warrant to search the house and grounds. Don't forget the berry thicket at the end of the cul-de-sac. She'd be just cute enough to bury him there on city property."

"West Bloomfield won't even need a warrant for that."

"Thanks, John."

He looked around, at the marble and velvet and stained glass and gold leaf and painted plaster. "Big place, huh? My old man would say a person could store a mess of cotton in here."

"Not really. It's already full."

Forty

AUTUMN BEGAN bang on schedule, with starchy winds and needles of rain and the first chill of death from Alberta. The leaves on the trees planted in boxes along Woodward turned brazen and bloody—in River Rouge they remained black as the coke in the ovens in the foundry—and the Tigers fell out of the run for the pennant at the point where they usually fell out when they had any shot at all. In September, officers from Detroit and West Bloomfield working jointly turned up Neil Catalin's decomposing remains in the soft soil under the untended brush at the end of the street in front of his house. His widow, Gay Catalin, was arrested, arraigned in Detroit Recorder's Court on a charge of open murder, and scheduled for trial in October.

The circumstances of the crime were bizarre enough to inspire a theme show on one of the afternoon TV talkfests— "Men Who Obsess and the Women Who Love Them"—and to interest a national cable network, which covered the trial, borrowing personnel and equipment from Gilda Productions, currently in receivership with Judy Yin acting as general manager. A well-known feminist attorney took charge of the defense pro bono, arguing for acquittal on the grounds of temporary insanity brought on by the victim's infidelity and virtual desertion. The trial lasted two weeks. The jury deliberated for five days, then reported itself deadlocked, seven to five in favor of conviction. A mistrial was declared.

Orvis Robinette was recovering under police guard in a room at Detroit General Hospital. He awaited arraignment for felony homicide in the death of Leo Webb during the commission of a burglary.

The night of the day the jury hung in the Catalin case, Vesta and I had dinner at the Downtown London Chop House, caught a concert at the Ford Auditorium, and afterward walked along the riverfront, which was well lighted and filled with strollers dragging the last good out of the season before the long gray coma of winter. We were comfortable in our light cotton jackets, but there was a coppery smell of change in the air. The weather reader on Channel 4 was predicting snow for Halloween.

"Do you think they'll try her again?" Vesta asked.

We had stopped to watch an ore carrier steaming under the Ambassador Bridge, its coal-shovel prow gleaming greasily in the lights strung along the cables between the spans.

"Maybe not," I said. "Prosecutors are always running for something and want that feminist vote. Apparently the right to murder your husband is in jeopardy. If they do go again it won't make television. The networks already have reruns to spare."

"I didn't even watch myself when they repeated my testimony on the late news. It's the first time I ever played myself on camera. I'm pretty sure I was wrong for the part."

"The D.A. loved you. If I were you I wouldn't read any notices from the defense."

"I walked out during a taping of *Hard Copy* last week.

The interviewer kept referring to me as the 'Delilah from Detroit.' I signed a release, so they're threatening to sue."

"I wouldn't sweat it. Next week some high school algebra teacher in Delaware will seduce a student into murdering her husband and they'll forget all about you. Warhol was right."

"Maybe not."

We resumed walking. She had on cream-colored pleated slacks with a top and jacket to match. It looked yellow under the lamps. Her long black hair was gathered into a loose ponytail and she wore no jewelry and little makeup. She might have been a mature senior in high school. She was quieter than usual.

I said, "Something happened."

"Something." She nodded.

I lit a cigarette without offering her one and tossed the match toward the river. It made a short orange arc and spat when it struck the surface.

"A producer called," she said then. "He saw me on *Court TV*. He wants me to fly to L.A. and audition for a part on *Days of Our Lives.*"

"Did he call you Chickie and talk with a lisp?"

"He wasn't one of those. I called SAG. He checks out as far back as *Playhouse Ninety*. It's a genuine offer. He sent me a plane ticket and everything."

"What's the part?"

"A homewrecker."

I said nothing.

She moved a shoulder. "So I'm typecast. Neil used to say that's what makes a star shine."

"I hope he was right. You've earned it."

We passed an old man in a light blue suit, narrow-brimmed hat, and black-and-brown wingtips, holding hands with a white-haired woman who walked with an aluminum cane.

Vesta said, "You could go with me."

"To the audition?"

"To L.A. I mean, if it works out. To live."

I shook my head. "Southern California's crawling with P.I.'s. Here I'm a small frog in a small pond. Out there I'd just drown."

"There's loads of security work. Every ten-year-old who shoots a cereal commercial thinks he needs a bodyguard."

"That's appealing. A babysitter with a Motorola."

She stopped and hugged herself. There was no wind and the air was mild. "Work with me here. I'm trying to find out if we have anything worth hanging on to."

"When do you leave?"

"Tomorrow."

"I'm relieved. For a minute there I was worried you weren't giving me much notice."

"You could come out later."

"I'd have to work up contacts, memorize a whole new set of streets. My Spanish isn't that good."

"I probably won't get the part anyway."

"You probably will."

A breeze came up then, moist from the water and edged with sulphur from the smelters downriver. A radio was playing on the Canadian side. The notes Dopplered over in a warped glissando: a slide trombone with tonsils. Sarah Vaughan. Vesta reached up and pulled a stray lock of hair away from her face. "Tell me where I screwed up so I'll know what to avoid next time."

"You didn't. I'm as bad as Neil in my way. You'd spend most of your nights watching television alone or reading a book, not knowing if I picked up a tail job that took me all the way to Seattle or if I was floating facedown in La Brea.

Maybe it's not worth killing over, but nobody should have to put up with it either."

"There are other jobs. You've got a college education."

"You could model."

She made a face. Then she smiled. Then she looked away. The slight bump on her nose gave her the profile of an Indian princess. "If this is right, how come I feel so crummy?"

"That's how you tell."

Next day I drove her to the airport. She kissed me at the curb, tipped a skycap to carry her bags inside, and followed him through the automatic doors without looking back. I went to see a movie.

More
Loren D. Estleman!

Please turn this page
for a
bonus excerpt
from

THE WITCHFINDER

a new
Mysterious Press hardcover
available at
bookstores everywhere.

One

THERE ARE MORNINGS, just after dawn on unseasonably hot June days when every breath you draw is filtered through forty pounds of wet laundry, that you welcome the clear cold icicle of the telephone bell ringing.

You sit on the edge of your bed for a while waiting for the overcast to clear, uncertain whether you were preparing to rise or retire, then the ringing comes again, an hour behind the first, and you get up and squish out into the living room where the air from the open window chills you in your damp underwear, and the second ring is just ending. Everything you hear and see and do is at quarter-speed. It's a kind of brownout of the brain.

"Is that Amos Walker?"

A man's voice, ageless and tweedy, with Big Ben chiming on the consonants. I'd tapped into an episode of *Upstairs, Downstairs*.

"It was last night. I can't answer for it now." I sounded like a low-revolution drill even to myself. "What time is it on my side of the Atlantic?"

"Shortly after six. Did I wake you?"

"Hold the line, please."

Hearing the birds now—they were singing at normal speed, which in my present condition sounded like a chorus of slipping fan belts—I found a box of matches and a butt longer than an inch in the ashtray on the telephone stand and lit up. The chased the bees out of my head. "Okay, I checked the bed and I'm not still in it. Who am I speaking to?"

"My name is Stuart Lund. I'm an attorney."

"Not a barrister or a solicitor?"

One of those screwy computer scales you hear on the telephone played in the pause on his end. "No, I'm a naturalized American citizen and have been for fifteen years. I'm prepared to offer you a retainer in the amount of one thousand dollars if you'll agree to meet me this morning here in my suite at the Airport Marriott."

"Which airport?"

"Detroit Metropolitan, of course. Did you think I was calling from England?"

"The accent threw me off."

"Indeed. I wasn't aware I still had one."

"You don't need one if you're going to use words like *indeed*," I said. "Okay, make the offer."

2

"I believe I just made it."

"You said you were prepared to. I thought you people were more careful with the language than us born Yankees." The filter ignited. I punched out the butt. The stench of scorched rubber hung on the stagnant air. "Pardon the impertinence, Mr. Lund. Also the effrontery. I'm experiencing a power surge. My standard retainer is fifteen hundred."

"There will be a substantially larger sum involved if I decide to employ your services as an enquiry agent. The thousand is merely for coming out. It's yours whether or not we agree to do business."

"Are you acting on behalf of a client?"

"More accurately, in compliance with a client's wishes. I'm representing the estate of Jay Bell Furlong."

"Jay Bell Furlong the architect?"

"The same. Can I expect you?"

"I haven't read or seen the news since last night. Has he died?"

"As of my last call to Los Angeles five minutes ago, no. Although my use of the term *estate* is technically premature, as his executor I'm under instructions to waste no time. Which is precisely what I seem to be doing." His tone acquired a measured amount of impatience, as if he'd raised one of a series of internal floodgates an inch.

3

"I'll be there in less than an hour, Mr. Lund."

He gave me the number of the suite and broke the connection.

I showered, toweled off, and shaved, feeling fresh sweat prickling out of the open pores as I stood in the cross-draft between the window and the bathroom doorway. Dressing, I selected a blue shirt, dark blue knitted tie, the tan summerweight, and brown mesh shoes, on the theory that if I looked cool I might at least make someone else feel cool and maybe he'd return the favor. I combed my hair and reconnoitered the gray. The beard underneath the skin was as blue-black as ever, but my temples were beginning to resemble the Comstock Lode.

There was no time for breakfast, even if I were in the habit. I swigged orange juice straight from the carton, overcame the urge to climb into the refrigerator with it when I put it back, and went out to the garage. I drove with all the windows down and the wind lifting my combed hair, which the hell with it. When that model of Cutlass roared off the line, air conditioning was for Rolls Royce.

My clientele had taken a stylish turn. At eighty and change, Jay Bell Furlong was the last of the legendary school of American architects who had cast away the posts and lintels and marble scroll-work of the Old World. They had substituted hori-zontal lines for vertical, invented the concept of harmony with the environment, and fought a desperate and ultimately losing battle against the Xeroxed glass, girder, and reinforced-concrete designs rolling out of the cost-effective East. Theirs was the last dying bellow of art in a field seized by accountants and the low bid. For a heartbeat their bold innovations had swept a continent. Now Louis Sullivan was forgotten, Frank Lloyd Wright was dead, and Furlong was about to be, rigged as he was with tubes and insulated wire in the cancer ward at Cedars of Lebanon Hospital in Los Angeles, the elephants' graveyard of forgotten movie stars, one-hit rockers, and disgraced presidents. The media deathwatch had been going on for a week. Furlong's rallies and relapses made the Eleven O'Clock Report as regularly as the box scores.

What his attorney was doing in Detroit, where impressive architecture was looked upon as an empty lot in the making, was foggy.

As I swung into the short-term lot at the airport, a leviathan of a 757 shrieked overhead at a steep angle, sucking its wheels into its belly and dragging its shadow over the car like a coronation train. The sky the jet was headed for didn't look any more inviting than the ground. A low dirty cloudbank had been stalled over the metropolitan area for days, trapping the kind of temperatures and humidity normally associated with the

Philippines. Old people die like goldfish in that weather, also high school juniors at fast-food restaurants with hundred-dollar sneakers and short tempers.

The lobby air hit me like a bucket of ice water after the convector of the pavement. That particular Marriott may be the only hotel in the vvorld built directly onto an airport terminal. Certainly it's the only one this side of Beirut where you have to pass through a metal detector to check in or visit. I said something on that order to the guard at the gate, who scowled and tipped his head toward a sign that informed me my First Amendment rights were suspended on the premises. I told him what I thought of that, but by then I was two floors up in the elevator.

Stuart Lund came in at six-two and three hundred pounds in gray silk tailoring with a large head of wavy yellow hair, blue eyes like wax drippings, and a black chevron-shaped moustache he hadn't bothered to bleach. He was about fifty. After opening the door to his suite, he shifted a mahogany cane with a cast-silver crook to his left hand and offered me his right. "You're punctual. Very admirable."

I stepped past him into a large room that would have been cheerful if the drapes weren't drawn, with fat armchairs and a free-standing refrigerator under lock and key. A television on a swivel was tuned in to CNN with the sound very low. Lund asked me to sit and approached the refrigerator, leaning a little on the cane.

"I never shall get over the way they see to one's creature comforts in this country's hotels. I'm sinfully well stocked. It's early, but I understand all you detectives are seasoned imbibers."

"That's fiction," I said. "Make mine a Bloody Mary."

"One of the more fascinating queens." He used the key, married the contents of a toy vodka bottle and a miniature can of tomato juice in a barrel glass, and brought it over. "I apologize for not joining you. The lag," he explained, lowering himself into a chair that for anyone else would have been a loveseat.

"Did you fall off the ramp?"

He lifted his eyebrows, then glanced down at the cane. "Gout, I'm afraid. The complaint of colonial governors and certain kings of France. I'm under physician's instructions to lose a hundred pounds, but I'm in revolt. People who have been fat all their lives and suddenly become thin are pathetic to see, like polar bears wasting away in the wrong climate. The stick belonged to an ancestor: Sir Hudson Lowe, Governor of St. Helena and Bonaparte's gaoller for the last six years of the Corsican's life." He pronounced the word the same as jailer, but he wouldn't have spelled it that way.

"My grandfather rode shotgun on a beer truck."

He wiggled his moustache, then hooked the cane on the arm of the loveseat and produced a fold of paper from an inside breast pocket.

The check bore Jay Bell Furlong's name and address in the upper left corner. Lund had signed his own name. I pocketed it. "Power of attorney?"

"The privilege did not come cheap. I've been Jay's legal adviser, secretary, business manager, confidant, and frequently his whipping post ever since he brought me here from Gloucester. He disengaged me from a firm of solicitors that represented William Pitt, and which another ancestor of mine helped establish. It was quite the family scandal at the time; although I daresay dear old Uncle Nigel's decision to attend a meeting of the House of Lords in a chiffon evening dress and diamonds has supplanted it."

"Was it before or after six?"

He worried his moustache with a row of small perfect teeth. No English dentist was responsible for those. "Do you know, I never asked. I hope the old boy hadn't cast of all of his breeding."

Now that I was there his impatience seemed to have ebbed. I picked up the pace. "Who gave you my name?"

"A colleague, Arthur Rooney. He hadn't many flattering things to say, but what wasn't good was

8

irrelevant. I'm chiefly interested in your ability to maintain a confidence."

"I've been to jail over it four times." I spelled it jail. "That's public record. No sense telling you how much it's cost me in ace bandages. That isn't."

He weighed me. The waxy eyes looked as if they would retain thumbprints. "Do you know the historical definition of the term witchfinder?"

"I do if it's anything like witch hunter."

"They're not the same. Not quite. The Puritans of your— excuse me, our—New England colonies employed hunters to rid them of witches. The hunters in their turn engaged witchfinders to gather evidence against them, or rather to manufacture it. I'm not at all convinced that there weren't such things as witches, but I do question the statistics of the time."

He rested a hand on the crook of his cane, clouding the shiny silver with his personal humidity. "In the country of my birth we were quick to condemn the Pilgrims for fleeing England in search of religious freedom only to impose a far more repressive creed upon themselves. But they behaved as they did out of a sincere belief in the forces of good and evil, Christ the Redeemer and Lucifer the Tempter. The witchfinders did not share that belief. They were paid commissions on the witches they managed to expose; not an incomprehensible arrangement when you consider the state of colonial finances, but it was scarcely fertile ground for verdicts of innocence. The tests these finders conducted upon the wretches who stood before them accused were barbaric. Those who survived were judged guilty and hanged."

"Burned, I thought."

He shook a finger at me.

"You really should know at least as much about your native country's past as a newcomer. They burned werewolves. They hanged witches."

I looked down at the glass in my hand. He looked too comfortable to get up and fix me another, and at the rate he was going I would touch bottom long before he reached his point. But he'd hired the audience along with the hall. Behind him on CNN, a brief tape biography of Jay Bell Furlong ended and the camera cut to a reporter standing on the sidewalk in front of Cedars of Lebanon Hospital. You know it's a slow news week when builders long more air time than destroyers.

"When witches passed out of fashion," Lund went on, "the finders lost their comfortable posts, but not forever. In a culpable society there will always be employment for the bearers of false witness. They're less flamboyant now, more difficult to identify. They no longer hang out shingles and they've burned their black cowls. That's why I called you. Your assignment is to find the witchfinder."

"Speak American, Windy. You're wearing the man out."

This was a new voice in the auditorium. The door to the suite's adjoining bedroom had opened. The famous Furlong bone structure was on the screen, and as I craned my head around I thought at first those Lincolnesque features had burned into my retinas, moving with my eyes. The man the nation's press waited to photograph on his horizontal way to the Los Angles County Morgue was standing in a hotel doorway in Detroit with a drink in his hand.